The Hanging in the Hotel

Simon Brett

The Hanging in the Hotel

A Fethering Mystery

MACMILLAN

First published 2004 by Macmillan
an imprint of Pan Macmillan Ltd
Pan Macmillan, 20 New Wharf Road, London N1 9RR
Basingstoke and Oxford
Associated companies throughout the world
www.panmacmillan.com

ISBN 0 333 90853 8

1 3 5 7 9 8 6 4 2

A CIP catalogue record for this book is available from
the British Library.

Typeset by Intype London Ltd
Printed and bound in Great Britain by
Mackays of Chatham plc, Chatham, Kent

to

Sophie and Jeremy

with lots of love

Chapter One

As the taxi entered the gates, Jude looked up at Hopwicke Country House Hotel, a monument to nostalgic pampering. The mansion had been built in the early eighteenth century by George Hopwicke, a young baronet who had increased his considerable inheritance by 'the successes of his plantations in the West Indies', or, in other words, by his profits from the slave trade. The main building was a perfectly proportioned cube, the ideal echoed in so many late twentieth-century developments of 'exclusive Georgian townhouses'. The elegantly tall windows on the three floors at the front of the house looked down from the fringes of the South Downs, across the bungalow- and greenhouse-littered plain around Worthing, to the gunmetal glimmer of the English Channel.

Stabling and utility buildings were behind the house, neatly shielded by tall hedges. The hundreds of acres in which George Hopwicke had built this testament to his taste and opulence had been sold off piecemeal for development over the centuries, and at the beginning of the twenty-first century only a four-acre buffer protected the upper-class elegance of the hotel from the encroachments of the ever-expanding English middle classes, and from the encroachments of the present. Even the brochure said, 'Leave the twenty-first century behind when you step through our elegant portals.'

It's remarkable, Jude thought as the taxi nosed up the drive, how much nostalgia there is in England for things that never existed. To escape the present, the English like nothing better than to immerse themselves in an idealized past. She felt sure the people of other nations – or other nations whose peoples could afford the luxury of self-examination – also venerated the past, but not in the same way. Only in England would the rosy tints of retrospection be seen through the lens of social class.

The taxi crunched to a halt at the furthest point of the gravel arc, which went on round to rejoin the road at a second set of tall metal gates. The semi-circle of grass the drive framed was laid out as a croquet lawn.

Jude paid off the driver, without calculating how large a chunk the fare would take out of her evening's earnings, and hurried through the classical portico into the hotel.

New visitors were intended to notice the artfully artless displays of impedimenta that tidily littered the hallway, but Jude had seen them all before, so she didn't pause to take in the coffin-like croquet box with the mallets spilling out, the randomly propped-up fishing rods, the brown-gutted tennis racquets in wooden presses, the splitting cricket bats and the crumpled leather riding boots. Nor did she linger to scan the walls for their hunting prints, mounted antlers, stuffed trout or ancient photographs of dead-looking tweedy men surveying carpets of dead birds.

Everything in the displays of which Jude took no notice supported her theory about English nostalgia. Hopwicke Country House Hotel aspired to an image of leisured indolence, set in comforting aspic somewhere between the late nineteenth and early twentieth centuries. It was a world of field sports and tennis parties, of dainty teas on shaven lawns, of large slugs of brandy and soda before many-coursed dinners. It was a world in which nobody was so indelicate as to think about money, and in which all the boring stuff was done by invisible servants. It was a world that had never existed.

But though the guests of Hopwicke Country House Hotel deep in their hearts were probably aware of this fact, like children suspending disbelief to their own advantage over the existence of Father Christmas, they willingly ignored it. None of the clientele, anyway, had the background which might qualify them to argue with the detail of the hotel's ambiance. Real aristocrats, whose upbringing might have contained some elements of the effect being sought after, would never have dreamed of staying in such a place. American tourists, whose images of England were derived largely from books featuring Hercule Poirot, Miss Marple and Lord Peter Wimsey, found nothing at all discordant. And, though the trust-funded or City-bonus-rich young couples who made up the rest of the hotel's guest list might occasionally assert themselves by sending the wine back, they were far too socially insecure to question the authenticity of the overall experience for which they paid so much over the odds. When they departed the hotel, they didn't blanch as they flashed a precious-metal credit card over the bill. In that detail, the image was sustained; no one was so indelicate as to appear to think about money.

As to all the boring stuff being done by invisible servants, here the hotel was on less certain ground. Though that was certainly the effect to which the management aspired, they didn't have at their disposal the vast armies of staff which would have ensured the clockwork precision running of an Edwardian country house. Economy dictated that there were never really enough bodies around to do everything that was required, that the hotel's owner ended up doing far more menial work than she should have done and that, when one member of staff failed to turn up on time, chaos threatened.

Which was why Jude had received an emergency call from the hotel's owner that April afternoon. There was no one at the antique reception table as she hurried past, just a tiny brass bell to summon service. Jude was making for the kitchen at the end of the hall, but noticed a door opposite the bar entrance was open, and moved towards it.

Steep steps led down to the hotel's cellar. The lights were on. As Jude peered down, a familiar face looked up at her.

'Thank God you've come!'

'What is it this time?'

4

'Bloody waitresses! Stella's cried off because she's going out with some new man, but she promised me her daughter'd come in. Bloody kid rang in at quarter to four to say she couldn't do it.'

'Any reason?'

'Didn't say. Told me and rang off.'

'Suppose you should be grateful she rang at all.'

'Why? God, Stella's going to get an earful when she next comes in!'

'Don't sack her.' Jude's voice was firm and cautionary. 'You can't afford to lose any more staff.'

'No.' Suzy Longthorne the hotel owner sighed, and held out two bottles of port. 'Could you take these?' She picked up two more, turned off the cellar light, came up the stairs and locked the door behind her. 'Going to need a lot of port tonight,' she said, and led the way through to the kitchen. Inside, she put the bottles down on the table and wearily coiled her long body into a chair.

Even though she had thickened out around the neck, Suzy Longthorne remained a beautiful woman. It was still easy to see why she had graced so many magazine covers, been a desirable trophy for so many photographers and pop singers, been so frequently pursued and so frequently won. The famous hair, which had been through every latest style for nearly four decades, almost certainly now needed help to maintain its natural auburn, but looked good. The hazel eyes, though surrounded by a tracery of tiny lines, were still commanding. And the lithe, full-breasted figure seemed to have made no concessions to the years, though less of its toning now came from the gym than from the extraordinary effort of running Hopwicke Country House Hotel.

Suzy was incapable of dressing badly. Other women in the same pale grey T-shirt, jeans and brown leather slip-on shoes would have looked ordinary, sloppy even. Suzy Longthorne could still have stepped straight onto a catwalk. On her even the blue-and-white-striped butcher's apron looked like a fashion accessory.

In fact, a perfect photo shoot could have been done at that moment – the chatelaine of Hopwicke House in her kitchen. Like the rest of the hotel, the room had been restored by expensive designers to a high specification. Without losing its eighteenth-century proportions or its wide fireplace, the kitchen had been equipped with the latest culinary devices. Hidden lighting twinkled knowingly on surfaces of stainless steel and the copper bottoms of serried ranks of utensils.

The two women had known each other since their late teens, when both had been picked up as potential 'Faces of the Sixties'. But Jude's modelling career had stuttered to a quick end. Though she didn't lack for offers of work (among other things), a couple of long photo shoots and one catwalk show had brought home to her the incredible tedium of the job and she had moved sideways into acting in the blossoming world of fringe theatre and television.

But Jude's relationship with Suzy had endured. Not on a regular basis – frequently years would elapse between contacts – but it was always there. Usually, Suzy was the one who contacted Jude at the end of another of her high-profile relationships. And the tear-stained famous face would be buried in Jude's increasingly ample shoulder, while the perfidies of men were once again catalogued and bold unrealizable ambitions for a relationship-free life were once again outlined.

Suzy never seemed aware of what others had observed in their encounters with Jude – that they were the confiders, she the confidant. Jude rarely gave away much information about herself and, though her own emotional life had been at least as varied – if not as public – as Suzy's, little of it was aired. There were friends to whom Jude did turn in moments of her own distress, but Suzy Longthorne was not one of them.

Yet the relationship wasn't one-sided. Suzy mattered to Jude. There was a core of honesty in the woman that appealed to her, together with a strong work ethic. And Jude was endlessly fascinated by the problems that accompanied the fulfilment of many women's dream – that of being born incredibly beautiful.

Suzy Longthorne had bought Hopwicke Country House Hotel with the proceeds from the breakdown of her longest marriage. For thirteen years she had stayed with Rick Hendry, as he metamorphosed from ageing rocker to pop entrepreneur to television producer, and as his tastes had shifted from the maturity of his wife to the pubescent charms of wannabee pop stars. Rick had made his name with a band called Zedrach-Kona, who produced supposedly profound sci-fi-influenced concept albums in the late seventies. The success of these, including the massive seller *The Columns of Korfilia*, had made him rich and famous for a year or two, then rich and forgotten. But in his fifties, Rick Hendry had found a new incarnation as an acerbic critic on *Pop Crop*, a television talent show which pitted the talents of manufactured boy and girl bands against each other. His own company, Korfilia Productions, made the show, and so once again for Rick Hendry the money was rolling in.

By that time, being back in the public spotlight meant his ego no longer needed the support of marriage. The divorce settlement had been generous and Suzy had invested it all in Hopwicke House.

The venture had started well. The conversion of the space from private dwelling to hotel had been expensively and expertly completed. The recollected glamour of its new owner gave the venue an air of chic. Well-heeled names from her much-publicized past booked in. Journalists who'd cut their cub-reporting teeth on interviews with Suzy Longthorne commissioned features for the newspapers and magazines they now edited. For a place that marketed itself as a discreet, quiet retreat, Hopwicke Country House Hotel got a lot of media coverage.

Suzy was by no means a remote figurehead in the enterprise; she was a very hands-on manager. Her money was backing the project, and she had always kept an eye on what her money was up to. She was punctilious about the quality of staff – particularly the chefs – who worked for her. The media may have started the ball rolling, but word-of-mouth recommendations ensured its continuing motion.

As the reputation of Hopwicke House grew, the hotel appeared more frequently in brochures targeted at the international super-rich – particularly Americans. Soon the breakfast tables in the conservatory resounded to Californian enquiries as to what a kipper might be, or tentative Texan queries about the provenance of black pudding. The hotel was included in an increasing number of upmarket tours, and played its part in nurturing the delusion of wealthy Americans that England had been created by P. G. Wodehouse and Agatha Christie.

So Suzy Longthorne had cleverly carved her niche, done the appropriate niche-marketing, and looked set fair to reap great riches from that niche.

Until 11 September 2001. Among the many other effects of that momentous day, as Americans ceased to fly abroad and the bottom fell out of the tourism market, bookings at Hopwicke Country House Hotel immediately declined. Unfortunately, the transatlantic market was not alone in drying up. A collective guilt about over-indulgence had struck the Western world, and no amount of inducements in the form of weekend breaks with suicidally low profit margins seemed able to reverse the downturn for Suzy's business. She had been forced to abandon the exclusivity that had been her cachet and selling-point, and accept bookings from anyone who wished to stay.

It was with this knowledge, on that April afternoon,

that her friend Jude asked, a little tentatively, 'Who have you got in tonight?'

Suzy's perfect nose wrinkled with distaste. 'The Pillars of Sussex.'

'Oh.' Jude grimaced in sympathy. Though she had never met any members, she recognized the name. Like most British clubs and institutions, it had been founded in the second half of the nineteenth century. Originally, under the grand name of 'The Pillars of Society', the group had been initiated for philanthropic purposes, and was still involved in local charity work and Christmas fund-raising. As with many such associations, however, the initial worthy intention soon took a back seat to procedures, rituals, ceremonies, elections, all of which had the same general aim: that those who had achieved membership of the Pillars should feel eternally superior to those who had not. Nothing had changed since an 1836 publication, *Hints on Etiquette*, had observed that, 'the English are the most aristocratic democrats in the world; always endeavouring to squeeze through the portals of rank and fashion, and then slamming the door in the face of any unfortunate devil who may happen to be behind them.'

Needless to say, meetings of the Pillars of Sussex involved a great deal of drinking.

What made all this worse, from Jude's perspective, was that the Pillars of Sussex was an exclusively male organization. She had grown up suspecting that in the absence of female company men get increasingly childish, and experience had turned the suspicion into a conviction. She did not relish the evening of raucous misogyny ahead.

But her views didn't matter; she was there to help out her friend. 'What do you want me to do, Suzy? Bar?'

'No, I'll handle most of that. Part of being the hostess. Might need some help with the drinks orders before dinner.'

'Trays of glasses of wine?'

'I think this lot'll probably be drinking beer. No, basically, I want you to help with the waitressing.'

'OK.' That was what Jude had been expecting. 'Is it just me?'

'No, I'll help, of course. And I've got Kerry . . .'

Suzy spoke as if this possession was a not unmixed blessing. Jude had met the girl on a previous visit – a sulky, rather beautiful fifteen-year-old supposedly destined for a career in hotel management. Since Kerry was in her last year at private school and without much prospect of making any impact academically, her parents had arranged for her to spend her Easter holiday doing 'work experience' at Hopwicke House 'in order to get some hands-on training'. The girl's commitment to her career choice was not marked – her only interest seemed to be pop music – but Suzy endured Kerry's flouncing and inefficiency with surprising forbearance.

Perhaps any help was better than none. Finding steady waiting staff was a continuing problem for Suzy. 'Don't suppose you know anyone looking for some part-time work?' Jude was asked, not for the first time.

She shook her head, not for the first time, and once

again had the mischievous idea of mentioning the job to her neighbour. It wouldn't be a serious suggestion. Carole Seddon, with her civil-service pension and her hide-bound ideas of dignity, would be appalled at the notion of acting as a waitress. But Jude was playfully tempted to unleash the inevitable knee-jerk reaction.

'Max is cooking for them, presumably?'

'Yes.' Suzy looked at the exquisite Piaget watch Rick Hendry had lavished on her for one of their happier anniversaries. 'He should be in by now. I'm afraid the Pillars of Sussex aren't his favourite kind of clientele. Still, how else are we going to get dinner for twenty and most of the rooms full on a Tuesday evening?' She spoke with weary resignation.

Max Townley, Jude knew, saw himself as a 'personality chef'. He was good at his job and, so long as Hopwicke House attracted high-profile guests, he had enjoyed mingling, and identifying himself, with celebrity. Since the downturn of the previous year, Max had been less at ease, and Suzy knew that each 'ordinary' restaurant booking she took made him more unsettled. The fact that fear of drink–driving convictions would guarantee most of the hotel's rooms were booked for the night carried little weight with the chef. From Max's point of view, as clientele for a restaurant where he was cooking, the Pillars of Sussex were about as bad as it could get.

'Are you worried about him not turning up?' asked Jude.

'No, he'll be here. Max is enough of a professional to do that. But he'll make his point by being late . . . and

resentful.' Her voice took on the chef's petulant timbre.
'A load of bloody stuffed shirts who wouldn't recognize
good food if it came up and bit them on the leg, and
who will have blunted any taste buds they have left
with too much beer before dinner, and then be allowed
to smoke all the way through the meal.'

'Really?' asked Jude, amazed. One of the strictest
rules of the Hopwicke House restaurant had always
been its non-smoking policy. Mega-celebrities of the
music and film business had succumbed meekly to
the stricture, and retired to the bar for their cigarettes
and cigars. The fact that the prohibition was being
relaxed for a group as undistinguished as the Pillars of
Sussex showed, more forcibly than any other indicator,
the levels to which Suzy Longthorne's aspirations had
descended.

But it didn't need saying. Jude leant across the
kitchen table and took her friend's hand, still soft from
its years of expensive lotioning.

'Things really bad, are they, Suzy?'

There was a nod, and for a moment tears threatened the famous hazel eyes.

'Everything rather a mess, I'm afraid,' the 'Face of
the Sixties' admitted.

'Anything you can talk about? Want to talk about?'

'Some things, maybe. Certainly this.'

From a pocket in her apron, Suzy extracted an
envelope. It bore the Hopwicke House crest, but no
name, address or stamp. The back had not been sealed,
just tucked in, and the envelope was slightly bent from
its sojourn in the apron.

'Kerry found it in one of the rooms she was checking. She said she opened it because she thought there might be a tip inside . . . though I think she was just being nosy.'

Jude picked up the envelope. 'May I?'

Her friend gave a defeated nod.

There was only one sheet of paper inside. Of the same quality as the envelope, again it bore the Hopwicke House crest. Centred on the page were three lines of printed text.

ENJOY THIS EVENING.
IF YOU'RE NOT SENSIBLE,
IT'LL BE YOUR LAST.

Chapter Two

The phone call had disturbed Carole Seddon. Her life was rigidly compartmentalized, and many of its compartments had, she hoped, been sealed up for permanent storage. To have one of those old boxes opened threatened her hard-won equilibrium.

Having retired from the Home Office early (and the earliness still rankled), moving with her Labrador Gulliver to a house called High Tor in the seaside village of Fethering had seemed an eminently sensible solution to the problem posed by the rest of her life. And, though the arrival of her next-door neighbour had added extra dimensions to that life, in her more po-faced moods Carole could still feel nostalgic for the acceptable dullness of Fethering pre-Jude.

There was a sharp division in Carole Seddon's mind between the life she had lived in London and now lived in West Sussex. Although she was happy to discuss her career as a civil servant, she had kept few London friends, and never talked about her personal life. Jude was one of the very few people in Fethering who knew her neighbour had once been married and was a mother.

Had the phone call come from David, Carole would have been less flustered. Her relationship with her ex-husband had now settled down to something totally inert, its only remarkable feature being the fact that two people with so little in common had ever spent time together. Mutual financial interests, or news of long-lost relatives' deaths, necessitated occasional phone calls, which were politely conducted without warmth, but without animosity.

It was Stephen, however, who had rung Carole that evening, and she wasn't so sure what her relationship with her son had settled down to. On the rare occasions when she could no longer keep the lid on that particular compartment battened down, its contents prompted a mix of unwelcome emotions. She felt guilty for her lack of maternal instinct. Stephen's birth had been a profound shock to her, shattering the control which up until then she had exercised over all aspects of her life. A woman who indulged in any kind of self-analysis might have deduced she had experienced post-natal depression, but for Carole Seddon that was territory into which she did not allow her mind to stray. She had been brought up to believe that giving in to mental illness was self-indulgent. Life was for getting on with.

All she knew was that, from the start, Stephen had represented a challenge rather than a blessing. She could not fault herself on the meticulous attention she had given to his upbringing, but she knew she had never felt for him that instinctive love about which so many parents wax lyrical.

So when, as an adult, Stephen drifted further away from her, Carole felt no extra guilt, no regret, possibly even an inadmissible degree of relief.

They never lost touch. Present-givings at Christmas and birthdays were meticulously observed. They rarely met in London, but at least twice a year Stephen would come down to the Fethering area and take his mother out for lunch. The meals were eaten in anonymous seaside restaurants or pubs, and passed off amiably enough.

On these occasions Carole would say the minimum about her local doings, but Stephen seemed quite happy to monopolize the conversation. He talked almost exclusively about his work, which involved computers and money in a combination his mother never quite managed to grasp. She should have taken more interest when he first started his economics course at Nottingham University; then maybe she would have been able to follow the subsequent progress of his career. As it was, when they met she felt increasingly like someone at a party who hadn't caught the name of the person to whom they were talking initially, and had left it too late to ask.

So, if a question about their relationship had been put to them, both Carole and Stephen would have said they 'got on'. In spite of the divorce, theirs could by no means be classified as a 'dysfunctional' family; it was just one that lacked spontaneous affection.

Inside Carole grew the suspicion, which she was unable to voice – even to herself – that the entire contents of her son's gene-pool derived from his father, and that Stephen Seddon was, in fact, a deeply boring man.

But exciting things happen even to boring men, and that evening Carole's son had had exciting news to impart.

'Mother . . .' he'd said. As a child, he'd always called her 'Mummy'. When he left for university, the word seemed to embarrass him. 'Mother' was safer, less intimate. He'd stuck with it.

'Mother, I'm engaged to be married.' The wording, too, seemed formal, distancing.

It was the last thing Carole had been expecting. For Stephen to ring was unusual enough; for him to ring with anything to say beyond vague pleasantries was unheard of. 'Ah,' she had responded, caught on the hop. 'Wonderful.'

Funny, she'd never really thought of her son as having a sexual identity. He'd certainly never brought any girls home. Though maybe, given the state of his parents' marriage, he might have considered that an unnecessarily risky procedure.

'Her name's Gaby. I met her through work.'

'And what work is that? Remind me again.' Of course she didn't say the words, but Carole was surprised how readily they came into her mind. The unspoken response struck her as funny, and she knew it would have struck Jude as funny too.

She managed to come up with a more socially acceptable, 'So how long have you known each other?'

'Three years. But we've only been going out together for the last seven months.' Stephen spoke of

18

his fiancée with exactly the same seriousness as he did about the work that Carole didn't understand.

'Does she do the same sort of thing as you do? Is she in the same company?' Whatever that's called.

'Oh no, no, she was a client. We set up a financing package for the agency she works for,' he continued, confusing his mother even more. She understood the individual words; they just didn't seem to link together into anything that made sense.

'Ah.' Carole tried desperately to think what potential mothers-in-law were supposed to say in these circumstances. 'So have you thought yet about when you're going to get married?'

'September the fourteenth,' her son replied, surprisingly specific.

'Well, that sounds fine.'

'It fits in with Gaby's parents. They always spend August in the South of France.'

Oh yes, of course. The fiancée would have parents. Presumably at some point Carole would have to meet them. She shrank instinctively from the thought of contact with these unknown people. If their daughter was called Gaby, and they spent their summers in the South of France, then perhaps they weren't even British?

'Also,' Stephen went on, 'that date suits Dad fine.'

Carole was shocked by how much that hurt. Not just Stephen continuing to call David 'Dad' while she had been relegated to 'Mother', but the implication of her ex-husband's complicity in her son's life. David had been told about the wedding before she had. He'd probably met Gaby. They all lived in London, after all. (At least, presumably Gaby lived in London.) Perhaps David was regularly included in social excursions with the young couple.

Her marriage, the event Carole thought she had locked away for ever, was evidently still capable of breaking out and reviving her pain.

'I'd like you to meet Gaby,' Stephen pressed on doggedly.

Carole felt new guilt. She should have said that before he did. 'I'd love to meet Gaby soon' – that's what she should have said. And yet, in the shock and smarting from the hurt, she was forgetting even her most basic good manners.

'Oh yes, I'd love that!' Trying to make up the lost ground, she only managed to sound over-effusive.

'We want to come down the weekend after next.' As her son spoke, Carole realized he was following an agenda. His and Gaby's lives between now and the wedding were rigorously planned. Telling his mother the news and introducing her to his bride-to-be were duties that had to be performed and fitted into their schedule. 'We've got to be in the area.'

'Oh, why?'

No answer could have surprised her more than the one Stephen came up with. 'We're looking at some houses down your way.'

'Really?'

'Gaby's very keen to get out of London. We're looking for a big family house in the country for the next stage of our lives.'

So formally did her son speak these words that Carole knew, had Jude been there to hear them, they would both have giggled. But, on her own, Carole was too winded by the implication of Stephen's words to offer any response.

'So I was wondering, Mother, whether you'd be free for Sunday lunch that weekend.'

'Lunch? Sunday week. Yes, that sounds fine.' Uncharacteristically gushing, she added, 'I'm simply thrilled at the idea of meeting Gaby!'

'She's longing to meet you,' Stephen asserted, with all the enthusiasm of a weatherman announcing a cold snap. But he hadn't finished. 'There is one thing, Mother.'

'Yes?'

'I am very keen that you and Dad should both be at the wedding. Will that be all right?'

'Yes,' said Carole Seddon. 'Yes, of course it will be.'

That was only one of her worries after she had put the phone down. A lot of moribund emotions had been stirred up, reminding her they were still far from dead. And she knew they wouldn't go away. September the fourteenth would be a climax, a day of maximum stress, but that would not end the process. She was reliving the myth of Pandora's box. Now it had been opened, Carole was made aware of its fragility, and felt foolish for the misguided reliance she had placed on its security.

Another troubling thought occurred to her. It was rare for Stephen to come down to Fethering, and even rarer for him to stay overnight. On the few occasions when he wasn't just down for a quick pub or restaurant lunch and away, she had put him up in her spare bedroom. But if he was coming with a fiancée . . . The spare room only had a single bed. Oh dear, would she have to arrange for a double to be brought in? Worse than that . . . would she actually have to ask Stephen what sleeping arrangements he and Gaby favoured? The potential embarrassment loomed large enough to cloud Carole's entire horizon.

Seriously shaken, she wanted to talk to Jude. But even though the April evenings were drawing out, it still went against Carole's nature to knock on the front door of Woodside Cottage.

She telephoned instead. Jude was out.

Chapter Three

The outside door of the kitchen clattered open and, as Max Townley entered, Suzy slipped the sheet of paper and envelope back into her apron. The chef was dressed in black leathers; he'd parked his worshipped motor bike outside. He had once tried to impress Jude with the fact that this was a Ducati, but her patent lack of interest hadn't allowed him to get far. As he came into the kitchen, he removed a crash helmet, revealing short bluish-black hair. He was as lithe and jumpy as a Grecian cat, his eyes piercingly pale blue, and his thin mouth permanently tight with discontent.

He nodded acknowledgement to the two women, and focused sneeringly on Suzy's Piaget watch. 'It's all right. They'll get their precious dinner in time. Fat lot they'll notice, though.' He moved angrily across to a butcher's block, on which stood a box of vegetables and flicked through it. 'Still no celeriac.'

'They hadn't got any celeriac,' said Suzy evenly.

'I know they hadn't this morning. You said you'd ring them.'

'I did ring them, and they still didn't have any celeriac.'

'Well then, get a bloody different supplier! How am I supposed to produce a celeriac remoulade without bloody celeriac?'

'You'll have to do something else.'

'I thought you'd agreed a menu with the guests.'

'They won't notice.'

The chef's head snapped back and he faced his employer, but the retort on his lips died in her stare. He returned to the vegetables, mumbling, 'No, hardly matters what I give them, does it? Might as well nip down and get them takeaways from Macdonald's. Bloody peasants'd probably prefer that.'

Morosely, unzipping his leathers, he went through into the pantry to change into his freshly laundered white jacket, black-checked trousers and clogs.

Jude knew she had just witnessed a battle of wills, and also knew Suzy had won it beyond doubt. The triumph might simply be a credit to strength of person- ality, or maybe there was some other source of power. There had been rumours of an affair between the chatelaine of Hopwicke House and her chef, but Jude doubted their veracity. Such rumours clung around Suzy and every attractive man she met, but she was too shrewd an operator to put her business at risk by an unprofessional liaison.

Kitted out in his chef's gear, Max slipped a couple of heavy-bladed knives out of their slots, like a cowboy drawing his six-shooters, and started to chop fresh carrots on the butcher's block. His movements were slick from experience, and flamboyant by choice. He was a chef who, when he was working, welcomed – and played up to – an audience. Jude recalled some talk of his being considered for a television series, of a pilot programme about to be made, but she'd never heard the outcome. She could imagine Max successful in the role. His sulky good looks, his showmanship and waspish tongue might be just what a television scheduler wanted in the ever-more-desperate search for new ways of dressing up images of food.

Wearily, Suzy stretched out her long, perfect body till it was a straight line between chair seat and back. Then she snapped upwards to her feet. 'Must get on. They'll be coming soon. Kerry's supposed to be laying the tables. She should be finished by now.'

'Anything I can do?'

'Thanks, Jude. Yes, give me a hand with a bit of set-dressing.'

Max Townley was now singing to himself. Quite a tuneful version of 'Boiled Beef and Carrots'. Maybe that was another part of his sales pitch for the television moguls. The Singing Chef. God knows, thought Jude, as she followed Suzy out into the hall, they've tried every other kind.

Some of the tables in the restaurant had been locked together to make a twenty-seater for the Pillars of Sussex. The basic laying-up had been started, but apparently abandoned. The table settings were certainly not yet ready for those final touches which Suzy alone could provide. Of Kerry, the table-layer, there was no sign. Suzy and Jude exchanged a puzzled look.

Alerted by a clink of glass, Suzy led the way through to the darkened bar area. In the dim light behind the bar, Jude could see a slight blonde girl in a black-and-white waitress's uniform, standing guiltily with a balloon of brandy in her hand.

'What the hell are you doing, Kerry?' Suzy snapped. 'I've told you before, you're not to drink on duty!'

'I h-had to,' the girl stuttered. 'I was so shocked.'

She pointed across to an armchair where the substantial figure of a balding elderly man was slumped.

'I've never seen a dead body before.'

Chapter Four

Suzy appeared unfazed and reached for a light switch. As she did so, the crumpled figure in the armchair stirred blearily.

'Dead body, Kerry?'

The girl shuffled awkwardly and put down her glass. 'It was dark. I just thought . . . He looked dead. I'll go and help Max.' Seizing the excuse like a lifeline, she rushed out of the room.

Suzy's beautiful eyes narrowed. 'Little liar,' she murmured. 'Mind you, that was a new excuse.'

Then why do you keep her on? Jude was about to ask, but the man in the armchair had risen to his feet, embarrassed at having been caught – literally – napping. He swept his hand across his forehead as if to straighten the hair that was long gone.

'I'm so sorry, ladies. Arrived early. Must've nodded off.' His voice aspired to, but didn't quite achieve, a patrician bonhomie.

He was in his sixties, dressed in a striped three-piece suit of an earlier generation, and wore a tie with red, blue and white striations, which didn't quite manage to look regimental. The watch-chain bridging his waistcoat pockets established him as something of a poseur. In his lapel buttonhole gleamed the dull gold of a badge which neither woman recognized as the prized insignia of the Pillars of Sussex.

'I'm Suzy Longthorne. And this is Jude.'

Fastidiously, he took the hotelier's hand. Unlike most men she met, he didn't add that extra pressure that beautiful women learn to live with. 'Donald Chew. We spoke on the phone. I'm outgoing president.' He left a gap for an impressed reaction. Receiving none, he went on, 'And of course we have met here before, haven't we?'

Suzy smiled polite acknowledgment of this, though she didn't look as though their previous encounter had made much impression on her.

'Always know we'll be well looked after at Hopwicke House. Excellent food – ' he nodded across the hall ' – and of course your wonderful cellar.' He cleared his throat. 'Thought I'd come along a little early to check the arrangements. No one around, so I toddled through here and . . . just d-dozed off.'

The slight hesitation suggested he had got himself in training for the evening's dinner with a heavy lunch.

'I think you'll find everything is as we agreed, Mr Chew. The table isn't fully set yet, but we're just about to do it.'

'Fine. I wasn't really worried. Just felt I should check, you know . . . as outgoing president.'

'Of course. Well, we'll serve drinks to your members in here.'

A glint came into his eye. 'Is the bar actually open now?'

'The bar's open to residents at all times,' said Suzy, moving behind the counter. 'Could I get you something?'

'Large one of those wouldn't hurt.' He pointed to the bottle of Famous Grouse. 'With the same amount of tap water.' He guffawed meaninglessly. 'Start as I mean to continue, eh?'

'And then would you like to check into your room, Mr Chew?' asked Suzy, as she handed his drink across.

'No hurry. If you just let me have the key, I'll find my own way.'

'Of course.' She went to fetch it from the set of pigeonholes on the wall behind the reception desk. In the brief ensuing silence, Donald Chew made no attempt to say anything to Jude.

Suzy returned and handed him a key with a heavy brass fob. 'Would you excuse us, Mr Chew? I'll just finish the table settings and when they're done, I'll call you and you can check everything's all right.'

'Fine.' Slumping back into his armchair, he tapped his breast pocket. 'Got the seating plan in here. Very important. Can't have a New Pillar sitting nearer the president than an Ancient Pillar.'

Suzy Longthorne smiled acknowledgement of what a solecism that would be, and returned to the dining room, with Jude in tow. Donald Chew's voice followed them, 'And if I want another drink, I'll just shout.'

'Yes. Or ring the bell at reception.'

Once again Jude was struck by the dignity with

which her friend fulfilled her menial role. Even in her most high-flying days, Suzy had maintained a core of pragmatism. Though many men had spoiled her, she had never let herself be spoilt. Suzy was well-enough grounded to bear stoically whatever fortune might throw at her.

She looked at the unfinished table setting without overt annoyance, and started to align knives and forks from the cutlery tray. 'Could you ask Kerry to come and help?'

Jude nodded. 'And should I be getting into my kit?'

'Yes. Sorry.'

'It's all right.' Jude grinned. 'I always wanted a part in *Gosford Park*.'

As she approached the kitchen door, she could hear Kerry talking about her favourite subject.

'I mean my voice is definitely good enough, and I know I'm better-looking than most of the girl singers you see on *Top of the Pops*, but in television you've got to get that one lucky break.'

'Tell me about it,' Max was saying, as Jude entered the kitchen.

The relaxed way in which Kerry lolled at the table, chatting to the chef, confirmed what Jude had suspected, that the girl's talk of a dead body in the bar had been a spur of the moment fabrication, a cover-up for her brandy-sipping. According to her boss, Kerry, in spite of her age, had a propensity for sampling the goods in the bar; she had been ticked off more than once about it.

'Suzy wants some help in the dining room.'

Elaborately lethargic, the girl rose to her feet. She was wearing the uniform Jude was shortly to don, a long black dress with a white, lace-fringed apron. By the time the guests arrived, they would both be wearing white lacy mob-caps as well. Kerry's confidence about her looks was justified. She was a little below average height, but generously rounded, with that glow young women exude when they've finally put the awkwardness of adolescence behind them. Her naturally beautiful skin and blonde hair were enhanced respectively by skilful make-up and expensive cutting. Her manner implied a precocious sexuality, though Jude had no idea whether the image was backed up by actual experience. In her Edwardian black, Kerry looked good and knew it, Lolita in fancy dress.

Jude herself wasn't particularly keen on being kitted out like a refugee from *Upstairs, Downstairs* and a thousand other television series, but that was Suzy's house style, so she went along with it. The only advantage she could see, with an evening of drunken Pillars of Sussex ahead, was that none of them could put a hand up her skirt.

'All right. I'll go,' said Kerry, as if the most unreasonable request in the world had just been foisted on to her, and slouched out of the kitchen.

As the door swung back and forth in her wake, Jude caught the sardonic eye of Max Townley. 'Attitude problem?' she suggested.

'Whatever it is, Suzy's stuck with it.'

'Oh?'

'Don't you know who Kerry's Dad is?'

Jude shook her head.

'Well, stepfather, actually. Bob Hartson.'

'Doesn't mean anything to me.'

'Big local property developer. Often seen buzzing around in a chauffeur-driven Jaguar. You'll see him tonight. He's one of the bloody Pillocks of Sussex. And he's bailed Suzy out.'

'What?'

'She's had a bit of a cash crisis in the last six months.'

'I knew that, but I didn't know how serious it was.'

'Serious enough for her to look for an investor. Bob Hartson obliged. Which means that if he wants Suzy to teach his useless daughter the hotel trade – or if he wants her to do anything else for him – then that's what Suzy has to do.'

While Jude was taking in the implications of this, the chef changed tack. 'How long have you known Suzy?'

'Goodness . . . Thirty years? Nearly forty now, I suppose.'

'And did you know her through media connections?'

'It's so long ago that in those days the word "media" was hardly invented. But, yes, I suppose I met Suzy through the fashion world.'

'Did you work in television too?'

'A bit.'

'And are you still in touch with people from those times?'

'A few, yes. Friends like Suzy. Some others—'

'Because what I really wanted to ask you, Jude, was—'

But Max Townley never got to his question, because the door banged open to readmit a heavily sighing Kerry, suffering the unjust imposition of having to fetch more side plates.

As Suzy had anticipated, for drinks before dinner most of the Pillars of Sussex favoured pints of beer. At least, maybe some of them would have preferred something else, but drinking pints of beer before dinner was a necessary component of their masculine ritual.

So Suzy was kept busy behind the counter, pulling pints, and Jude was kept busy handing them round and taking orders, a system that avoided a crush at the small bar. Dinner was scheduled to start at eight, and at ten past Suzy asked Jude to warn Max she was about to usher the Pillars through to the dining room.

In the kitchen, Max and the spotty youth who gloried in the title of *sous-chef* were rushing around in a panic of preparation, while Kerry sat at the table pontificating on the merits of the current Top Twenty. In front of her, there was an open bottle of wine the chef had been using for cooking. As Jude came in, Kerry pushed it away, as though she hadn't just been taking a surreptitious sip.

'Are you set, Max? Suzy wants to send them through.'

'Bloody hell! Why doesn't she ever give me enough notice?'

'The dinner was meant to be at eight.'

'Yes, but . . . Kerry, have you put all the bloody starters out?'

'I *will*,' replied the girl, once again put-upon.

'They should already be bloody there!'

'I'll help,' said Jude, and passed Kerry a tray of stuffed field mushrooms from one of the heated cupboards.

Kerry rose complaining from her seat, but at that moment the door from the hall opened and she lost all interest in the dinner. 'Hello, Geoff. Is Dad here?' she asked excitedly.

The man who had entered without knocking did not wear a uniform, but his dark suit instantly spoke the word 'chauffeur'. He was short, thick-set and balding; his features sagged, as though they had melted in excessive heat.

Kerry's manner towards him was one of indifferent acceptance, treating him like some kind of fixture or fitting.

'Your Dad's just freshening up in his room. I'm wondering where I'm going for the night.' He nodded at Max Townley. 'I'm Geoff, Bob Hartson's driver.'

'And what do you think you're doing, just walking into my kitchen?'

'It's where the chauffeur always goes, in the kitchen,' the driver replied evenly. 'It's his proper place. While the boss eats the posh grub in the dining room.'

'Oh, shit!' said the chef gracelessly. 'I'm not meant to be feeding you too tonight, am I?'

34

'No, I don't want your ponced-up nosh. I'll go down the pub and get something with chips. Then I'll come back and play on my Gameboy, so if anyone can show me which room I'm in, I'll be fine.'

'Be in the stable block,' said Kerry. 'I'll show you.'

'Bloody stable block?' the driver objected. 'What's this? Staff quarters? I thought if I got to stay in this poncy gaffe, at least I'd get a decent room.'

'That's where Suzy's put you, Geoff. I suppose I could have a word and see if there's a room in the hotel where—'

'No,' Jude interposed firmly. 'Suzy's got quite enough on her plate. If that's the room she's allocated, then you'd better stick with it.'

The driver shrugged, unworried. His protest had only been for form's sake. Always worth trying, like asking for an upgrade on an aeroplane. Sometimes it actually worked.

Kerry took him out through the back door to the stable block.

At that moment, Suzy came in from the dining room. 'OK. We're off!'

Chapter Five

'I am Bob Hartson, a Pillar of medium height ...' a
ripple of knowing laughter greeted this sally. Kerry's
stepfather was a tall man with the muscle-bound body
of a retired wrestler. The corrugated face beneath his
corrugated grey hair was red and unvisited by
imagination.

'... and I would like to introduce to the Pillars of
Sussex my guest – Mr Nigel Ackford.'

His sponsor looked on indulgently, as the young
man at the far end of the table rose unsteadily to his
feet. His suit was perhaps a little too sharp and his tie a
little too pastel for the tastes of some of the guests, but
he said what protocol demanded of him.

'I am very honoured to be here, even at the pedi-
ment of the great Pillars.'

The formula was greeted by raucous laughter and
wild applause, disproportionate to any possible interest
or wit in what had just been said. Jude doggedly continued clearing the dessert dishes.

In the remains of one sherry trifle a cigarette butt
had been stubbed. Max wouldn't like that. It wasn't the
first thing of the evening Max wouldn't like. Normally,

he would have returned home by this time, and missed seeing the latest insult to his cuisine, but that evening he had tried to neutralize his anger by drinking vodka. The ploy hadn't worked – the alcohol seemed to make him even testier – but it had ensured he'd have to stay the night in one of the staff rooms. He might not have cared about the dangers to himself, but there was no way he was going to put his precious Ducati at risk from drunken driving.

Donald Chew, by now almost comatose with drink, smiled approvingly as the new president rose to his feet to reply to the young guest. James Baxter wore the heavy, over-elaborate chain which had, until recently, hung around Donald Chew's neck. Baxter had spent his life in local government, working mostly in the planning department, and was seeing out his last couple of years before retirement in a job where, in spite of a fine-sounding title, he could do little harm. His main professional duty now seemed to be lunching, and he took disproportionate pride in being president of the Pillars of Sussex. He cleared his throat portentously before his reply.

'Your words are pleasing to the highest Pillar of Sussex. Welcome, and may you enjoy our dinner.'

Since they'd already finished eating, this didn't seem to make sense, but Jude had, much earlier in the evening, realized logic played little part in the protocol of the Pillars of Sussex.

'And tell me, Mr Ackford,' the President rumbled on, 'a little of yourself . . . or of those details which you are willing to share with the Pillars of Sussex.'

This was greeted by another automatic ripple of hilarity. Not for the first time, Jude wished she understood the rituals of male laughter. Its triggers seemed to have nothing to do with the humour of what had just been said; there were just certain prompts which, in an all-male assembly, required an immediate responsive guffaw. How to recognize these prompts Jude had no idea; she reckoned she never would – having been born the wrong gender.

Trifle dishes balanced up her arm, a skill mastered in her late twenties when she'd run a cafe, Jude made her way back towards the kitchen. As she left, she heard Nigel Ackford begin to present his professional credentials to the assembled Pillars.

'After being educated at Portsmouth Grammar School, and studying law at Bristol University, I was articled to Renton and Chew in Worthing . . .' A rumble of appreciative recognition greeted the name. Donald Chew was his boss. The young man moved in the right circles. He was one of them. 'I qualified as a solicitor two years ago, and was fortunate enough to be kept on by Renton and Chew, working mostly at the moment on the conveyancing side, though I hope in time to expand my portfolio of skills to include . . .'

When Jude and Suzy returned to the dining room with the coffee, the rituals were over. Guests had been welcomed, a new member initiated, and a toast drunk to 'Pillars past, Pillars now standing, and Pillars yet to be erected.' The wording of this last invocation, innocently coined in the late nineteenth century, was followed by the obligatory sniggering guffaw that in such company greets any form of the word 'erect'.

This was the sound that met the two women as they entered. Then the rituals gave way to speeches. Expressionless, Suzy and Jude set out cups, saucers and coffee pots as, sycophantically and with a few limp jokes of his own, James Baxter introduced the evening's guest speaker, the president of a local rugby club, 'Who I've heard speak before and who I know will give us all a lot of good laughs. So, if any of my fellow Pillars suffer from weak ribs, be warned you're likely to crack a few!'

The guest speaker started with a reference to the wives and girlfriends marooned at home by the Pillars' dinner, and took this as a springboard for a sequence of quick-fire jokes about women, of a crudeness Jude found hard to credit. She caught Suzy's eye and received the unspoken message to grin and bear it.

Jude realized she and Suzy had become invisible. They were merely functionaries, fulfilling their task of serving coffee. The fact that they had identities, the fact that they were women, the fact that one of them was a great beauty of her generation and was now dressed in a stunningly expensive designer black dress, had no relevance at all.

The jokes continued, each cruder than the last, and the raucous responses to them fed the communal hatred and fear of women. As Jude and Suzy slipped, unnoticed back into the kitchen, the fumes of misogyny rising from the Pillars' table were almost visible.

*

The clearing-up took a long time, though fortunately the Pillars of Sussex did not keep very late hours. There had been much bold talk of 'staying in the bar all night', but their stamina did not match their bravado. Most of the men had had two or three pints before dinner, plenty of wine with the meal, and were pretty incoherent before they started on post-prandial Scotches, brandies, ports and further pints.

The drunkest of the lot was Nigel Ackford. Bob Hartson kept plying his guest with more drinks, and seemed to take pleasure in watching the young man's movements grow more random, and in hearing his speech become more slurred.

'Are you staying tonight, Bob?' Jude heard Nigel say at one point. 'Or are you being driven home?'

'No, I'm going to stay. Geoff's kipping down here too. He can drive me back in the morning.'

Nigel Ackford waved his glass. 'Time I bought you one, Bob.'

'No. This evening's my treat, and that means everything. Here, sexy Suzy, same again, please!'

Jude was once again impressed by Suzy's forbearance, as she watched her behind the bar, dispensing orders with efficiency and an automatic smile. Even Suzy's automatic smiles were beautiful.

None of the men noticed this. Though their conversation was still largely composed of jokes predicated on rampant lust, the presence of a real woman seemed not to impinge on their collective consciousness.

With Suzy cornered behind the bar, Jude found she was doing the initial stages of clearing the dining room on her own. Kerry, who should have been helping, was sitting with her adoring stepfather, Bob Hartson, who, apparently amused by her precocious relish for alcohol, kept plying the girl with drinks. At no stage did Suzy make any attempt to remind Kerry of her duties.

The atmosphere in the bar was raucous, and the conversation degenerated into ever more misogynistic jokes and playground insults. Only Donald Chew seemed marginalized from all the banter. He smiled and joined in the automatic guffaws which greeted every punchline, but looked aloof, not quite one of the boys, as he continued steadily to drink and unsteadily to sway. He was the first to say he was off to find his bed.

'Ooh, sweetie!' someone shrieked after him in a mock-camp voice. 'Hope you find someone nice in there waiting for you!'

And the Pillars of Sussex roared their obligatory laughter.

'Spoilsport!' shouted someone else, as the retiring president left the bar. 'The rest of us have only just *started* drinking!'

Again the Pillars guffawed.

But, in spite of bold protestations about staying up all night, Donald Chew's departure served as a signal to the others. Jude got the impression the Pillars were not drinking on out of enjoyment, but simply as some kind of endurance test. Now one of their number had given in, it was all right for the others to do the same. Within twenty minutes, the bar was empty. The clock showed a quarter to one.

Kerry had somehow contrived to vanish too. When Jude mentioned this, and the fact that the girl should be helping with the clearing up, Suzy just grimaced and said, 'It won't take us long.'

But it did. The hotelier's high standards would not allow any detail to be left till the morning. So the two of them worked dourly on. The only interruption came when Suzy's mobile phone rang. She answered it. 'Hello. Oh, are you? See you then.'

She said no more, and offered no explanation for the call or the lateness of the hour at which it had been made. It was not in Jude's nature to ask for such information, but she noticed there seemed to be a new tension and impatience in the way Suzy continued with the tidying up.

It was nearly half-past two by the time they collapsed in the kitchen.

Suzy moved to one of the fridges and took out an open bottle of Chardonnay. She filled two glasses and raised hers to Jude. 'First of the day,' she said. 'And last of the day. It's the only time I have a drink. Just one glass. I usually feel I've earned it.'

'You certainly have tonight.'

'Yes.' Suzy sighed. The tracery of lines between her eyebrows bunched together.

'What is it?' asked Jude, returning to their conversation of earlier in the evening. 'Money?'

'Oh, there's always money – when I can't think of anything else to worry about.'

'And can't you think of anything else to worry about at this precise moment?'

42

But Suzy wasn't going to be drawn. She grinned bleakly. 'Things will get better. Or they won't. Either way, life will continue . . . at some level.'

Recognizing a barrier to a subject when she heard one, Jude moved on. 'That note Kerry found . . .'

'Oh yes?'

'Which bedroom was it in?'

'I didn't ask her. I'll ask in the morning.'

'Where is she? Asleep in her staff room?'

'Presumably. Have you put your overnight stuff in the stable block yet?'

'Haven't had time.'

Suzy looked across at the rack, from which only one key still hung. 'Well, just be careful you don't walk into the wrong room.' She gave Jude a tired grin. 'Otherwise Max or Bob Hartson's chauffeur will think Christmas and their birthday's come on the same day.'

Jude grinned too. 'I'll be careful.' But there was something she couldn't let go. 'Suzy, do you mind if I have another look at the note Kerry found? Just rather intrigues me.'

'Look away.' The hotelier rose wearily to her feet and crossed to the row of hooks from which a range of overalls and aprons hung.

She reached her hand into the pocket of the blue-and-white-striped one. A shadow crossed her face.

'It's not there.'

Chapter Six

Suzy Longthorne lived in a barn conversion behind the hotel, and the staff quarters were in a converted stable block. The rooms were functional rather than luxurious, but each had its own walk-in shower and tea-making facilities.

Because her friend looked so suddenly exhausted and keen to leave, Jude said she'd lock up. She'd stood in at the Hopwicke Country House Hotel often enough to know the routine. The internal fire doors had to be checked and then the external doors locked. There was an alarm system, but it had been triggered so often by insomniac guests it was very rarely activated. If any of the residents should require anything during the night, bells rang in Suzy's barn and the staff quarters. They were rarely sounded; it was made clear to the guests on arrival that they were staying in a country house hotel; what was being mimicked was the genteel life of the upper classes, rather than the corporate luxury of twenty-four hour room service.

As she climbed the stairs to check that the fire doors were closed, Jude was struck by how quickly the raucous camaraderie of the Pillars of Sussex had been switched off. From some rooms snores rumbled; no doubt later in the night, as ageing bladders protested against the many pints that had been poured into them, toilets would flush. But at two-thirty in the morning the overall impression was of silence.

She was on the top landing when she heard the noise. It sounded like a gurgling at first, but after a few moments she identified it as singing. Not particularly sophisticated – or indeed varied – singing. Just one little nursery rhyme phrase endlessly repeated, circling round and round.

The sound came from behind one of the fire doors. These were a legal requirement, but took no account of the architectural values. Though designed as sympathetically as possible, they still spoiled the proportions of the elegant top-floor landing.

Jude opened the fire door to reveal the source of the singing. Nigel Ackford, still in his sharp suit, was propped up, his body slack as if boneless, against the wall of the corridor. There was a silly smile on his mouth, out of which the strange, circular song still dribbled.

Jude tried to wake him up, but he was too far gone to respond properly. He was aware she was there, and tried to focus his grin on her, but the effort was too much. He was amiably, rather than aggressively, drunk, and made no objection to her rummaging in his suit pockets. Jude quickly found his key. Its number matched the room outside which he had collapsed, so he had only just failed to make it all the way to bed.

She unlocked the bedroom door, lifted the young

man with difficulty, and manoeuvred him inside. His limbs were slack and powerless, and there seemed to be a disproportionate number of them; Jude's mind formed the image of handling a drugged octopus.

Nigel Ackford had been given one of the best rooms in the hotel, presumably at the expense of his sponsor, Bob Hartson, who, from what Max Townley had said about him, could well afford such extravagance. The room was dominated by a high four-poster bed, with heavy brocade curtains gathered around the uprights by silken ropes. The windows were covered with the same brocade, and when the curtains were drawn back in daylight, they would reveal a perfect view down to the English Channel. As she manhandled the comatose guest onto the bed, Jude reflected that, when he woke up the next morning, he wouldn't be in much of a state to appreciate the vista.

She decided to take some of his clothes off, so he wouldn't have a creased suit to add to the embarrassment of meeting the Pillars at breakfast. Though his body was unresisting, she had difficultly extracting his limbs from the jacket. Once she'd removed his shoes, the trousers slipped off more easily. The pastel tie came off too, and she undid the top couple of buttons of his shirt, in case he twisted in the night and constricted his throat.

Jude put the suit on a hanger in the heavy dark-oak wardrobe, then turned to look at the figure on the bed. In his rumpled shirt, striped boxer shorts and socks, there was something boyish about Nigel Ackford. Despite the heavy late-night shadow on his chin, and the dark hair on his legs, the posture of his body suggested a five-year-old crumpled in sleep.

She decided he'd be more comfortable under the covers and managed to extricate the duvet and quilted bedspread from under the deadweight of his body, and flip them over him. Surprisingly, this, the gentlest of the manipulations he had undergone during the previous ten minutes, woke Nigel Ackford.

He looked around in benign confusion, and took a moment or two to register Jude's presence. His confusion intensified.

'It's all right,' she said, remembering her strange garb. 'You're not in some dream of being tended by an Edwardian nanny. You're in your room at the Hopwicke Country House Hotel. I'm Jude. I've just helped you get into bed.'

'Ah.' Nigel Ackford giggled, reinforcing his childlike image. 'I'm sorry I needed helping.'

Jude let out a non-judgmental 'Well . . .'

'No, really sorry. I found the evening rather a strain. Very important to make the right impression with the P-Pillars of Sussex.'

'They seemed quite impressed with you.'

'Yes.' He smiled beatifically. 'Yes, I think I did all right.' His smile grew broader. 'Bob Hartson said he thought he might be able to put me up for membership soon.'

'To become a full Pillar?'

As soon as she had said the words, Jude realized how ridiculous they sounded, but Nigel Ackford was unaware of any incongruity.

'Oh yes, that'd be good. I'm quite young to be a Pillar of Sussex.'

Jude nodded, because that seemed to be the appropriate thing to do. The young man's eyes gyrated in their sockets, and his lids flickered. He would soon be asleep.

But he overcame drowsiness for another mumbled communication. 'Going to be a good year, this one. All my troubles are over. All sorted out. I've made up my mind which way I'm going. This is going to be a good year.' His head nuzzled luxuriantly back into the soft pillow. 'I'm going to ask Wendy to marry me. And I'm pretty confident she'll say yes . . .'

He was asleep. Jude left the room quietly, but she needn't have bothered. Nigel Ackford was so deeply under nothing would wake him until, presumably, the crushing agony of the morning's hangover.

Jude was used to the routine of the staff quarters. She took the remaining key from its rack and went out into the deep blue calm of the April night. In the last light before she locked the kitchen door, she saw from her watch that it was nearly three o'clock.

There was no bulb in the hall light of the stable block, so Jude couldn't see the number on her key tag. With an internal grin, she remembered Suzy's warning about not gatecrashing the dreams of the chef or the chauffeur, but if she didn't take the risk, she wouldn't have anywhere to sleep. So she pushed against the nearest bedroom door, which gave easily.

It was the wrong room, but not as embarrassingly

wrong as it could have been. A small bedside light had been left on to reveal the usual chaos left by a teenage girl. Distinctive T-shirts thrown down on the unmade bed left no doubt as to the occupant's identity. But of Kerry herself there was no sign. The room was empty.

The next door was locked. Jude's key fitted, so no worries about chefs or chauffeurs. She let herself in. Suddenly aware of how tired she felt, she had only the most perfunctory of washes and fell into bed. The alarm was set for seven, so that she'd be back on duty to serve breakfasts to the Pillars of Sussex. She wondered, after the excesses of the night before, how many of them would feel ready to face the full English. Most, she reckoned, as she fell instantly into sleep.

Chapter Seven

Suzy, sensible as ever, recognized that Edwardian nanny costumes would look incongruous at eight o'clock in the morning, so the staff's daytime uniforms were neat blue suits. Jude always found at least two in the uniform cupboard which fitted her, suggesting that a lot of the hotel's staff were mature matronly women.

As she had surmised, almost all the Pillars of Sussex went for the full English breakfast option. One or two looked a little sweaty and greenish about the gills, but they managed to keep up a diluted version of the night-before's banter. The misogyny certainly remained. There were many shouted exchanges along the lines of 'Don't get sausages this big at home!'

'That's what your wife was saying to me only the other day!'

And each such sally would be rewarded by its statutory guffaw.

Because the Pillars came down to breakfast in dribs and drabs, and because Suzy was busy at reception collating their bills, it was a while before any kind of head-count could be done. And since eating breakfast was not mandatory, guests who chose to could stay in their rooms until the ten-thirty check-out time.

So it wasn't until then that the absence of three of the previous night's diners was observed. Jude checked the names against a printout of the guest list, which showed who had been allocated which room. Two gaps were quickly explained. Donald Chew, for reasons of his own, had gone early. He'd demanded his bill at seven-thirty, and left before breakfast. Next, after a couple of slices of toast and a cup of coffee on the dot of eight, Bob Hartson had been driven away by his chauffeur.

But no one had seen Bob Hartson's guest, Nigel Ackford.

Having witnessed the state of the young man the night before, Jude wasn't surprised. Either he was still sleeping it off, or he was simply immobilized by his hangover. Stupid boy, she thought as she climbed up towards the top floor. She wasn't judgmental about people who over-indulged; she just reckoned they made life unnecessarily difficult for themselves. Jude drank a lot of white wine, but she very rarely got drunk. In spite of her laid-back manner, there was within her a steely core of discipline. Perhaps it was recognizing the same quality in Suzy that had kept the two of them friends.

She climbed up the hotel stairs, pushing the folded guest list into the pocket of her blue suit. On the top landing, she took out a pass-key, and opened the door of Nigel's room Inside it was still pitch dark. As the sprung door clicked shut behind her, the brocade curtains squeezed out every glimmer of daylight.

'Time to get up, I'm afraid, Mr Ackford.' She crossed to the curtains and grasped the pull-string. 'Shield your eyes, because I'm about to let the day in.'

Jude pulled the curtains wide, and turned back to face the bed.

Nigel Ackford had not shielded his eyes. They stared, prominent in their sockets, their whites discoloured with specks of red. His face was congested to the colour of claret. His body hung still, sock-clad feet dangling over the edge of the bed. Around his neck, suspending him from the end crossbar of the four-poster, was one of the silken ropes that had tied back the curtains.

Nigel Ackford had been spared his hangover.

Chapter Eight

Carole couldn't believe how relieved she was to see Jude on her doorstep the following afternoon. She hadn't slept well. The news from Stephen had upset her, and the fact that it upset her, upset her more. She should have been ecstatic. The announcement of a son having found the woman with whom he wishes to spend the rest of his life is something for which every mother should be waiting. There was potential for a new generation and all kinds of old-fashioned things, like hope. Joy should be unconfined.

And yet joy was not Carole's predominant emotion; it was confusion, closely followed by guilt. This defining moment in family life had left her examining the shortcomings of that family life, had highlighted the failure of her marriage, and had reminded her of her lack of maternal instinct. She needed to talk to Jude about it. Jude was sympathetic. Jude was a constructive listener.

But that particular afternoon Jude was not in a listening mood. Her priority was the news she had to impart. And when she had imparted it, Carole realized her neighbour was shaky, perhaps even in shock.

Jude's customary serenity was so ingrained that Carole was surprised to see her in this state. She quickly supplied them both with glasses of white wine and sat Jude in an armchair in the sitting room. To avoid delay, she even resisted her instinct to put out a little table beside the chair for her friend's wine glass.

'Presumably you've talked to the police?'

'Yes, they sent me home. There weren't any cabs available, I had to get two buses. That's why it's taken me so long.'

'You should have called me from your mobile. I'd have picked you up.'

'Sorry, I didn't think.' Unwontedly twitchy, Jude looked out of the window into Fethering High Street. 'The police said they'd be round later to talk more. Suzy wanted the minimum of fuss at the hotel.'

'One can understand that she would.' Carole couldn't quite keep disapproval out of her voice when Suzy Longthorne's name came up. They'd never met, but the former model's public image predisposed Carole against her. Being splashed over papers and magazines, having high-profile lovers, building a career simply from being pretty . . . all of it offended Carole Seddon's Calvinist work ethic. Deep down, there was also the natural, inescapable resentment of a plain woman towards a beautiful one.

Feeling guilty for her disapproval – everything was making her feel guilty that day – she compensated with solicitude. 'You must be feeling terrible – awful for you to have actually found the body.'

Jude nodded. 'It was nasty. Particularly as I'd talked to the boy only a few hours earlier.'

'And he hadn't sounded suicidal then?'

'Far from it.'

Carole grimaced wryly. 'Who can tell what goes on inside another person's mind?'

Jude felt confident she quite often could tell, but all she said was, 'True.'

'Was there a suicide note?'

'Apparently. Well, not necessarily a suicide note, but some document which made the police pretty certain it was suicide. I didn't see it. As soon as I found the body, I rushed straight down to tell Suzy. She went up to the room to check it was locked, and then called the police. Apparently they found a letter in the bedroom – under the pillow, I think.'

'And did they immediately question all the guests?'

'They had all gone by then. Had breakfast, checked out by ten-thirty.'

'Who were they again? You did tell me.'

'The Pillars of Sussex.'

Carole made a face. 'Oh yes, I have heard of them. Some kind of back-scratching organization for local businessmen, isn't it?'

'That's right.'

'And this poor young . . . you know, the one who died . . . was he a member?'

'A guest. But he seemed quite excited at the prospect of becoming a member.'

'Hm. Lucky for your friend Suzy' – Carole was incapable of saying the name without the preface of 'your friend' – 'that all the guests had gone before the news broke.'

'I suppose so.'

'Well, it's the kind of thing you'd want to keep as quiet as possible. You're hardly going to advertise a suicide in the hotel brochure, are you?'

'No.' Jude was preoccupied, still uncharacteristically subdued. Her mind was full.

'Though there's no way it won't get out soon enough,' Carole went on. 'People gossip. The hotel staff are bound to talk.'

'I don't know that they will. Suzy commands a lot of respect. So if she asks them not to tell . . .'

'I doubt if even Suzy Longthorne's fabled charms could stop this getting out.' The resentment was back in Carole's voice.

'No. Probably not.'

'Did the police speak to the staff?'

'Yes. A quick word with each of us individually; then they'll follow up.'

'Have they closed the hotel down?'

'I'm not sure what's happening. There aren't any bookings for the next couple of nights. Some at the weekend – a wedding reception and quite a lot of people staying over. By then I would imagine they'd have completed any investigations they're going to make.'

'Hm. Well, that's very sad. Horrible shock for you . . . and a terrible waste of a young life.' Carole reckoned she had shown an adequate amount of sympathy, and could move the conversation on. 'I actually had some rather surprising news. From Stephen, my—'

But she got no further. Jude was on her feet, looking out of the window. A car was parking outside Woodside Cottage.

'It's the police. I'd better go and let them in.'

Carole's face set in an expression of frustration.

There was an apologetic fastidiousness about Detective Inspector Goodchild, as if he would rather have been doing any job other than his own, and actually regretted the necessity of dealing with criminal matters. He was tall, and his pale grey pin-striped suit reinforced his image of pained decency. His sidekick, Detective Sergeant Fallon, was either awestruck by the presence of his senior or silent by nature. Beyond a 'Hello again' on arrival, he didn't speak during the interview.

'Once more, I'm very sorry to have to take you through all this, Miss—'

'Jude, Inspector. Everyone calls me Jude.'

'Right. Well, Jude, I'm aware you've had an unpleasant experience, so I will try not to dwell on it, but there are of course certain details . . .'

'I understand.'

'In any case of an unnatural death – particularly a suicide, we—'

'Are you sure it is a suicide?'

The Inspector smiled indulgently. 'Jude, I know you expressed doubts back at the hotel, and I can assure you we will be investigating every angle. The verdict of the cause of death will have to wait for the inquest.'

'When's that likely to be?'

'Within the week. The preliminary inquest, anyway.'

Jude was alerted by the adjective. 'Oh?'

Patiently, Inspector Goodchild explained. 'It's entirely possible we won't have gathered all our evidence together by then. The coroner may well adjourn the inquest to give us time.'

'And that's when you'll get your suicide verdict?'

He smiled the smile of someone accustomed to recalcitrant and emotional witnesses. 'Jude, I'm sorry. I simply used the word "suicide" for convenience. It looks like a suicide, but I suppose, until the coroner's verdict, I should really be saying "*apparent* suicide". Would you be happy if I referred to the unfortunate incident as "the death"?'

'I don't mind what you call it, so long as you haven't made up your minds about what happened.'

'Of course not. That would be very unprofessional for people in our job.' This made her feel even more patronized. 'Now, I think we've got the details of how you discovered Mr Ackford's body this morning – though, if any other recollections come to you, we would be most grateful to hear them.'

He reached into the inside pocket of his smart suit for a card. 'While I think of it, this has got my numbers on it. The mobile, the office . . . I'm based in Worthing, so if there's anything you wish to communicate, don't hesitate . . .' She took the card, while the Inspector went on, 'I'd like to talk, Jude, if I may, about the conversation you had with the deceased in the early hours of this morning.'

'Yes.'

'You say Mr Ackford was very drunk.'

'Extremely. They'd all drunk a lot right through the evening.'

'Ah yes.' Detective Inspector Goodchild smiled fondly. 'Always enjoy their drink, the Pillars of Sussex.'

Something in his manner alerted Jude. He seemed to know all about the association. Was it even possible he was a member? Had someone from the group already been in touch? Had someone pointed out how awkward it might be for the Pillars of Sussex to be contaminated by the merest whiff of scandal? They had a lot of local influence, which might easily reach up to the highest echelons of the West Sussex Constabulary.

But she didn't vocalize her suspicion. 'Nigel Ackford was singing. He wasn't a maudlin drunk, not self-pitying and self-hating. He was cheerful.'

'So you're saying that's a reason why he was unlikely to have killed himself?'

'Possibly, yes. He seemed far from suicidal when he talked to me. His mood must have changed pretty violently in a few hours.'

'People's moods do, Jude. I don't know if you're familiar with the symptoms of depression?'

The condescending tone made her want to snap back, but she curbed the instinct. 'I *am* familiar with the symptoms of depression. I have done some work as a healer and alternative therapist.'

'Ah.' It could have been Carole responding. She would have put exactly the same mixture of disbelief and contempt into the monosyllable. 'We did find anti-depressants in the dead man's sponge bag, Jude.'

She hadn't expected that, but didn't allow the information to put her off track. 'Nonetheless, I still don't think Nigel Ackford was suicidal the last time I saw him. He was full of hope. He reckoned he was a shoo-in to join the Pillars of Sussex, and he seemed very excited about that.'

' "Excited" is a good word, Jude, in the circumstances. Manic depressives are subject to violent mood-swings. Not to mention a loose grasp on reality. And if Nigel Ackford seriously thought someone of his age had any chance of becoming a Pillar . . .' Goodchild let out a dismissive grunt. 'I'm no psychologist,' he admitted generously, though still implying that he put such experts in the same category as alternative thera-pists. 'No, I'm not, but from everything I've heard about Nigel Ackford – just in the very brief time that I've even known of his existence – he seemed to display all the symptoms of bi-polar disorder.'

'Well . . .'

'Up when you saw him at two-thirty this morning,' the Inspector persisted, 'and down when he woke up with a crippling hangover some few hours later.'

'But you don't know—'

'Jude, Mr Ackford had a history of mental illness. He broke down at university. Last year he had three months off from his employers, Renton and Chew. He also—'

'Inspector, he was going to get married. He was about to propose to his girlfriend.'

This did stop him in his tracks. 'Might that girlfriend's name be Wendy?' he asked.

'Yes.'

He nodded, and exchanged a look with the impassive Detective Sergeant Fallon. 'We've just come from talking to Miss Wendy Fullerton.'

'And she's Nigel Ackford's girlfriend?'

Jude's enthusiasm was quickly dashed. 'She *was* Nigel Ackford's girlfriend.'

'Well, I know. Obviously he's dead and—'

'She was Nigel Ackford's girlfriend until four months ago. Then she broke off the relationship.'

'Oh. But if he'd asked her to marry him, she might have felt—'

'If he'd asked her to marry him, I got the impression Mr Ackford would have received a very dusty answer. Wasn't that the impression you got, Fallon?'

The Detective Sergeant nodded.

'So,' the Inspector continued, 'while the *thought* of proposing to the young lady might have buoyed Mr Ackford up when he was drunk, he would still have woken up to the reality that she had in fact – not to put too fine a point on it – dumped him. Which,' he concluded with satisfaction, 'is exactly the sort of thing that might make any man contemplate topping himself.'

'But, I still think—'

'Jude!' Inspector Goodchild's veneer of urbane fastidiousness was wearing thin. 'We found a letter.'

'Yes, I heard about that. What did the letter say?'

'I am not at liberty to reveal the contents.'

'Was it handwritten?'

'There is a tradition,' Inspector Goodchild said coldly, 'that in situations like this, the police ask the questions, and we—'

Jude interrupted as a sudden, welcome recollection came to her. 'But of course there was another letter! The note that was found in one of the bedrooms.'

'I'm sorry?'

'There was a note, a threatening note.' Jude's words tumbled over each other in her excitement. 'Printed on Hopwicke House headed paper. Suzy showed it to me. Kerry had found it in one of the bedrooms. It said: "Enjoy this day. You won't see another one" – something like that.'

The Inspector looked sceptical. 'Rather strange, wouldn't you say, that Miss Longthorne didn't mention this *note* to me?'

'She must have forgotten. In the shock of everything that was happening.'

'We did ask Miss Longthorne more than once whether anything unusual had happened yesterday, either before or after her guests arrived.'

'It must have slipped her—'

'We put the same question to the young lady, Kerry.'

'And she didn't remember finding the note in the bedroom?'

'She didn't mention it, no.'

'But there was a note. I swear there was.'

'Right, right.' Inspector Goodchild nodded slowly. 'I'm not disbelieving you, Jude. I should think you're probably right. Miss Longthorne forgot about it in the excitement of the moment.'

'And I'm sure, if you asked her specifically about the note she showed me . . .'

'Just what I was about to do.' He produced a mobile phone from his pocket and, as he keyed in a number, said, 'Wonderfully neat little gadgets, these, aren't they? Makes you wonder how we ever managed without them. They've made such a difference to—' He raised a hand, indicating that he had got through. 'Miss Longthorne? It's Detective Inspector Goodchild. Sorry to be back to you so soon, but there is a detail I need to check. Thank you. Very kind.'

He looked around the clutter of Woodside Cottage as he listened to Suzy, but Jude could not hear what her friend was saying. Then Goodchild spoke again. 'I've just been talking to your friend Jude, and she was telling me about this note that was found in one of the bedrooms yesterday. Found by the girl, Kerry, apparently? The contents were of a threatening nature, I gather. Ah, thank you. Thank you very much. I'm afraid I probably will have to be in touch again, but only on minor details. It shouldn't take long. Thank you. And I hope you manage to get a good night's sleep tonight. Goodbye.'

He ended the call and smiled. She didn't need him to spell it out, but he did.

'I'm sorry, Jude. I'm afraid your friend Suzy Long-thorne doesn't have any recollection of ever seeing the note you described.'

Chapter Nine

'I just do not believe that that boy committed suicide,' said Jude, as they approached the Crown and Anchor.

'If he had a history of depression . . .' Carole argued.

'He may well have had a history of depression, but I saw him that night. He wasn't depressed then. He was just drunk.'

'Drink is a notorious depressant,' said Carole primly.

'But he wasn't drunk and depressed. He was drunk and incapable. He couldn't have organized a suicide, he could hardly stand.'

'Then maybe it happened by accident.'

'You do not remove a curtain rope, tie it to a crossbeam and put it round your neck by accident.' Jude pushed open the clattering doors of the pub.

Carole followed her in, surprised to see so much anger. She was the uptight one; Jude always seemed to emanate an almost unnatural laid-back calm. But the interview with Detective Inspector Goodchild had clearly got to her.

'Well, there's a sight to brighten up a dull evening. Two large Chardonnays if ever I saw them.'

Ted Crisp stood in his usual position behind the bar. His beard and hair showed their customary ignorance of grooming. The sweatshirt he wore was so faded that its original colour could have been black, blue or green; the advertising logo it had once shown off was now an incomprehensible blur. The idea that she had had an affair with him – however brief – still seemed incongruous to Carole. But not distasteful. She was glad their relationship had now settled down to a kind of joshing affection.

He was pouring the drinks before they ordered them. There was some comfort in that, thought Carole. Though she still didn't think of herself as a 'pub person', it was good to have a haven where one was known and recognized.

'How're you, Ted?' she asked.

'Mustn't grumble. Doesn't stop me, though. Guess what this is an impression of.' Suddenly he turned a full three hundred and sixty degrees behind the bar.

'No idea.'

'A counter-revolutionary.'

They gave the joke the groan it deserved. In a previous incarnation, Ted Crisp had been a stand-up comedian. If the one he'd just cracked was representative of his jokes, it was no wonder he'd sought alternative employment.

'So you two got any news, have you?'

'Well . . .' Carole scoured her memory, without much optimism that she'd find anything interesting. Then she suddenly remembered. 'Actually, my son's getting married.'

'Fancy,' said Ted.

'You didn't tell me that,' said Jude.

'I've hardly had a chance to get a word in.'

'True. Sorry.'

'I keep forgetting you got a son.' Ted scratched his chin through the thatch of beard. 'Forget you'd been married, and all. Still, we divorcees have to stick together, don't we?'

Carole didn't like that. Her marriage was a private failure. She didn't want it to be lumped together with all the other broken relationships.

'What's your potential daughter-in-law like?' asked Jude.

'I haven't met her yet.'

'But you must have got an impression from what Stephen said.'

Carole had. Her son had engendered an impression of someone she wouldn't get on with. Someone whose agency had had a financial package set up for it, who had rich parents who were possibly not even British. Someone who had the rather affected name of Gaby. Of course she didn't say any of that. She knew it was just prejudice. But then Carole, like most middle-class English people, had ingested prejudice with her mother's milk.

'Not really. Her name's Gaby.'

She tried to keep disapproval out of her voice, which was just as well, because Jude said, 'Gaby. That's a nice name.'

'She'll probably talk your head off.' In response to

curious looks, Ted explained, 'Gaby by name, gabby by nature.'

Yes, it was a blessing for everyone, really, that he'd not continued with the stand-up.

'Anyway, I'm going to meet her soon,' said Carole, with what she hoped sounded like enthusiasm. 'Weekend after this.'

'It's very exciting,' said Jude. 'The prospect of grandchildren.'

That was the consequence of the marriage about which Carole hadn't allowed herself to think. In spite of Stephen's talking about buying a large family house, she had not followed the logic through. Grandchildren – they would provide another opportunity for her maternal skills to be found wanting. It was all daunting – and very confusing.

She was relieved that when they'd sat down, having ordered Ted Crisp's recommendation of Dover sole, the conversation reverted to the events at Hopwicke House. A suspicious death was always so much more interesting than wedding plans.

'I've a feeling there's a kind of cover-up,' said Jude.'

'Aren't you being a bit melodramatic?'

'I got the firm impression from Detective Inspector Goodchild that he'd be very happy with a suicide verdict.'

'From what you say, the death did look like suicide. And presumably the police like things nice and straightforward.'

'Yes, but I got the feeling there was more to it. As if Detective Inspector Goodchild had been talked to by someone . . . and that someone didn't want the investigation to go any further.'

'What makes you say that? Do you have any evidence?'

'No.' The idea was quickly dismissed. Jude had always placed more reliance on instinct than evidence. 'Those Pillars of Sussex are an incestuous lot. All scratching each other's backs. They've got a lot of influence locally. If they wanted something kept quiet, I'm sure they could arrange it.'

Carole went into wet-blanket mode, a position that came distressingly easily to her. 'Jude, you don't know any of the people involved. You only met them last night – and that was hardly *meeting* in any meaningful sense. You may not have liked the Pillars of Sussex setup – I don't like secretive all-male associations either – but that doesn't mean they're in a conspiracy to pervert the course of justice.'

'No, I agree. But there's one person I do know up at the hotel, and she's behaving totally out of character.'

'Your friend Suzy?' This was said with the inevitable flicker of disapprobation.

'Yes. She denied having seen that threatening note. I know she saw it – she showed it to me. So somebody's been putting pressure on Suzy. And I want to know who.'

Although she was not convinced by them, Jude's suspicions had at least kept Carole's mind off thoughts of her son and his fiancée. But it couldn't last. When she got back to High Tor from the Crown and Anchor, there was a message on the answering machine.

'Hello, Mother. It's Stephen. Just a few details about the weekend after next, when we're going to be in Sussex. We want a good base for looking at property, and we wouldn't dream of landing on you, so we wondered if you'd check out a place Gaby's heard about near Worthing called Hopwicke Country House Hotel. Could you just look at it, see if it'd be all right for us? Could you confirm you've got this message? Thank you.'

Carole's first thought was: there's a coincidence.

Her second was: what does he think I am? 'Could you just look at it, see if it'd be all right for us?' Yes, sir, of course, sir, three bags full, sir.

And her third was: At least I don't have to worry about sleeping arrangements here at High Tor.

Because she was Carole Seddon, the relief from the third thought brought her more comfort than the second thought had brought her discomfort.

Chapter Ten

'Listen, Jude, if there's one subject I know about, it's publicity. Good and bad.'

It was true. Suzy Longthorne had suffered the attentions of the press pack ever since she was in her teens. She had been flattered by them, fawned on, extravagantly praised, worshipped even. Then she had been criticized, carped at, pilloried, vilified. She, of all people, knew how quickly a media darling could become the target for all the mud that could be slung. And she knew how irrelevant the actual behaviour of a celebrity was to the press's treatment of it. Suddenly, on a whim, they could turn against you, at the flick of a switch converting every positive to a negative.

'I've put a lot of time and money into building up Hopwicke House,' she went on at the other end of the phone. 'I'm not about to throw all that away because of a burst of bad publicity.'

'What are you saying?'

'I'm saying that a suicide at the hotel is about the worst thing that can happen. But it's containable. The poor young man's family won't want it blazoned all over the papers. The Pillars of Sussex certainly won't want that either. And the police, for once, seem quite inclined to be discreet. OK, there may be some publicity when the inquest happens, but hopefully that can be kept to the minimum too.'

'So you're saying "Don't rock the boat".'

'Exactly.'

'You can't deny you saw that note.'

'I can't deny it to you, Jude, no, because you saw it too. But I can sure as hell deny it to the police . . . or anyone else who asks.'

'That's lying, Suzy.'

'So? For God's sake, Jude, don't come on to me like some sort of moral guardian. There are worse things in the world than lying. I happen to think that a murder enquiry at Hopwicke House would be one of them.'

Jude seized on that. 'So you think it was murder too?'

'I don't think anything,' her friend replied wearily. 'I think what happened yesterday morning was another piece of incredibly bad luck, and I don't know how many more of them I and this business can survive. I will do anything to keep the wrong kind of publicity for Hopwicke House down to a minimum. If that involves a little lying . . . then so be it.'

'But don't you want to know the truth about what happened?'

'No, Jude, I really don't.'

It was true. Suzy wanted to protect her business and her reputation. Not everyone, Jude reflected wryly, was like her, desperate to get to the bottom of every mystery that life offered.

'Listen,' the voice on the phone went on, 'over the years I've had enough prying into my private life. I don't want to put at risk—'

'This is hardly prying into your private life.'

Suzy sounded thrown by this, as if she were covering up. 'No, I . . . well, I didn't mean—'

'You had nothing to do with Nigel Ackford.'

'Try telling that to a tabloid journalist. They'll have fabricated an affair between us within seconds. And no doubt, along with that, the implication that I murdered him when he tried to break it off. In a fit of jealous rage. I can see the headlines now. "Fading sixties beauty Suzy Longthorne . . ." '

'Are you telling me you will never admit to the existence of the threatening note Kerry found?'

'Yes, Jude. That is exactly what I'm telling you.'

After she had put the phone down, Jude felt troubled. Not because she feared the disagreement might end her friendship with Suzy – Jude was not prone to flouncing – she knew they'd stay in touch. What had troubled her, were Suzy's words about prying into her private life. The guard had dropped then; she had sounded vulnerable, ill at ease. Almost guilty. As if concern for her business was not the only reason why she wished to minimize the level of investigation into Nigel Ackford's death.

The local phonebook had proved surprisingly helpful. There was only one 'Fullerton, W.' and the address was in Shoreham, a few miles along the coast from Fethering.

'Is that Wendy Fullerton?'

'Yes.'

'You don't know me. My name's Jude.'

'Oh?'

'I'm calling in connection with Nigel Ackford.'

This news prompted an entirely different 'Oh'. A metal shutter had come down.

Jude rushed ahead before she could be cut off. 'I was working at Hopwicke Country House Hotel that night. I think I was probably the last person to see Nigel Ackford alive.'

'I'm not interested in—'

'He said something about you.'

'He said something about me?'

Jude had the girl's attention now. 'I wonder if it would be possible for us to meet?'

Wendy Fullerton's consent was grudging, but, intrigued in spite of herself, she did want to know about her former boyfriend's final hours. She worked for a building society in Worthing. She could nip out for a coffee the following afternoon. Three o'clock. Only for a quarter of an hour, mind. She was keeping her escape routes covered.

'It's good I've got an excuse to go up to Hopwicke House, to check it out for Stephen.'

'Yes.' Jude agreed distractedly.

'So maybe I could do some follow-up investigating?' Carole suggested.

'I'll tell you for free, you won't get anything out of Suzy.'

'Another member of staff might be more forthcoming.'

'If you see another member of staff. The one I
really need to talk to is Kerry.'

'What's all this "I", Jude? I thought we worked
together.'

'Yes. Sorry. It's just . . . since I know the set-up at
Hopwicke House . . .'

'Of course.' But Carole didn't sound completely
mollified.

'What we really need to do,' said Jude, trying to
make up for the unintentional slight, 'is to find out
more about the Pillars of Sussex. I wouldn't be surprised if Nigel Ackford's death had something to do
with one of them.'

She crossed to an old bureau, and from its crowded
surface produced the guest list she had retrieved from
her apron before leaving Hopwicke House, and handed
it across.

'Any of these names mean anything to you?'

'There's one I know,' said Carole.

Chapter Eleven

'Hello. Could I speak to Barry Stilwell, please?'

There was a slight delay, during which Carole visualized the solicitor. Thin. Thin face. Lips thin almost to the point of absence. And so eternally pin-striped that she had idly wondered whether his flesh was pin-striped too. Fortunately, she had never been put in the position of verifying that speculation – though not for want of trying on Barry Stilwell's part. The recollection of his face-flannel kisses could still send an involuntary shudder through her body.

'Well, well, well, Carole. This is a voice from the past. An unexpected bonus in my boring day.'

'Good to talk to you again too, Barry,' she lied.

'To what do I owe this? Business or pleasure?'

Well, it wasn't really business. She was neither getting a divorce, nor moving house, nor sorting out a will, and those were the three areas of limited expertise from which Barry Stilwell, as a solicitor, made a very good living.

'Can we have a third category?' asked Carole. 'It's not business, it's not pleasure. It's really, I suppose, brain-picking.'

He sounded disappointed at that, but was still eager to meet. An unexpected cancellation (oh yes?) meant he was actually free for lunch that day. Could Carole make it? Wonderful. Why not go back to the Italian in Worthing? Yes, Mario's. 'Of happy memory?'

Carole's memories of dinner with Barry Stilwell at Mario's weren't particularly happy. As she put the phone down, she wondered if the solicitor had once again misinterpreted her interest in him. Surely not, though. When they'd last met, he'd been a widower. Now he was remarried to the widow of a fellow Rotarian. Surely he wouldn't be looking for other female company, would he?

Oh yes, he would. The enthusiastic – though dry – kiss he placed on her lips when he greeted her, the hand in the small of her back guiding her to their table, the grin of masculine complicity to Mario as they sat down, all suggested that perhaps Barry Stilwell wasn't totally fulfilled in his new marriage.

Carole reckoned the best deterrent was to bring up the subject of his wife straight away. 'Congratulations. I heard you had remarried, but I don't know any of the details.'

'Oh, thank you,' he said dismissively. 'Now tell me about yourself. What have you been up to during this age since we last met? We mustn't leave it so long next time,' he added, with a chilly squeeze of her hand.

Removing her hand from the table, Carole persisted, 'I don't even know your wife's name.'

'Pomme.'

'Pomme?'

'Pomme.'

They were in danger of sounding like an entry for the Eurovision Song Contest. 'It's French for apple,' Barry elucidated unnecessarily.

'Yes. I know that. So where did you meet?'

'At a Rotarian event,' he said hurriedly. 'Her late husband was a past president, like me.'

'Oh?' Carole hoped she sounded impressed. She was trying to.

'But enough of—'

'And does Pomme have children?'

'Yes. Three. They're all grown up now.' Barry Stilwell was keen to dispel the hovering shadow of his wife from their dining table.

'So how do you like being a stepfather?'

'Well, it's . . . well, it's fine. I don't really see a lot of them.'

'Because, of course, you didn't have any children with – ' damn, the name had gone completely ' – with your first wife.'

'No. Vivienne and I were not blessed.'

Thank you for the name check, thought Carole, as she went on, 'So how's married life second time around?'

'Fine.' The word was as thin as his lips. 'And what about you? Any new men on your horizon?'

'No.' As she thought about it, Carole realized how little she regretted the fact. She liked the slightly anti-septic exclusivity of High Tor. A man's presence would only impinge on her privacy. That was one of the reasons why her skirmish with Ted Crisp couldn't have lasted. But she was not about to mention that to Barry Stilwell.

'So I'm in with a chance?' he responded with misplaced roguishness.

'You're married, Barry.'

'Yes, but—'

Fortunately the appearance of Mario, flourishing menus the size of billboards, cut short the predictable litany about some men really *liking* women, his wife being very understanding and how, given the diminishing time available to them, people of their age should live life to the full.

The routine had been stalled once. Carole was determined not to give him another chance to run it before the end of the meal.

Exactly as he had on their last tryst at the restaurant, Barry Stilwell made much of ordering, indulging in a lot of coy consultation with Mario as to the quality of the day's specials. Since the owner – as he would – said that everything on the menu was wonderful, this seemed a rather pointless ritual. But it was an essential part of the Stilwell restaurant protocol.

So was his elaborate tasting of the Italian Chardonnay he had persuaded Carole to share. 'I enjoy my wine,' he volunteered, as if she might be interested. 'Never drink spirits – I don't like the taste. But I do enjoy my wine.'

She'd told him if he ordered a bottle he'd have to drink the bulk of it, as she was driving, but the prospect did not seem to worry him. She got the impression he

drank most lunchtimes, probably in the same restaurant, to ease the tedium of an afternoon of divorces,
wills and conveyancing. And she would have put
money on the fact that the lunch bills were somehow
claimed as legitimate expenses. She wondered how her
consultation with him would be described when it was
put through the firm's books.

About time, though, that she defined the real
purpose of their meeting. 'I always remember you
saying, Barry, that your local connections were pretty
good.'

He beamed, taking this as an undiluted compliment. 'I think I could be said to know my way around
the West Sussex network, yes.'

'So you know everything about your fellow solicitors here in Worthing?'

'Oh yes, I certainly do. Though, Carole, I might
quibble with your use of the word "fellow". We are
rivals, you know.'

'Of course.' Only so many divorces, wills and conveyancing jobs to go around. 'The firm I want to know
about is Renton and Chew. Do you know them?'

He smiled complacently. 'I certainly do. Knew old
Harry Chew, but he's long dead. His son Donald took
over as senior partner, but he's no chicken. Pushing
seventy, must be. I know him very well.'

'And are there any Rentons still around?'

'No. I do know some of the junior partners, though.
I could give you names if you're interested. A couple of
them are in the Rotary.'

'And are any of them Pillars of Sussex?'

A flicker of caution crossed his face. 'No, not the junior partners. The Pillars of Sussex tend to be a bit higher up the career ladder. I'm surprised you know about them.'

'It's the kind of organization you hear about if you live down here any length of time. Pretty high-powered and exclusive, I gather?'

The flattery worked. Barry positively preened himself as he replied, 'You could say that. It's a recognition of substantial achievement when you become a Pillar.'

'And is it a secret society?'

'That makes it sound rather sinister. I prefer the word you used earlier. "Exclusive". Yes, that'll do.'

Carole continued the line of flattery. 'I've heard it said that the Pillars of Sussex are the most powerful organization in the entire county. That only the really important movers and shakers get elected.'

He was enjoying this buffing of his self-esteem. 'I can't deny that's pretty accurate.'

'And, needless to say, you're one?'

He chuckled acknowledgment of this, then looked at her with a new shrewdness. 'So what have the Pillars of Sussex got to do with your enquiry about Renton and Chew?'

Carole was faced by a dilemma. According to Jude's conjecture, the Pillars of Sussex might well be co-ordinating a cover-up of what happened to Nigel Ackford. If that were the case, any mention of his death would make Barry clam up instantly. She decided to pretend ignorance of the apparent suicide at Hopwicke House.

'Well, you may have answered my question already – about how easy it is to become one of the Pillars of Sussex.'

'Extremely difficult.'

'Yes. I'm asking this for a friend.' That much at least was true. 'For reasons of her own, she wanted to find out something about the Pillars of Sussex.'

'I'd better warn you. There are a lot of details about the association's affairs that I'm not allowed to divulge.'

Though of course it's still not a secret society. Carole had the thought, but didn't voice it. 'Just . . . this friend of mine . . . well, there's someone she's having business dealings with . . .' this was where the lies began. 'And this person told her that he was about to become a Pillar of Sussex.' That bit almost went back to being truthful. 'And she was just wondering whether that was a likely possibility . . . or whether – this person – was just lying to impress her.'

'It would depend very much who the person we are talking about is, what kind of status he has.'

'He works for Renton and Chew. That's where that connection comes in.'

Carole wouldn't have thought it possible for Barry Stilwell's lips to get thinner, but they did, as he drew in a sceptical breath. 'The only person at Renton and Chew who is a member of the Pillars of Sussex is Donald himself. As I said, nobody below senior partner level would stand a prayer.'

'Oh. Well, it sounds like my friend may have been spun a line.'

'I'd say so. Can you give me the name of the man who's been having her on?'

'Nigel Ackford.'

Confirmation of Jude's suspicion couldn't have come in more convincing form. Barry Stilwell's face closed over completely, and a moment passed before he had fully recovered himself.

'Nigel Ackford?' he repeated, doing a bad impression of someone who'd never heard the name before.

'Yes,' Carole lied blithely on. 'He told my friend he was about to become a Pillar of Sussex. I think the expression he used was "a shoo-in".'

'He couldn't have been more wrong. Nigel Ackford was – is – a very junior solicitor.' The correction was a complete giveaway. Carole had offered no indication of knowing the young man was dead, and Barry Stilwell was not about to tell her. 'He's not even, I believe, a very good solicitor, so I would have thought the chances of his ever becoming a Pillar of Sussex are as likely as mine are of going to bed with Nicole Kidman.'

The leer with which he accompanied this suggested that the loss was all Nicole Kidman's.

'Is it possible for bad solicitors to get jobs these days?' asked Carole, all innocence.

'Not a lot changes in the world,' Barry replied sagely. 'As ever, it's not what you know, it's who you know. With the right contacts, even bad solicitors can still get taken on.'

'So did Nigel Ackford know Donald Chew? Is that how it happened?'

'No.' The solicitor looked uncomfortable, but was saved from further explanation by the arrival of the starters. Or rather, of his starter. Carole, always a light luncher, had, in spite of her host's blandishments, insisted that all she required was *pasta con vongole* as a main course.

As she watched the familiarity with which Barry tucked into his *tonno e fagioli*, she was even more convinced that he knew the whole menu intimately. She waited till he had chomped his first mouthful before asking, 'So, is there anything else you can tell me about Nigel Ackford?'

'No. Just know the name. Never met him.'

'But I thought you both attended the Pillars of Sussex dinner at Hopwicke Country House Hotel earlier this week.'

The shock effect was very rewarding. Two beans and an arc of onion shot out onto Barry's plate as he reached for his napkin. He wiped his mouth, and tried to curb his agitation, as he asked, 'How do you know about that?'

'Got a friend who was working there.' Carole was enjoying juxtaposing the occasional truth with her lies.

'Yes. Well, we were both there, but I didn't meet Mr Ackford.'

'There were only twenty of you. And I gathered he had to introduce himself formally to the whole group.'

'Maybe. But I didn't actually talk to him personally. Not on a one-to-one basis.'

She let the silence run, and he looked relieved, hoping she was about to change the subject. Dashing his hopes, she revealed she knew about Nigel Ackford's death in the hotel. 'Were you aware at the time of what had happened, Barry?'

He squirmed. 'No. I had an early breakfast and left. Had to get into the office. I heard the news later.'

'Someone phoned you?'

'Yes.'

'As no doubt they phoned round all the Pillars of Sussex?'

'Presumably.'

'What did they say?'

'Just that the poor young man had been found dead; so we would know the news before it came on to the radio or television.'

'It hasn't yet come on to either the radio or the television, has it?'

'Has it not? I don't know.'

'No. Don't you think that's odd?'

'What?'

'Unexpected death in a public place like a hotel. You'd have thought the media'd be on to it by now.'

'I hadn't really thought about it.'

'Unless of course someone was deliberately trying to suppress the news.'

He shrugged, suggesting that her conjecture was possibly true, but that he had far more important things in his life to worry about.

'Who rang you?' asked Carole. 'Was it someone from the Pillars of Sussex who told you to keep quiet about the death?'

'I really can't remember. And I was just given the

information, told about what had happened. I wasn't told to keep quiet.'

'But who was it who rang?' Carole persisted. Her slight inhibition about being directly rude to the solicitor had long since vanished. She didn't like the man. She'd never liked him. She didn't care what he thought of her.

Barry Stilwell, however, was not to be drawn. For the next part of the lunch there was a distinct *froideur* between them. As he tucked into his *saltimbocca à la Romana*, he talked impersonally about local topics: the state of the beach at Worthing, the problem of vagrancy in Brighton, the prospects for the long-awaited by-pass at Arundel. And he resisted Carole's every attempt to return the conversation to the subject of Nigel Ackford.

She thought at least she'd dampened his romantic ardour, but he reverted to flirtatious mode as he pressed her – unsuccessfully – to have a dessert and ordered *tiramisu* with cream for himself. (Did he eat like this every day? Why on earth didn't he put on weight? Carole decided that Barry Stilwell had a metabolic thinness of spirit that denied his body the comfort of fat.)

She'd incautiously left her hand on the table again, and he picked it up as they waited for Mario to bring the coffee. 'It really means a lot to me, seeing you again,' he simpered. 'You know I've always had a thing about you.'

Carole found this hard to believe. She was a thin, grey-haired woman in her mid-fifties. Even at her supposed peak, she had had little of the sultry temptress about her. Still, there was no accounting for tastes. Maybe Barry was just desperate. She found herself wondering what Pomme was like, and what kind of married life they shared. The speculation was distasteful, but it wouldn't go away.

His hand was wrapped around hers like a slice of smoked salmon, but since she could not get free without overt rudeness, they stayed linked.

'I'd like to think,' Barry went on, 'that there's not such a gap before the next one.'

'The next what?'

'Meeting. Lunch. Whatever. I think it's very sad we lost touch last time.'

'Not that sad. You went off and got married.' Which was a huge relief to me, she might have added.

'Yes.' He brought a boyish hangdog expression into his eyes. It didn't suit him. 'Who knows whether I'd have done that if I hadn't lost touch with you?'

Oh, no. This was getting beyond a joke.

'Anyway, I'll ring you. We must meet again.' The smoked salmon tightened around her hand.

'Are you talking about another lunch?'

'Some evenings are also possible,' he said cautiously. 'Pomme does line-dancing on Thursdays. And I've got the Rotary on Tuesday evenings.'

'But you couldn't take me to the Rotary. I thought that was an all-male organization.'

'It is,' he agreed. 'Except for our ladies' nights.' Then, with a shameless wink, he went on, 'I do, however, have some very good friends in the Rotary.

They wouldn't rat on a chap if he didn't turn up to the odd meeting.'

Carole was flabbergasted. Their last encounter should have left Barry Stilwell in no doubt that she couldn't stand him. Yet here he was coming on to her, unambiguously proposing they should have an affair. An affair whose logistics he seemed to have worked out in considerable detail.

Fortunately, Mario's arrival with the coffee got her hand unwrapped from the smoked salmon. For the rest of their lunch she contrived to avoid making an illicit assignation with her host. At the end, she managed to escape with only the lightest brush of face-cloth across her cheek.

But, as she drove the Renault back to High Tor, Carole found herself shuddering with disbelief at what had just happened. The idea of being attractive to a man was not totally repellent to her. But being attractive to Barry Stilwell . . .

Yuk.

Chapter Twelve

As she sat sipping her cappuccino and waiting for Wendy Fullerton, Jude reflected on the coffee-shop boom and how one clever idea could suddenly take over the world. People had drunk coffee for many centuries, but it was only in the late twentieth that they had started drinking overpriced and variegated coffees on sofas in chains of identical cafes. And so, many millions of pounds were made. But it couldn't last, the boom must be nearing its end. The fact that there was such a coffee shop in Worthing seemed to prove her point. By the time trendy outlets start to open in dowdy venues, the smart money has already moved on.

The girl was only a little late. She wore a blue suit over a patterned blue-and-red shirt. Though better tailored than building society uniforms used to be, the ensemble still expressed little personality. Short dark hair with a reddish colouring and heavy make-up, which should have made her stand out, somehow seemed to have the opposite effect. They provided a mask, a perverse kind of anonymity.

Wendy Fullerton recognized Jude from the description given over the phone. All she wanted to drink was still mineral water. She sat impassively by while Jude fetched a bottle and glass from the counter. There was no expression behind the mascara or the perfectly outlined metallic claret lips. Wendy's hands, nails varnished in the same colour as the lips, lay still on her lap. She was giving nothing away; any effort would have to be made by Jude.

After another sip of cappuccino, Jude embarked on her mission. 'As I said, I was working up at Hopwicke House the night Nigel Ackford died.'

'Doing what?' asked Wendy Fullerton.

'Waitressing.'

The girl nodded, as if this were significant information.

Quickly, and without sounding judgmental, Jude told her how she had found Nigel drunk in the corridor in the small hours.

'He always drank a lot when he was nervous,' Wendy volunteered, almost as if this were a justification. 'And he was very worried about that Pillars of Sussex meeting.'

'You imply you knew he was going to it.'

'Yes.'

'I had heard your relationship ended four months ago.'

'We stopped living together then. It just didn't work, so he went back to his place.'

'How long did you live together?'

Jude's questions were so gentle that it didn't feel like an interrogation. The girl answered fluently, 'Only about nine weeks.'

'But you'd known each other for some time?'

'Oh yes, we'd been knocking around together for four years – longer – on and off.'

'And then he moved in?'

'Mm. But like I say, it didn't work. Nigel was too intense, too moody for me.'

'So was that the complete end, when he moved out?'

'No. We stayed in touch. Lots of phone calls, texting each other. Met for the odd meal, but it wasn't really working.'

'Because of his moods?'

The doll-like head nodded. 'Yes. And I was sort of thinking, time's moving on. I'm twenty-eight next birthday, and Nigel was, like, drifting. Still living in a rented flat. He wasn't looking ahead. He didn't really have any ambition.'

Jude could see it all. Perhaps too young to be worrying about her biological clock, Wendy was worried about her aspirational clock. No doubt she had contemporaries who were getting married, contemporaries with impressive boyfriends carving out careers for themselves. Nigel Ackford wasn't providing her with that kind of prospect. Her work probably didn't help either. Building societies are magnets for young couples, full of plans to set up home together, to get their stake in the booming property market, to mortgage their lives away. Wendy would be dealing with people like that every day. And Nigel was still living in a rented flat. If the relationship wasn't going to go the distance to the destination of fitted kitchens, integral garages and babies, then Wendy had thrown away four years of her life, and had better move on quickly to find an alternative prospective partner.

'But Nigel was doing well, wasn't he?' Jude suggested.

Before the girl could answer, she was interrupted by the trill of a mobile phone. She took it out of her pocket, checked the number calling and pressed a button.

'Don't worry. I'll take it later. Just seeing if it was for me.'

'Sorry?'

'My phone got stolen. While I was waiting for a replacement, Nigel lent me his. Well, he gave it to me, said he was going to get another . . . so I have to check whether a call's for me rather than him.' This thought was too forceful a reminder of her boyfriend's absence, so she drove it away. 'You were saying, about Nigel doing well?'

'Yes. Well, I would have thought . . . qualified solicitor, good job at Renton and Chew. I actually heard him start to tell the Pillars of Sussex his life history that night. Sounded as if he was doing fine.'

A grimace spoiled the perfect outline of Wendy Fullerton's mouth. 'In some moods he was. He must've already had a lot to drink to be so positive that night. Other times, he – well, he had no self-confidence at all.'

'He got depressed?'

The girl nodded, a little flicking movement that seemed both to acknowledge and to dismiss the idea at the same time.

'Do you think he got depressed enough to kill himself?'

'He talked about it,' she admitted. 'I never took that literally. I knew he got low, but I never thought he'd actually do it.' A tremor ran through Wendy Fullerton's body, and Jude realized the immense effort that was required to maintain her impassivity.

'Shows how wrong I was,' the girl said eventually.

'Did you know any of the people involved in the Pillars of Sussex?' A negative flick of the head. 'He didn't talk to you about them?'

'He may have mentioned the odd name. I didn't really take it in.'

'But he was excited about being invited to the dinner?'

'Oh yes. He saw it as something very positive, like, perhaps his luck was changing. He was very young to be invited to something like that, even just as a guest.'

'Did you know his host for that evening? Bob Hartson?'

'Used to know him. We lived quite close, before he started making a lot of money and moved upmarket. I sometimes used to baby-sit for them, make a bit of pocket money while I was still at school.'

'Would that be for Kerry? Or did they have other children?'

'No, Kerry's the only one. She's not his daughter. His wife's. How come you know her?'

'She works up at Hopwicke Country House Hotel as well.'

'Does she?' The idea seemed to surprise Wendy. 'I can't imagine her working anywhere.'

'Why not? Most people have to.'

'Yes, but I thought, with Daddy's money . . .' She couldn't disguise the envy in her voice. 'I heard he'd set her up in a flat in Brighton – and she can't be much more than sixteen. Not even that, actually. I remember, it's her birthday quite soon. She's still only fifteen – and got her own flat. No mortgage, nothing – lucky little bugger. Surprised to hear she's working. I suppose I'd always seen Kerry as a kind of trust-fund kid.'

'She's doing work experience up at Hopwicke House, with a view to learning hotel management.'

A short, cynical chuckle. 'And then no doubt Daddy'll buy her her own hotel to play with.'

'Maybe. Do you still see her?'

'Might bump into her in the street, say hello, that's it.'

'And what was she like as a child?'

'Spoilt little madam. Only had to ask for something and she got it. I think her new Daddy was buying her affection in the old traditional manner.' Again, undisguised resentment.

'How did Nigel come to know Bob Hartson?'

'Through work. Renton and Chew handle all Bob Hartson's legal stuff. He's very in with the senior partner there, Donald Chew. Nigel was very impressed that Bob Hartson seemed to be, sort of, taking him under his wing as well.'

'Yes.' Jude was thoughtful for a moment. What was it the property developer had hoped to get from the young solicitor? Why had he bolstered the young man, even suggested he might become a member of the Pillars – which, from what Barry Stilwell had told Carole, was extraordinarily unlikely. Oh well, worth asking. 'Apparently, Wendy, Hartson was even suggesting that he might put Nigel up for membership of the Pillars of Sussex.'

'I didn't know that.'

'No, well, he only told me on the night—' Jude wished she hadn't embarked on that sentence, and quickly changed direction. 'So you don't know why Bob Hartson might have wanted to cultivate Nigel?'

A quick shake of the head, then a silence. The girl took the first sip of her water, and looked at her watch. Jude hadn't got long.

'Thank you very much for seeing me, Wendy.' She scribbled a number on a paper napkin. 'That's my mobile. Do give me a call if—'

'If what?'

'If you find out anything else about how Nigel died.'

The girl looked blank. 'That's not very likely, is it?'

Jude had to admit that it probably wasn't. 'No. I know this must be a difficult time for you.'

After a moment of bemusement, the girl said, 'Oh, you mean because of Nigel.' She considered the idea, as if it hadn't occurred to her before. 'Yes . . . I don't think it's really sunk in yet. I'm afraid my first reaction was, like, relief. Awful, but maybe that's what he wanted. He won't be unhappy any more.'

'No.'

'And . . . well, it has, like, made certain decisions for

me. Our relationship wasn't going anywhere, it had to end at some point and . . .'

She looked at her watch again. Jude wondered what further information she could get before this particular window closed.

But Wendy had already slipped off her stool and was saying, 'I'd better be getting back. End of the week, things to tidy up.'

'Yes. Once again, thank you very much for making the time to see me.'

The girl lingered, though. There was something else she wanted to say, but she wasn't finding it easy to get the words out.

'Jude . . . you mentioned on the phone that Nigel said something about me – you know, when he was drunk.'

Of course. Jude had completely forgotten the pretext on which she had arranged their meeting.

'Yes. I'm so sorry. He did.'

'What did he say?' The question tried to sound casual, but failed.

'He said he was going to ask you to marry him.'

Wendy Fullerton winced, as though she had just been stabbed.

'And he said he felt pretty confident that you'd say yes.'

The facade of insouciance cracked. Tears welled and spilled, making rivulets in the girl's thick armour of make-up.

Chapter Thirteen

'I've fixed to go up to the hotel tomorrow morning,' Carole announced. 'To have a look around. So any thoughts as to what I should look out for would be welcomed.'

'Well . . .' Jude buried her fingers in her bird's nest of blonde hair as she concentrated. 'Certainly ask to see the four-poster room on the top floor. The murder scene.'

'We don't know that it was murder,' Carole reprimanded her puritanically.

'Don't nitpick.'

'But the girlfriend wasn't surprised by the idea that he'd committed suicide.'

'No, I know that. He was depressive, he had threatened to kill himself. I'm just convinced he didn't.'

'I agree with you completely.' Behind the rimless glasses, there was a rare twinkle in Carole's pale blue eyes. 'But we mustn't get carried away.'

'Why not?' asked Jude pugnaciously. 'Why is everyone in this bloody country always so terrified of getting carried away?'

Carole looked across the cluttered sitting room at

her friend. Jude didn't usually behave like this. Normally she was very grounded, secure in her own space.

Reading her thoughts, Jude explained, 'I'm sorry. I'm letting this get to me. It must be because I saw the boy so soon before his death. I can't stop thinking of the waste. And that's sort of mixed in with my distaste for all-male organizations like the Pillars of Sussex. I'm sorry, it's just . . .' Tears glistened in the large brown eyes.

Carole found herself in a rare role reversal: she was calming Jude, rather than the other way round. 'Don't worry. We'll find out what really happened to Nigel Ackford. That's the only thing that's going to make you feel better.'

Jude nodded gratefully.

That Saturday morning the South Downs glowed in the spring sunshine, as Carole's Renault made its sedate way up to Hopwicke Country House Hotel. There were no other buildings nearby, no other cars on the road, nothing to betray the passage of the centuries. The perfectly proportioned square mansion must have looked like this, Carole thought, when George Hopwicke first took possession of it.

She left the car in the guests' car park, and walked round to the main entrance. As ever, the set-dressing of the hall was perfect, transporting her back into a BBC costume drama. The props placed her in the eternal afternoon of the Edwardian period, innocent of the coming horrors of the Great War.

The only discordant note was the soundtrack. From

the bar, the latest ersatz girl group squeaked away on Radio One. Carole rang the small silver bell on the antique reception desk.

Nothing happened. The music continued.

She moved across the hall towards the open door of the bar. A small portable radio on the counter was revealed as the source of the noise. In front of it, side-on to Carole's view, a slight blonde teenage girl in blue skirt and white smock overall was gyrating in time to the music. Her right hand held a feather duster in lieu of a microphone, into which she lustily sang along with the radio.

'Good morning. You must be Mrs Seddon. Excuse me.'

Carole hadn't heard Suzy Longthorne's entrance. She watched as the slender hotelier crossed to the bar. 'Could you switch that off, please, Kerry.'

The words weren't said with much emphasis, but there was no doubt they represented an order rather than a request. The music vanished in mid-squeak.

No one could have lived through the years Carole had without seeing images of Suzy Longthorne. Even someone as resistant to trendiness as she was could not have avoided that iconic figure. On many occasions Suzy had progressed from the fashion sections of the press to the news pages.

And, despite her innate resistance to the person who Carole thought of as 'Jude's friend Suzy', she could not help being impressed seeing her in the flesh. The auburn hair gleamed, the hazel eyes sparkled, and it cost a lot to get a black wool trouser suit that looked that casual.

'Yes. I hope you don't mind my coming. My son's thinking of staying here and asked me to have a look round.'

Whatever Suzy Longthorne may really have thought about having her premises vetted, she was far too well-bred and professional to let any negative feelings show. Maybe in better times she would not have agreed to guided tours. When Hopwicke Country House Hotel was the sought-after destination of the glitterati, perhaps its qualities could be taken as read. In the current, American-free, chillier climate, Suzy Longthorne could not risk losing a single booking.

She led her potential customer through into the bar. Kerry was now assiduously dusting the racked bottles behind the counter, but Carole got the impression her industry was solely for her employer's benefit. The moment Suzy was out of sight, the movements would become more lethargic. And the moment she was out of earshot, Radio One would probably reassert itself.

Carole tried to think of a pretext for speaking to the girl, but none came to her. Jude would have thought of something. But then of course Jude knew Kerry, anyway, so she wouldn't have needed a pretext.

Carole was duly appreciative of the bar and adjacent dining room. She cooed at the conservatory where she was told breakfast and afternoon tea were served, and admired the wonderful views up over the Downs. She was suitably impressed by the residents' lounge and the library. Though she was fairly certain her son wouldn't need to take advantage of the conference suite, she thought that, too, was very well appointed.

Next came the test. 'And could I see some of the bedrooms as well?'

Suzy Longthorne made no demur. There was apparently no part of her hotel which was closed to scrutiny. As she pointed out the various facilities, she let drop a few well-practised gobbets of information. But they all concerned the early history of Hopwicke House; she was not so indiscreet as to mention any of its more recent – and more newsworthy – guests.

A front bedroom and a back bedroom on the first floor had been inspected, and Suzy stood on the landing looking quizzically at her visitor. The moment had come.

'I understand,' said Carole, 'that there is a room with a four-poster as well?'

Suzy Longthorne did not blanch. 'Yes, there is. It is rather more expensive than the others. Popular for honeymoons and that kind of thing. Special celebrations.'

'I don't think money's a problem for my son.' As she said the words, Carole realized she had no idea whether or not they were true. Stephen had never shown any particular signs of extravagance. He had always managed his finances carefully. But maybe being engaged to Gaby had raised his aspirations. Maybe it was her money he was budgeting with. There were certainly any number of cheaper options in the area than Hopwicke Country House Hotel.

Suzy pointed out the wonderful view from the top

landing. 'If I had a telescope, I could probably see my house,' said Carole.

'Oh. Where do you live, Mrs. Seddon?'

'Fethering.'

'Well, you can certainly see the route of the Fether as it reaches the sea.'

Carole looked at the thin ribbon of water threading down through the coastal plain. The river shone in reflected sunlight with a duller gleam than the surrounding rectangles, glasshouses of local nurseries.

'Come and have a look at the four-poster.' Suzy Longthorne pushed through the fire door into the corridor where Jude had found the drunken Nigel Ackford. She unlocked the bedroom door.

Inside, everything was immaculate. The curtains around the bed were neatly roped back. Sunlight beamed cheerfully through the tall windows. Nothing betrayed the room as a scene of death.

'It's beautiful,' said Carole. 'I'm sure my son and his fiancée would like this.'

'Getting married, are they?' Ever the business-woman, Suzy Longthorne picked up the cue. 'We've had some wonderful weddings at Hopwicke House. If they were looking for somewhere for the reception . . . If your prospective daughter-in-law's local . . .'

'No, I'm afraid she isn't,' said Carole, realizing she hadn't a clue where Gaby lived. She'd assumed London, but she didn't actually know. Nor did she know where her prospective daughter-in-law might want to get married. Hopefully, such details would become clearer once she had lunched with the happy couple on Sunday week.

Carole was now faced with a dilemma. The hotel tour having ended, it was clearly her cue to leave, and she could do that. On the other hand, she felt she should take something back for Jude. So, resorting to bad acting, she announced, 'I've suddenly remembered. This must be the room where that poor young man died.'

Suzy was far too controlled to react violently, but her beautiful face hardened as she said, 'I'm sorry?'

'I should explain. I'm a friend of Jude's.'

'Ah.'

'She's my next-door neighbour.'

'Of course. Fethering. I've been to her house. What did she tell you?'

'Just that there had been this . . . sad incident up here. I'd forgotten about it until . . . actually being in this room . . .'

The explanation sounded implausible even to Carole's own ears, but Suzy did not pick up on it. Calmly, she said, 'Yes, it was very unfortunate. I'm afraid that's one of the hazards of the hotel trade. Apart from the cases they're carrying, you don't know what other baggage your guests bring with them. Maybe the anonymity of a hotel room appeals to people in that condition. Certainly doesn't show much concern for others, but then I suppose suicide is the ultimate act of selfishness. Just as people who throw themselves under buses don't think of the effect of their actions on the driver and passengers, so the reactions of the staff are not uppermost in the mind of someone who chooses to end his life in a hotel room.' An expression of concern crossed Suzy's face. 'Jude is all right, is she? It must have been a terrible shock for her.'

'She was a bit shaken, but she's fine.'

'Good.'

As she was escorted down the splendid staircase, Carole plucked up her courage and asked baldly, 'There is no doubt that the death was suicide, is there?'

'No,' Suzy replied firmly. 'No doubt at all. And, incidentally, Mrs Seddon . . .'

'Yes?'

'I would be most grateful if you didn't say anything about the young man's death to your son – or indeed to anyone else. Word of mouth is so important in a profession like mine. It would be very damaging for me if news of this unfortunate occurrence were to get around.'

As she nosed the Renault gently over the gravel of the Hopwicke House drive, Carole mulled over her recent conversation. Suzy Longthorne had certainly closed her mind to the possibility that Nigel Ackford's death had been anything other than suicide. And it looked as though the police shared that opinion. Surely, if they had any doubts on the matter, the four-poster room would still be under forensic examination, not open to receive the next guest.

For a moment, Carole's own conviction wavered. She had seen nothing untoward, she only had Jude's suspicions to animate her own. And even Jude's customary serenity had been shaken by the shock of what she'd found. Maybe at such a time her responses weren't entirely reliable.

These thoughts were interrupted by the blare of a hooter, suggesting the Renault was nearer the crown of the road than it should have been. As she steered closer to the hedge that lined the lane, Carole was overtaken by a throatily roaring motorcycle, driven by a man in black leathers.

Clinging round his waist, a helmet crammed down over her blonde hair, was the unmistakable figure of Kerry Hartson.

Chapter Fourteen

Jude was not one of those women for whom the visit was an essential weekly ritual, but she did enjoy going to the hairdresser. She had been blonde for so long that she'd almost forgotten her original hair colour, though she was relieved to observe her roots were not yet showing white. For her the signal to go to the hairdresser was not the blondness creeping away, but a sudden sensation one morning that there was too much hair to pile on top of her head. That was when she'd book in, or more often just appear without an appointment.

She wasn't particularly bothered who did the cutting, being able to find subjects for conversation with most people. As usual, she did more listening than volunteering information. She found the process restful, the washing, the application of the colour, the cutting.

But the most enjoyable part was waiting for her hair to dry after the colour had been applied. Jude liked lying back in a chair, secure in the knowledge that there was nothing else she could be doing at that point. The drying process would take as long as it took, at such times the hairdresser would be busy with another client so conversation would not be required. And Jude could either let her thoughts wander, or idly skim through a variety of magazines which did not impinge on the normal course of her life.

The Saturday after Nigel Ackford's death, she was in the hairdresser's enjoying one of those weeklies that have redefined – and considerably lowered the qualifications for – the status of 'celebrity'. In the inevitable synchronistic way that relevant events have a habit of bubbling to the surface at the right moment, she found herself looking at a picture of Suzy Longthorne.

The photograph dated back to the prime of Suzy's marriage to Rick Hendry, and the accompanying text was all about him rather than her. She was mentioned as a 'former model', too old to ring many bells among the youthful demographics of the magazine's target audience. Rick Hendry would have suffered the same fate, had his career not been revived by new television fame. Famous for his acerbic dismissals of the talents of teenage pop wannabees, he had now reached the coveted status of 'the man the public love to hate'.

His new celebrity had brought him all the bonuses attendant on television popularity – appearances on chat-shows, at awards ceremonies and in highly paid commercials. The words – 'I wish I'd been born deaf' – with which he greeted the worst of the aspirants on the talent show had become a recent national catchphrase. He had even reached the giddy heights of being caricatured by cartoonists and lampooned by satirical television impressionists. The old rocker had certainly reinvented himself for the new millennium.

The photograph of Rick with Suzy was one of a sequence evoking his previous career. There were also shots of him leaving for international tours with his band, squiring other forgotten women, looking beat-up and past-it in the early nineties. These shots framed the main picture which showed Rick with his arms around nineteen-year-old twin girls who had survived the rigours of the talent show to become over-hyped one-hit Number Ones. His famously large teeth were revealed in a lascivious grin, which deepened the engraving of lines on his long thin face. His hair was short and grey. The caption read: 'As young as the women he feels.'

Jude had met Rick Hendry a few times while he had been married to Suzy. He had always worked hard on his image. The 'wild man of rock' was a cunning self-marketer, shrewd about business, tight with his money, ruthless in getting what he wanted. The new incarnation – poison-tongued, ageing enfant terrible – was, Jude felt sure, quite as carefully manufactured as any of the previous ones.

And whoever wrote the text which accompanied the magazine's photo-spread had clearly bought into Rick Hendry's self-image.

TV's Mr Nasty has never made any secret of the fact that he likes beautiful women. 'And when beauty and talent come together,' says Rick, 'the combination is a total knockout.' Currently single, the

'Black Mamba of the Box' isn't sure where he's going to strike next. 'I'm having such a good time playing the field, why should I ever go back to an exclusive relationship? There's life in the old dog yet.' And for an old dog who's made a career out of bitchiness, who can doubt that what he says is true?

Good luck, Rick – and I think we can put that prescription of Viagra on hold for a while yet!

Carole didn't notice her friend had had her hair done. Jude never emerged with that crisp salon-fresh look. Her hair was just piled up again on top of her head, secured by whatever clips or combs were her current favourites. Only the very observant would have detected a change in its degree of blondness. And that Saturday afternoon as she came rushing round to Woodside Cottage, Carole was far too preoccupied to take in that kind of detail. 'I've just had a call from Barry Stilwell,' she announced.

'Oh?'

'From his golf club.'

She sounded so bewildered that Jude giggled. 'I see. Not wanting to ring his mistress from home.'

'Don't be stupid!' But there had been something conspiratorial in Barry's tone, which had almost suggested they were sharing an illicit secret.

Jude scratched her newly blonde hair thoughtfully. 'I'm surprised men bother with that these days. Ringing from the golf club. You can use a mobile to ring from anywhere. You know, mobile phones have really changed the whole complexion of adultery.'

109

She sounded almost wistfully regretful of the fact, as though some of the fun had been taken out of the game. In other circumstances, Carole might have pressed her for amplification, but she was currently too shocked by her recent phone conversation with Barry.

'But he wants to meet me again,' she said.

'Go for it.'

'Jude, I can't. For one thing, he's repulsive. And for another, he's married.'

'Can't let details like that stand in your way.'

'I am not the kind of woman who has affairs with married men.' She knew she sounded terribly pompous, so she added, 'Or with anyone else, come to that.' Which somehow didn't sound right either.

'Carole . . .' Jude's brown eyes fixed hers in an expression of mock-seriousness. 'There are times when you mustn't think about yourself. You must set aside your own feelings and prioritize the greater cause.'

'I don't think having affairs with married men you can't stand could ever be defined as a greater cause.'

'It could if it brings a benefit with it.'

'What benefit could an affair with Barry Stilwell possibly bring?'

'Information.' The lightness had dropped from Jude's tone; she was completely serious. 'Barry Stilwell is the only link we have to the Pillars of Sussex. We need to keep in touch with him if we're going to find out what really happened to Nigel Ackford.'

'But—'

'Whether you have to go to bed with him to get that information is up to you – ' Jude grinned ' – Mata Hari.'

Chapter Fifteen

The emergency call came through at four. Four on a Saturday – Jude had a pretty good idea it would be Suzy Longthorne.

'I've been let down again.'

'What is it?'

'Wedding reception.'

'Who've you got?'

'Max, obviously. The boy who insists on calling himself the *sous-chef*, and Stella. It's one of the other girls who's let me down. Well, not really let me down. Her mother's ill.'

'And have you got Kerry?'

'Oh yes, I've got Kerry. For what it's worth.'

'OK. I'll get a cab.'

Suzy Longthorne's own chequered marital history did not stop her from putting on a good wedding reception at Hopwicke House. In keeping with the new fashion for four o'clock weddings, the guests would not arrive from the church before five-thirty, and by then Jude was neatly packaged in her Edwardian waitress kit,

111

standing in the hallway with a tray of champagne to greet the arrivals.

In this instance, the Edwardian theme had been picked up for the wedding itself. The men were dressed in frock-coats and the women in high-waisted long dresses with lots of buttons. This was quite flattering to most of them, though not to the bride, who didn't have a waist. Nor could a frock-coat be said to have done much for the groom, accentuating his shortness and making him look like a cross between Groucho Marx and Toulouse-Lautrec.

But it was not the place of Jude or any of the other hotel staff to comment on such things. The whispered bitchiness of the assembled guests was quite sufficient.

Jude was surprised to find she recognized two of those guests. The father of the bride, it turned out, was none other than the president of the Pillars of Sussex, James Baxter. Her godfather was Donald Chew. He was there with his wife, a small thin woman, who exuded disapproval of everything, particularly her husband.

Jude wondered whether the presence of the two men, and the family's unwillingness to spoil the day's celebrations, had anything to do with the perfunctory investigation of Nigel Ackford's death. Or indeed its hushing-up. An unnatural death in a hotel the week before a wedding reception might not be seen as the best omen for the future of a marriage.

She was determined to exploit the opportunity of her unexpected presence at Hopwicke House and speak to Kerry. There were a lot of questions she wanted to put to the girl about the night of Nigel Ackford's death. But the interrogation would have to wait. At the moment they were all too busy refilling champagne glasses and circulating the delicately delicious nibbles that Max Townley and his *sous-chef* had produced.

The format for the reception was a merciful one, in that a decision had been made to have the speeches before the meal rather than after. This was welcomed by the groom and the best man, who were among that large section of the community for whom public speaking ranks as a horror above noticing that the passenger in the seat next to you on a plane has plastic explosives strapped to his body.

James Baxter, of course, with his wide experience of chairing Pillars of Sussex meetings, had no such inhibitions. He thought of himself as a natural public speaker.

In this opinion he was misguided. He also believed himself to be such a natural public speaker that he did not require the support of notes. In this he was even more misguided. Notes might at least have imposed some structure on his maunderings.

He started, safely enough, by welcoming the guests, but immediately blotted his copybook by repeating one of the jokes which had been delivered by the rugby club speaker earlier in the week. It had been a bit iffy at the Pillars of Sussex dinner; in mixed company it could not have been less appropriate. His wife flashed him a look of iced venom, and when the groom laughed loudly, the bride shot *him* a look of iced venom, suggesting he had a long, hard marriage ahead.

Fortunately, Jude's waitressing duties meant she didn't have to listen to all the speeches, but as she slipped in and out of the kitchen she heard enough to suggest she wasn't missing much.

The groom said, without much conviction, that he was very lucky to have captured such a lovely bride, and he knew all his friends were envious of him. All his friends, who hadn't eaten since breakfast, and who had started the day's drinking at noon in the pub, were perhaps injudiciously honest in their assessment of the bride's charms.

The best man had bought a book on best man's speeches, and tried to reproduce some of the jokes he had read there. He interlarded these with stories of a blueness which made the rugby ones sound entirely innocent. But, since he spoke throughout in an inaudible monotone, he caused no offence.

Finally, the speeches were over, the cake was cut, and the photographer had finished his posings of the bride and groom, praying that the camera might work miracles. The guests then went through to the dining room, expertly decorated by Suzy Longthorne to resemble an Edwardian conservatory, and Jude had a chance to pursue her investigation.

In its heyday, Hopwicke Country House Hotel had had a restaurant manager and a *maître d'* to oversee dining arrangements, but staffing economies had left Suzy in charge. She controlled the flow of food delivery and removal with her customary efficiency, and proved that in the right circumstances it was possible even for a beautiful woman to become invisible. Once the diners got into their stride of eating, drinking and talking, they became completely unaware of the stage management around them.

During the preliminary seating of the guests, the waiting staff were kept busy. But as soon as the pre-prepared starters had been served, Jude found herself alone in the kitchen with Max Townley, as he plated up the main courses and put them in a heated cupboard to await their summons to the dining room.

'Did the police talk to you?' asked Jude. 'You know, about the boy who died?'

A flicker of panic crossed his face, but was quickly controlled. 'Yes. Had I heard or seen anything unusual during the night? No, I hadn't. I'd been heavily into the vodka and just passed out . . . not that I told the police that bit.'

'It's not like you to drink that much, Max. At least not here. Is it?'

'No. I'd had some bad news that day, that's all.'

'Oh?'

But he didn't rise to the bait and specify what the bad news had been. Instead, he went on, 'Presumably the police asked you rather more, since you actually found the body?'

'Yes.' She phrased her next question carefully. 'They didn't say anything, did they – about the possibility of the death not being suicide?'

The chef stopped ladling Cumberland sauce. The blankness in his face showed he'd never even contemplated the idea.

'No. What are you suggesting, Jude? Be pretty

115

difficult to do that to yourself by accident. One of these auto-erotic sex games that went wrong?'

She shook her head lightly. 'Just a daft thought.'

Max resumed his ladling. He was still twitchy and ill at ease. 'It's a first for me, you know. Someone topping himself in a hotel where I was working. You hear about it, but . . .'

'Does it upset you?'

He shrugged. 'Not my problem. Didn't even meet the bloke.' He moved away from the main courses and picked up a mixing bowl. He held a coated wooden spoon out to Jude. 'Have a taste.'

She did. 'Bloody marvellous. What's the liqueur in it?'

'Calvados. One of my specials. Goes over the apricot meringues.' He gave a dispirited nod towards the dining room. 'Not that they'll notice what it is. Far too pissed. That's the trouble with these late weddings.'

'You ever been married, Max?'

He laughed at the idea. 'Why would I want to do a thing like that?'

'Why does anyone want to do it?'

'A question, Jude, to which I've never found a satis-factory answer.'

'Max . . .' she lowered her voice, 'Tuesday night . . .'

'Mm?'

'The night Nigel Ackford—'

'I know the one you're talking about.' But he didn't sound as though he wanted to pursue the subject.

'Did you see Kerry?'

'Saw her when she was waitressing.'

'No. Later. After the Pillars of Sussex had gone to bed?'

He looked at her with undisguised suspicion. 'Why should I have seen her then?'

'She wasn't around to help tidying up.'

'Just gone to bed, I expect. Lazy little cow.'

'No. She wasn't in her room. I went in there by mistake.'

'And are you suggesting she was with me?' He was angry now.

'No, of course I wasn't.'

'I should bloody hope not. All right, I like women, but you'd never catch me going for jailbait like that. Kerry's trouble, let me tell you. She's a danger to—'

But who she was a danger to Jude did not find out. The door from the dining room clattered open, revealing Suzy, cool as ever in a long, seamless, light grey dress. 'Time to clear away the starters.'

Talking to Kerry proved more difficult. Jude was in the girl's company all evening, as they bustled back and forth with trays of fresh dishes and dirty plates, as they filled wine glasses and swept up breadcrumbs, but they were never just the two of them. And Jude needed to talk to Kerry on her own.

At last, in the pause before the coffee pots were taken in, they both arrived in the kitchen with armfuls of dessert plates. Max and his *sous-chef*, having set out dishes of petits fours, reckoned their evening's work was over and had set off home. Kerry looked anxious when she realized the room was empty except for the two of them.

As they unloaded the dirty dishes onto a table, she looked at Jude defiantly, like a schoolgirl who had been caught smoking. She was aware this was the first chance they had had to talk since Nigel Ackford's death.

Jude plunged straight in. 'On Tuesday, Kerry,' she said, 'you weren't around to help clear up after the guests had gone to bed . . .'

She could have predicted the monosyllabic response – a teenage, 'So?'

'I was wondering where you were.'

'I work for Suzy, not you, Jude. If she asks me where I was, I might tell her. I don't have to tell you anything.'

'No. But I happen to know you weren't in your bed at about three o'clock in the morning.'

'How do you know that? You been snooping in my room?'

'I walked into it by mistake.'

'Oh yes?' The words dripped adolescent sarcasm.

'Yes, I did. You weren't there. So where were you?'

'That's my business.'

'Usually that might be true, but at a time when someone was dying in the hotel, what everyone was doing becomes important.'

'What are you, Jude – an undercover police-woman?'

'No. Since you mention the police, though – did they talk to you?'

The girl nodded.

'And ask you where you were that night?'

Another nod.

'What did you tell them?'

For the first time, Kerry's defiance gave way to fear. 'I told them I went to bed.'

'What time?'

'I said twelve o'clock.'

'That was a lie, Kerry. I saw you still in the bar at twelve o'clock. With your father.'

'Stepfather,' came the automatic correction.

'All right. So were you still with him later on? At three o'clock?'

Fear in the girl's expression gave way to terror. 'No,' she insisted. 'No, I wasn't with him.' She looked very flustered. 'Look, I can't talk about this now. But please don't tell the police I wasn't where I said I was. You won't, will you?'

Jude had no intention of telling the police, but all she replied was a dubious, 'Well . . .'

'Listen, Jude, please don't tell the police. I'll tell you the truth. I promise I will. But not now. Not here.' She picked up a couple of coffee pots. 'Better take these through.'

'When are you going to tell me the truth, Kerry?'

'Tomorrow. Come to my flat in Brighton.'

'You really have got a flat in Brighton?'

'Why shouldn't I?'

'I'm sorry, but you're only fifteen and . . .'

'My parents have always encouraged me to be

119

independent,' she said sniffily. Then she gave Jude the address. 'I promise I'll tell you everything then.'

Which was, thought Jude, to put it at its mildest, intriguing.

Her one-to-one with Suzy Longthorne was in an even less glamorous situation: the gentlemen's toilet, in which one of the wedding guests had thrown up copiously. So extensive was the mess that the curious could have pieced together all the details of Max Townley's dinner from what was splattered over the tiled floor and walls. But it wasn't the food that had reacted with the guest's stomach; it was the excesses of alcohol he had been drinking since noon.

The individual who had caused the chaos had sidled quietly back to his seat and it had been left for the next visitor to the Gents' to find out and report what had happened. Suzy came through into the kitchen, as Jude and Kerry were piling up plates for the student who did the washing up. The hotelier's face was grim as she collected mops, buckets and disinfectant.

Jude asked what they were for, and was told.

'But you shouldn't have to do that, Suzy.'

'Everyone else is busy.' As ever, Suzy betrayed no resentment, just took the practical approach. It was all part of the job she had chosen for herself.

'I can do it. You'll ruin your clothes.'

'We'll both do it,' Suzy conceded, as she slipped a nylon overall on top of her designer dress.

So the circumstances weren't ideal, but it was the

first chance Jude had had that day to speak to her friend on her own.

As they mopped and swabbed, trying not to think about what they were doing, trying not to look at the debris or breathe in the noxious smell, Jude asked boldly, 'Why did you lie to the police about that note, Suzy?'

There was no pretence at incomprehension, just a straight answer – the answer she had given when asked the same question on the phone. 'Because I didn't want a murder enquiry at Hopwicke House. The place could have been closed for weeks. I certainly couldn't have done this wedding today.'

Jude wrinkled her nose grimly. 'At the moment not doing this wedding seems an attractive option.'

'I need the money, Jude.'

This prompted a characteristically blunt question. 'Why? Do you owe a lot?'

'Yes. I've borrowed like mad to keep this place going, but I don't think I can borrow any more. I need income. Otherwise I'll have to sell up.'

'Place must be worth a bit.'

'I wouldn't be destitute, no. But by the time I'd paid off my debts, I'd have lost massively on my investment. If I can keep going for a few more months, I'm sure I can turn this round.' There was a defiant set to her jaw. 'A few more years and I can sell it as a successful going concern. That'll be my pension.'

Practical as ever. Even through her years of fame and massive earnings, Suzy Longthorne had always kept a level head about her finances.

'And you're sure you can't borrow any more?'

The auburn hair trembled with a decisive shake of the head.

'Not even from Bob Hartson?'

The hazel eyes turned on Jude like the beam of a searchlight. 'How do you know about that?'

'Max mentioned it.'

Suzy nodded, as if she had assumed that to be the case. 'I'm not denying Bob's put some money into Hopwicke House. I'd hoped to be able to manage without investors, but that ceased to be possible. Better someone local, someone I know, than an impersonal bank or venture capitalist.'

'So you do know Bob Hartson well?'

'He's an acquaintance, not a friend.'

They had mopped up the vomit, the shreds of vegetable and other indefinable items from the walls and floor. Next they had to swab down the tiling with disinfectant.

After a few moment's rubbing, Jude asked, 'So what's the *quid pro quo*?'

'What do you mean?'

'With Bob Hartson. He lends you money. What do *you* have to do?'

'I have to pay interest. That's how money-lending usually works.'

'Nothing else?'

'What are you saying, Jude?'

'I was wondering why you continue to employ Kerry?'

This question seemed to bring Suzy relief, as if

she'd been expecting something worse. 'All right. There was a kind of agreement between Bob and me about that. But it's short term, just work experience. Soon, even a devoted a stepfather as Bob must realize that the girl has no aptitude for hotel work.'

'And will he then free her to fulfil her dreams of being a pop idol?'

'What do you mean by that?' asked Suzy sharply.

'I thought that's what Kerry wanted to be. I thought that's what all girls of Kerry's age wanted to be. That or a television presenter.'

'Ah. Yes. Well, you may be right.'

Again Suzy seemed relieved. What was the worse thing that she was expecting to be asked about? Jude hazarded a guess. 'And did Bob Hartson also put pressure on you to limit investigation into Nigel Ackford's death?'

The hotelier was really stung this time. 'No, he did not! I told you, I did that out of self-preservation. I can't risk bad publicity for the hotel.' The hazel eyes once again focused their unforgiving beam. 'Listen, Jude, you're a friend. A good friend. But I don't like the tone of your questioning. I have nothing to hide.'

Jude faced up to her friend. 'No?'

'No. Nothing criminal, anyway. We all have personal secrets.'

'Yes. Of course.' But Jude couldn't let it go. 'Suzy, I'm trying to piece together exactly what happened the night Nigel Ackford died.'

'Well, don't.'

'I'm sorry. I need to. I don't think he committed

suicide, you see. I think someone murdered him.'
There was a silence. 'Come on, tell the truth – what do
you think?'

Suzy's reply was very measured. 'I think some
things are better left undisturbed. You've no idea the
can of worms you could be opening up if you continue
digging away.'

'I'm sorry, Suzy. But I care about the truth.'

'Well, I don't,' she snapped back. 'I care about
keeping going, getting through the days. I care about
my privacy. If you'd spent a life like mine, you'd give
anything for a moment's anonymity.'

'I do understand, love,' said Jude gently. But she
still couldn't leave it. 'Just answer me one more
question . . .'

'What?'

'When we were tidying up that night after the
Pillars of Sussex dinner, your mobile phone rang. Who
was it?'

Suzy Longthorne started to unbutton her overall.
'I'd better get back to the guests. Would you mind
finishing up in here?'

After Suzy had left, Jude became suddenly aware of
the Parmesan vomit smell that surrounded her. She
nearly spoiled all their hard work by throwing up
herself.

Chapter Sixteen

It was early for the phone to ring on a Sunday morning. Barry Stilwell's tone was once again conspiratorial. 'Carole, I need to talk to you.'

She had no reciprocal need to talk to him, but, remembering Jude's exhortations, put a nuance of coyness into her voice as she said, 'Really, Barry?'

'Listen. Pomme's in the bath . . .' This is more information than I need to have, thought Carole. 'So I took the opportunity to call you to see if we could meet again?'

'Sure we could. At some point,' she replied lightly.

'This week. Lunch on Monday.'

'You're talking about tomorrow?'

'Mario's. You know it. And Mario's the soul of discretion.'

Objections rose within her. Not only did she find Barry Stilwell repulsive, she was also opposed on principle to extramarital affairs. (Though if Barry had any thought of actually starting an affair with her, he had another think coming.) 'Are you sure that'd be a good idea?' she asked, rather stiffly.

'I think,' he replied, deepening his voice in the

manner of some film star he had once seen, 'it's the best idea I've had for a long time.'

'Well . . .'

'Go on, say yes, Carole.'

She was torn between her instinct, her principles, and what Jude had said to her. Loyalty to her friend won. 'Very well.'

'Oh, thank you. You don't know how happy that's made me feel.'

If you knew why I'd said yes, you wouldn't feel happy, thought Carole. But she also felt a little frisson of excitement. Maybe she did have a bit of the Mata Hari in her, after all.

'Mario's, one o'clock, tomorrow.' A sudden panic came into Barry Stilwell's voice. 'Pomme's coming out of the bathroom! See you then.'

And the line went dead.

Later that morning, as she let Gulliver scamper around her on Fethering beach, Carole was once again struck by the incongruity of her situation. She, Carole Seddon, was apparently giving the nod to a married man who wanted to have an affair with her. Even more remarkable, to her way of thinking, there actually *was* a married man who wanted to have an affair with her. A repulsive one, true, but he did exist. That would have been a surprise to her former colleagues at the Home Office. And maybe to her former husband.

When they got back to High Tor, Gulliver was ecstatic to see their next-door neighbour, who had just rung the front door bell.

Jude wondered if it would be possible to have a lift to Brighton.

Brighton was looking its most beautiful that April Sunday morning. The white sea-facing frontages of hotels and apartment blocks reminded Jude of the previous night's wedding cake. The usual greeny-beige of the sea had made an effort and was giving a fair approximation to Mediterranean blue. People wandered along the promenade, holding sheaves of Sunday papers, some even anticipating summer in shorts and T-shirts.

Brighton in any season never failed to give Jude's spirits a lift. Carole was a little more old-fashioned about the place. Her thoughts of Brighton were dominated by newspaper headlines about gays and drugs and drunks and divorcees.

So early in the season and so early in the day, she had no problem parking the Renault on the front. Jude pointed up to a tall white monolith. 'That's Kerry's block. Did your parents present you with a flat like that when you were in your teens?'

'Certainly not.' The only exotic thing her parents had given Carole was the 'e' at the end of her name.

'I'd like to say come in with me, but I don't think I'd better. She might clam up.'

'No, of course not. I don't want to come,' Carole lied. 'I'll be fine with the paper.'

She had contemplated bringing Gulliver, but he'd already had a walk, and, besides, he sometimes got over-excited in a strange environment. The smells and sights of Brighton beach might well stir him into a frenzy of Labrador silliness. She'd decided she'd be better off with the *Sunday Telegraph*.

Jude got out of the car, and then looked back in disbelief at her friend, still sitting bolt-upright in the driving seat. 'Are you going to read the paper *there*?'

'Why not?'

'It's a lovely day. You're on one of the most beautiful seafronts in the country. I thought you might sit outside.'

'Yes. I *might*,' Carole conceded stiffly.

Kerry Hartson's flat was certainly splendid. A penthouse with a sitting room that looked out over the sea. Very expensive – and ridiculous, really, to be the home of a girl not yet sixteen. Jude wondered whether Kerry had been given it as a present by her doting parents, or if she had to pay rent. From what she'd heard of Bob Hartson, the answer would depend on the tax position. His stepdaughter might be living in the flat, but it was primarily his investment. So if a nominal rent would avoid paying tax on a gift, Kerry would be paying a nominal rent.

Like the girl's bedroom at Hopwicke House, the sitting room was very untidy, but not dirty. Jude could not imagine Kerry doing the cleaning herself, so no doubt some poor woman with dodgy immigration status was employed to dust round the detritus. CDs, DVDs and all the other essential acronyms of teenage life lay scattered over the floor, along with crumpled foil takeaway packs, dirty glasses and discarded garments.

Kerry herself was dressed in sloppy grey sweats that could have been nightwear or daywear. The room was stuffy and smelt of sleep. MTV pounded from the large screen in the corner, and the girl made no attempt to mute it as she shoved aside some clothes to make room for Jude on the sofa.

Nor did she offer any refreshment. Though on the surface she was her normal, laid-back, rather sulky self, there was a tension in Kerry that morning. Her invitation to Jude at the hotel may have sounded almost casual, but the girl knew something important was at stake.

First, though, she looked derisorily at the girl band sashaying away on the television. 'They're hopeless,' she volunteered.

'Are they?' Jude knew she wasn't qualified to pass judgement on that kind of music.

'Yeah. Manufactured,' Kerry continued knowledgably. 'Came up through *Pop Idol*.'

'Ah?'

'Telly show,' the girl elucidated. 'They haven't got any real talent.'

'Unlike you?'

This wasn't as rude as it sounded. In previous casual conversations Kerry had made no secret of her desire to make it in the pop world.

'I got a better natural voice than any of them.' She spoke as if this were an unarguable fact. 'With all the

129

right grooming – singing lessons, dance classes, designer clothes . . . yeah, I could make it.'

'Good luck. I hope it happens for you.'

The girl smiled slyly. 'Oh, I think it will.'

Was this just the confidence of a child whose parents had always told her she was wonderful? Or did she imagine that, like the flat, success in the music business was something her stepfather could buy for her?

Still, they hadn't met to discuss Kerry's career prospects. Since beating about the bush had never been Jude's favourite mode of approach, she moved on to the main agenda. 'You said you'd tell me what you were doing the night Nigel Ackford died.'

'Yes. I didn't see him – Nigel, the one who died – after I left the bar. He was drinking with all the others. That's the last I saw of him.'

'It wasn't his movements I was asking about, Kerry. It was yours.'

The girl was silent for a moment, then said, 'I went on drinking with my Dad. After the bar closed, he said he'd got a bottle of whisky in his room, so we went on up there.'

'Just the two of you?'

'No, there was another of Dad's friends with us.'

'Who?'

'I can't remember his name. He was one of those Pillars of Sussex.'

'Of course he was. They all were.'

'Yes. Anyway, that's what I was doing.'

The girl seemed relieved, and her eyes strayed

back to MTV. She had answered the question; so far as Kerry was concerned, the interview was over.

But Jude hadn't got enough information. Or rather, she was intrigued by the small amount of information she had been given. If that was all Kerry had to say on the subject, then why hadn't she answered back at the hotel? They had been alone in the kitchen. There was no one there to overhear or question Kerry's version of events. So why the mystery? Why had the girl dragged Jude all the way to Brighton for so little?

The only possible explanation must be that consultation had been required. Kerry had wanted to talk to someone before she detailed her whereabouts on the night of Nigel Ackford's death. And Jude had a pretty good idea of who had been consulted.

As if to confirm her conjecture, at that moment the door to the flat was opened with a key, and Bob Hartson walked in.

Carole was perhaps too protective of her independence. She had an inbuilt resistance to obeying another person's agenda, even when she knew it made good sense. So, although she did follow Jude's advice and read her *Sunday Telegraph* outside the car, perversely she sat in a shelter out of direct sunlight, and with her back to the sea. She therefore saw the Jaguar draw up outside the block opposite, and stay parked on the double yellow lines. She saw the large man get out, but since she'd never met Bob Hartson, had no means of identifying him.

As she allowed the *Sunday Telegraph* to confirm her

right-of-centre views, she occasionally looked up to see the Jaguar still there, its driver playing on a Gameboy. He looked absorbed, content to sit waiting. Presumably that's what being a chauffeur requires, thought Carole, infinities of patience, and always being at someone else's beck and call.

She didn't think it was a job that would suit her.

Bob Hartson's presence filled the room. He was wearing white chinos and a green polo shirt, tight against his biceps. Though beginning to give way to fat, his body was still deeply muscled, and seemed tense with unspoken threat.

'Hello, angel.' He grinned across at his step-daughter, who ran obediently to give him a big hug. Daddy's little girl.

He took in Jude's presence, but without surprise. She was convinced he knew she'd be there. Bob Hartson stretched a paddle of a hand towards her. 'Hi. We met at the hotel last week.'

'Hardly *met*. I was there waitressing.'

'Well . . .' The big man shrugged. He wasn't going to be picky about details. He was friends to everyone. The image he wanted to present that morning was of bonhomie, the magnanimous family man coming to visit his daughter.

'Just been playing golf,' he volunteered, and laughed. 'I didn't think it was possible, but I swear I'm getting worse at that game. When I'm standing over it with a club, the bloody ball seems to have a mind of its own. You ever play golf, Jude?'

That proved his appearance was a set-up. Bob Hartson wouldn't know her name, if he hadn't discussed the morning's rendezvous with his daughter.

'I'm afraid I could never see the attraction,' Jude replied.

'Oh, it's compulsive, you take my word for it. Like everything one can't do, eh? And don't let's pretend, it's also a very useful part of one's business life. Wouldn't believe the number of deals that get sewn up on golf courses, Jude.'

'I think I probably would.'

He chuckled. 'Well, if one can't mix a bit of business and pleasure, then what's life for?'

He really was going out of his way to be pleasant to her. But there was still an undertone of menace in his presence.

'So just dropped by on my way from golf – ' he grinned at Kerry ' – to pick this little lovely up. Geoff'll drive us home. Geoff's my driver,' he added for Jude's benefit.

'Yes, I met him at the hotel.' Since the name had come up, she wasn't going to miss the opportunity. 'Incidentally, on the relevant night at the hotel . . .'

'Mm?' The grin hardened on Bob Hartson's face.

'Geoff slept in the stable block, didn't he, just like I did?'

'Well—' Kerry began to reply, but her father's voice overrode her.

'Yes, that's right. Then he joined me for an early breakfast and drove me back to the office.' He gave his daughter another grin. 'Just as he's about to drive us back to get some of your mum's nice home cooking inside you. All very well, this independent living when you're just a teenager, but you need your parents to fall back on. I don't think you're quite up to doing the full Sunday roast with all the trimmings, are you, angel?'

Jude doubted whether Kerry was up to any meal preparation that involved more than picking up the phone for a takeaway. If she was, she had shown no signs of it in her work at Hopwicke House.

'Presumably, Mr Hartson,' said Jude, 'you know why I'm here this morning?'

He raised his eyebrows in what she knew to be false ignorance.

'Because of Nigel Ackford's death,' she prompted. 'Kerry asked me to come here, so she could tell me what her movements were on that particular night.'

'Oh yes, that's right.' He spoke as if he were pulling the recollection from the deepest recesses of his memory.

'Of course, it must have been very upsetting for you, Mr Hartson.'

'How's that?'

'Well, you must have known Nigel Ackford well. He was your guest, after all, wasn't he? At the dinner?'

'That's right. He was my guest, but he was more an acquaintance than a friend. I invited him along to the Pillars as a kind of favour to his boss who's been a friend of mine for a long time.'

'Why didn't Donald Chew take Nigel Ackford along as his own guest?'

Bob Hartson showed the tiniest of reactions to the

fact she knew the name, then shook his head indulgently. 'There's protocol involved in being a Pillar of Sussex. I could explain it to you, but . . . how long have you got? Just take it from me, it wouldn't have done for Donald to take along one of his own staff as a guest.'

Before Jude could ask for further elucidation, he went on, 'Tragic business, I agree, young Nigel. I read in the paper recently that more young men than ever are committing suicide. Most of them have probably got a better lifestyle than any previous generation, and yet they keep topping themselves. Never understand it . . .'

He moved across to the window, seeming to blot out a disproportionate amount of the view, and spoke more softly. 'So many lovely things in the world, and yet some people just can't see it. Look out there. Sea – beautiful spring day – who'd want to give up on all that, eh?' He laughed lightly. 'Do you know, Jude, this is one of the few views in West Sussex where you can't see anything that belongs to me.' Another little laugh. 'Well, except for Geoff down there in the Jaguar. What I mean is that from here you can't see one of my developments, and that's because all this flat looks out on is the sea. Of course, if you were out there in a boat, you could definitely see one of my developments.'

'This block?'

'That's right. Derelict when I bought the place. Bedsits. Totally run down. And look at it now. People say a lot of harsh things about developers. I like to think we do a lot to bring new life to old buildings.'

Since she hadn't accused him of anything, Jude was

finding this self-justification rather odd. He went on,
'Like most successful ventures, the development business is all about timing and spotting potential. You
have to be able to see what you can do with a site and
be bold and imaginative. Look ahead. There are places
that "informed opinion" says will never get planning
permission. Don't believe them. Governments change.
Policies change. Priorities change. Everything becomes
possible sooner or later.'

Having delivered himself of this property developer's credo while looking out over the sea, he turned.
Backlit against the window, his expression was invisible to Jude, but she could hear the new force in his
voice. 'Listen. I know you're upset by what happened
to that boy. We're all upset – me, Kerry, the other
Pillars – it's the kind of thing nobody wants to happen.
But it was suicide. In spite of any details that might
suggest an alternative scenario. Even that threatening
letter Kerry found, I'm sure there's an innocent explanation for that.' His voice became soothing, but did not
lose its strength. 'Jude, the police seem convinced it
was suicide. I would imagine the coroner will think the
same. So I don't really think it's a good idea to go
around stirring things up. I'm sure we all love the
thought of playing detectives, of proving wrong-doing –
all dramatic stuff. But not in this case. Here, what you
see is what you get. And what everyone sees, and I
think you should see too, Jude, is the tragic case of a
young man's suicide.'

There was nothing equivocal about Bob Hartson's

manner. She was being warned off. And, for that very reason, she couldn't let it rest there.

'Mr Hartson, could you just confirm what Kerry told me about where she was that night?'

Even though she still couldn't see his face, she observed the spasm of anger that passed through his body. But by the time he replied, he had regained control, and his voice was silky smooth. 'I don't know what Kerry's just told you. I can only give you my version of what happened, and if my daughter told you different, then she's lying.' Jude felt a surge of excitement, which quickly dissipated as he went on, 'After everyone left the bar, Kerry came up to my room with me and a friend. We all drank some whisky, then Kerry left us, my friend and I had a final noggin and he went off to his room about two o'clock, I suppose.'

'Thank you very much, Mr Hartson.'

He stepped away from the window and sat down, before looking smugly at his stepdaughter. 'So what did Kerry tell you? I've no idea.'

'I told her the same, Dad.'

'The truth. Good girl.' He turned back to focus the patronizing beam of his smile on Jude. 'Anything else I can help you with?'

'Yes, please.'

There was a twitch of annoyance at the corner of the developer's mouth. 'What?'

'Who was the friend, the other Pillar of Sussex, who came back to drink with you in your room?'

'His name,' Bob Hartson replied with suppressed annoyance, 'was Barry Stilwell.'

137

Chapter Seventeen

'But that's impossible,' said Carole as they drove back through the bungaloid sprawl that separated Brighton from Fethering. 'Barry doesn't drink whisky.'

'Are you sure?'

'He told me he never touched spirits. Doesn't like the taste.'

'He wasn't just saying that? Maybe he tells his wife – the sainted Pom-Pom – that he doesn't touch whisky, but when he's back with the boys . . .?'

'I don't think so. He volunteered the information to me when we had lunch at Mario's last week. Pomme wasn't there. He had no reason to feel pressured about it.'

'True. That's very interesting, Carole. I do hope you'll be seeing Barry Stilwell again soon.'

'Well . . .' In spite of herself, Carole blushed. 'I am supposed to be meeting him again for lunch tomorrow, but I'm not sure that I really should . . .'

'Of course you should. It's your duty, Carole. In the cause of truth.'

The spark in Jude's eye sent up the pomposity of her announcement, but there was a core of seriousness in what she said. Carole knew she had no choice but to continue betraying her sisterhood with Pomme.

'I wondered what your verdict was,' asked Stephen.

'What?' Carole couldn't imagine what her son was talking about. She was still getting over the surprise of his ringing on a Sunday evening. Their relationship was not on a relaxed enough footing to take that kind of event in its stride.

'Your verdict on the hotel. You said you were going to have a look at Hopwicke Country House Hotel for us.'

'Oh yes, of course.' So caught up had she been in what Jude would have described as 'the murder investigation' she had completely forgotten the real purpose of her visit.

'Well, the hotel's delightful. Lovely position, very nice rooms, wonderful menus. Of course, it is pretty pricey.'

'How much?'

'A lot. But if you stay two nights including a Saturday, there is a special deal for—'

'Gaby and I can only stay for the one night. How much would that cost?'

Carole told him the prices Suzy had quoted her.

'That's fine,' he said, without a moment's reflection. 'We'll go for that four-poster room.' Carole couldn't get used to the image of her son as a big spender. Maybe he'd always had it in him. Or was it just the influence – and income – of Gaby that had moved him up to another level of expenditure? Carole felt the familiar guilt at how little she really knew Stephen.

'Do you have the number there to hand, Mother? Save me the cost of a call to directory enquiries.' So down at the bottom end of the financial scale he was still capable of penny-pinching.

'Oh, by the way . . . did you ask about availability for the weekend? I don't want to waste a call if they're fully booked.' Once again the instinct for parsimony asserted itself.

'They certainly had rooms free when I was there. And I didn't get the impression they were expecting a sudden rush of bookings.'

'Fine. OK. Gaby and I will see you there for lunch on Sunday. Arrive twelve-thirty.'

And thus Carole was dismissed. As she put the phone down, she realized she should have said something about being very excited at the prospect of meeting Gaby. But the moment had passed.

Slightly mischievously, she wondered how her son would react to the news that tomorrow his mother would be having an illicit lunch with a married would-be lover.

'This is very soon after our last meeting,' Carole pointed out, after Mario had oozed them into their seats. This time he'd put them at a table for two in a little alcove at the back of the restaurant. Was this maybe the table where he always put couples who shouldn't be together? Indeed, had he put Barry here before with other female companions? The concept did not upset Carole; rather, it amused her. To imagine Barry Stilwell as a serial Lothario was so incongruous.

What was it with men? she reflected. Some of them seemed to be armoured in a self-esteem absolutely impermeable to logic, common sense or experience. Barry Stilwell's previous encounters with her should have made it clear that, not only did she not have any mildly romantic feelings towards him, she did not even wish to spend time with him. She found his company irksome. And yet here he was, surreptitiously squiring her at Mario's, apparently in the belief they would end up having an affair. Carole found herself baffled.

But his obtuseness did give her a kind of comfort. She would have felt bad stringing along someone less thick-skinned. Barry Stilwell, though, was fair game.

She indulged these thoughts while he went through his ordering and wine-tasting routines, and had to actually drag herself out of abstraction to concentrate on what he was saying.

Barry was talking about the success of his firm. Clearly things had been busy on the soliciting front. A booming housing market had meant an increase in people requiring conveyancing services; the cold snaps of the winter had satisfyingly decimated the geriatric population of the Worthing area, leading to more probate work; and of course the rise in the divorce rate could always be relied upon. It was, as ever, a good time to be working as a lawyer in a system devised by lawyers.

So good was business Carole gathered when she focused on Barry's words, that he was about to set up a second office along the coast in Shoreham. There were some empty premises he was going to inspect that very afternoon. Maybe Carole would like to come and cast her expert eye over them?

'In what way do I have an expert eye?'

'Well, you spent all those years working for the Home Office.'

'What's that got to do with anything?' Carole knew she should be more conciliatory, soften Barry up to extract information from him, but he got on her nerves so much she couldn't help the occasional sharp retort.

'You must have seen a good few offices in your time.'

'Yes,' she conceded.

'So you do have an expert eye when it comes to the business of selecting an office.' At this triumph of logic the thin lips curled into a smile.

'But, Barry, I have no particular expertise in solicitor's offices. You'd have a much better idea of what you need.'

'Yes.' he said cajolingly. 'But it's always good to have a second opinion, isn't it?'

'Surely it'd be better to get a second opinion from Pomme rather than from me?'

This had been the wrong thing to say. The thin lips straightened. 'Pomme's not a lawyer.'

'Nor am I. That's the point I was making.'

He moved off the subject of his new offices. 'So what's happening in your life, Carole?'

She didn't want to talk about her life. What she really wanted to do was to get Barry's conversation back to the night of Nigel Ackford's death. But certain civilities had to be maintained. He had asked her a straight question. It was her duty to come up with an answer. She tried to think what, if anything, had been happening in her life.

'Well, I'm meeting my son for lunch on Sunday.'

'I'd forgotten you had a son.'

'Yes. He's going to introduce me to his fiancée.'

'And I find it very hard to believe you have a son old enough to be contemplating marriage.'

She gave this arch automatic compliment a minimal smile, and moved on. She'd seen a useful way of redirecting the conversation.

'In fact, they're going to be staying at the Hopwicke Country House Hotel. I'm going to have lunch with them there.'

'I'm sure you'll enjoy it. Excellent food.'

'Oh yes.' She behaved as if a completely new idea had just come to her. 'Of course you were there for that Pillars of Sussex dinner, weren't you? We talked about it last time we met.'

'That's right.'

He didn't sound suspicious yet, so she pressed on. 'I get the impression those dinners are quite riotous occasions.'

'Well . . . I like to think decorum is always maintained.'

'Yes, but quite a lot of drinking goes on, doesn't it?'

Barry Stilwell smiled a bit-of-a-lad smile, and went into the elaborate circumlocution with which his type of man usually speaks about alcohol. 'Well, the occasional libation is certainly consumed. The odd noggin or tincture might pass the lips, yes.'

'More than "occasional" or "odd", from what I've heard. Drinks before dinner, copious wine during, sessions in the bar afterwards.'

The solicitor shrugged magnanimously, as if he were being complimented. 'A certain amount of that goes on, I suppose, yes. But,' he continued piously, 'everyone stays overnight at the venue, so there's no danger of drink-driving.'

'I wasn't suggesting that. I gather, though, with some of the Pillars, the drinking doesn't stop in the bar. It goes on up in their rooms.'

This prompted an indulgent smile of masculine complicity. 'I dare say that happens with some of the chaps.'

'Don't be so coy, Barry. It happens with you too.'

He looked surprised at this and said primly, 'I'm not one for excess, Carole. I know my limit. A couple of drinks in the bar, and then straight off to bed – that's me.'

Coyness was not a mode that came naturally to Carole, but she tried it this time. 'Ooh, Barry, you big fibber.'

He looked genuinely puzzled.

'A friend of mine met Bob Hartson yesterday.'

'Yes?' A look of caution came into his eyes at the mention of the name.

'He was telling her about the great night you all had at Hopwicke House last week.'

'Oh right, we did have a good time,' he agreed

heartily, before a sober recollection. 'Except, of course, for the tragic end to the event – which we didn't know about till the following day.'

'Anyway, according to Bob Hartson, you had quite a boozy session with him.'

This again was taken as a compliment. 'I suppose a few sherberts did go down the old gargle-chute in the bar, yes.'

'Not just in the bar,' said Carole, with another stab at coyness.

She felt sure the bafflement with which he greeted this was genuine, but went on, 'According to Bob Hartson, you were up in his room sharing a bottle of whisky with him.' – Barry Stilwell was silent – 'Which I thought was rather odd because you told me you never drank whisky.'

There was an almost imperceptible moment of thought before his smile became even more sheepish. 'My little secret is out, I'm afraid. Not something I advertise, because Pomme doesn't approve of my drinking whisky. She's of the view it gets me too drunk too quickly. But yes, I can't deny I do enjoy the odd snifter of the old Highland nectar.'

'And that's what you had with Bob Hartson that night in his room?'

He held his hands out, as if offering to be hand-cuffed. 'Can't deny it. If that's what Bob Hartson says I was doing, then that's what I was doing.'

'Just the two of you?'

'Oh yes.'

Now that *was* intriguing.

'You're sure Kerry wasn't with you? Bob Hartson's stepdaughter?'

'No,' Barry Stilwell replied with surprising vehemence. 'She certainly wasn't.'

Carole didn't reckon she was going to get much more relevant information, but what she had was good enough. Either Bob Hartson or Barry Stilwell was lying. Maybe they both were. Bob Hartson had possibly plucked Barry Stilwell's name out of the air to support his alibi, not knowing that Jude had a friend with a connection to the solicitor. Barry's reactions had suggested he knew nothing about the story he was supposed to be backing up, but had supported it out of solidarity to another Pillar of Sussex. Maybe he would soon get a phone call from Bob Hartson spelling out the party line on the events of that evening.

So, as Carole nibbled at her *insalata di frutti di mare* and Barry worked his way through his *bresaola, vitello alla Genovese* and *tartufi di cioccolota*, the conversation became more general, though the solicitor did constantly revert to his potential offices in Shoreham. He kept saying how pleasant and quiet they were, detailing the excellent amenities they offered, and emphasizing that they offered vacant possession.

It was only in the car park, when a leering Barry Stilwell actually dangled the keys to the offices in front of her, that Carole's rather slow perception caught up with his meaning. He had no interest in her views on the suitability of the premises for a solicitor's office; he saw it simply as a means of being alone with her. The excellent amenities, he spelled out, included a bed.

At this point, in the traditional style of the investigative journalist, Carole Seddon made her excuses and left.

Barry Stilwell, having seen her previous performance in the role, thought she was just once again being coy. And he determined to follow the old axiom of Robert the Bruce watching that extremely pertinacious spider: 'If at first you don't succeed, try, try again.' She'd come round. Of course she would. There was no possibility that she didn't find him attractive.

Chapter Eighteen

The Crown and Anchor had seats and tables at the front, looking across to where the River Fether ran out into the sea, but there was also an overgrown garden at the back, which Ted Crisp kept saying he was going to get tidied up and open for customers. But all that seemed to happen was that the garden, like his beard and his hair, just got more matted and messy.

'Hardly worth doing,' he said to Carole and Jude, as they looked through the window at the patch that Monday evening. 'Soon be next door to a building site, anyway.'

'What do you mean by that?' asked Carole.

The landlord pointed to the crumbling wall of a long, low structure on the other side of the pub garden. 'Old milk depot, that was. Used to be full of tankers and floats. Been empty for five years now. Soon be a nice shooshed-up residential estate, though.'

'Really?'

'Yes, I've seen the plans. Go on, have a guess how many houses they're going to fit on to that site.'

'Eight?' Jude hazarded.

He gave a derisory laugh. 'If only. The answer is twenty-four.'

'Twenty-four? On that space? Is there a lot of land the other side of the depot?' asked Carole.

'No. What you see is what you get. Within the perimeter of that existing building they are going to fit twenty-four residences. Starter homes, I think they call them. Two bedrooms and a pocket handkerchief of garden each.'

'Garages?'

'No. Won't be room for that.'

'So where are they going to park?' Carole instinctively asked the question any local would ask. 'Fethering High Street's already jammed solid. If High Tor didn't have a garage, I don't know what I'd do.'

'This is quite funny, actually,' said Ted, as he led them gloomily back across to the bar. 'Or at least it would be funny, if it weren't so bloody insane.' He took a bottle of Chilean Chardonnay out of the fridge. 'Come on, let me top you up. On the house.'

'You're pouring away all your profits,' Jude reprimanded him, as he filled the glasses.

'No way. Don't do this for everyone, you know. Only special customers.' He guffawed. 'And don't worry, I overcharge the rest, so it all evens up in the end.'

'You were talking about these starter homes,' Carole reminded him.

'Right. OK, well, what I'm about to tell you is government policy – if that's not a contradiction in terms with this lot in charge. One of the local architects comes to drink in here, he was telling me about it. You've probably heard there's a housing shortage in the south-east?'

'Yes.'

'So, the various possible solutions to that are: build new towns; extend the outskirts of existing towns and villages; start nibbling away at the Green Belt. But no. What the government, in its wisdom, has decided to do is not extend the area of existing housing, but to develop brown-field sites.'

'Like the old milk depot?'

'Exactly, Carole. And on these sites they want a greater density of housing.'

'More people living per square metre?'

'That's the idea, yes. But, of course, if you're going to do that, then you've got to keep the footprint of each house pretty damned small. No room for fripperies like garages.'

'Mind you,' Jude pointed out, 'it's not all bad, from your point of view. If you've got twenty-four new houses right behind you, that's not going to do any harm to your business, is it?'

Ted didn't seem to be persuaded. 'Maybe, maybe not. It'll certainly mean complaints about noise, kids thieving from my premises, cars clogging access to my car park.'

'Yes,' Carole, the proud Renault-owner insisted, 'where *are* the new residents supposed to put their cars?'

Ted Crisp grinned sardonically. 'Ah, now this is the clever bit. This is where the government suddenly does a little nod to the green lobby.' He pronounced his next words as though imparting the secret of life. 'Apparently, the fact that the new residents have nowhere to park *will encourage them to make greater use of public transport!'*

'But public transport round here's dreadful,' Jude objected.

'Yes,' Ted agreed. 'That is the small miscalculation the government has made. You'd think they'd realize they'd got the whole thing arse-about-face. The sensible plan, a naive person might imagine, would be *first* to get good public transport, *then* build houses without garages to attract people without cars. But no, that's not the way this government does things.' He ran an exasperated hand through his beard. 'Don't get me started on this government.'

'No, no, fine,' said Jude hastily. Ted Crisp had suffered a lot since the election of New Labour. A lifelong socialist, faced with a government of decidedly Tory tendencies, he had nobody left to vote for. Jude, herself without politics of any colour, could nonetheless sympathize with his frustration.

'Still,' he went on savagely, 'all be good news for the developers, won't it? They'll get a very cushy ride indeed – as ever. Nothing like a nice housing boom to boost the building trade, is there? Lots of profit for the developers, and the builders, and the decorators, and the plumbers, and the electricians, and their attendant army of local planners, and solicitors, and accountants and Uncle Tom Cobleigh and all. God, don't get me started!'

Though he kept asking to be stopped, Ted Crisp was clearly about to get started. 'When I think I grew up believing the Labour Party was the party of equality, that its principles encouraged the distribution of wealth to the less privileged members of—'

It was, in many ways, fortunate that at that point a large party of customers entered the Crown and Anchor. Once Ted did start on one of his diatribes, his listeners could be transfixed for a long, long time. With some relief, Carole and Jude crept away to one of the alcove tables. After that day's lunch with Barry Stilwell, Carole had become more aware of the significance of alcoves. She wondered how many illicit couples had exploited the privacy of the one where they now sat in the Crown and Anchor.

Jude was quickly brought up to date with what had been said during the lunch at Mario's. 'I'm certain,' Carole concluded, 'that he was just making it up. That dreadful male solidarity thing. Bob Hartson, a fellow Pillar of Sussex, had used Barry's name to establish an alibi, and Barry wasn't going to let another chap down. I'm sure he wasn't in that bedroom with Bob. Apart from the contradiction about drinking whisky, he didn't know that Kerry was supposed to be there with them.'

'Perhaps,' said Jude thoughtfully, 'he *did* know that Kerry was there.'

'What do you mean?' Carole looked at Jude, and the expression on her face told her exactly what her friend meant. 'That Kerry was alone in the bedroom with her stepfather. That— Oh, surely not?'

Jude shrugged. 'Wouldn't be the first time it had happened to a stepdaughter. She's a pretty girl. She greeted him very affectionately when he came round to her flat yesterday morning.'

The idea was still too extreme for Carole Seddon's hidebound mind. 'Surely not?' she repeated.

'Maybe not,' Jude conceded. 'But it's a possibility. Another idea to throw into the mix. What we now know for sure, though, is that there have been cover-ups about that night at the hotel. And I'm still intrigued about Bob Hartson's driver.'

'What?'

'You know – he's called Geoff. And he's supposed to have spent the relevant night in the stable block, as I did. But I wonder . . . When I asked about that at Kerry's flat, she could have been about to say something different when her father interrupted her.'

'Oh?'

'So perhaps we should check Geoff out.' Jude let an exasperated stream of air hiss through her teeth. 'The one thing that's clear is that somebody had something to hide. Either Kerry, or her stepfather.'

'Or possibly Barry Stilwell,' Carole added.

'How? Sorry, not with you.'

'Well, alibis work both ways. Suppose Bob Hartson knew that Barry was up to something that night. He might have volunteered the alibi to save suspicion pointing at his fellow Pillar of Sussex.'

'It's possible.' Jude sounded sceptical, but Carole was quite excited. The thought of Barry Stilwell as a potential murderer did at least make him a little bit more interesting.

Jude was up at the bar getting refills when she saw yet another photograph of Suzy Longthorne. In an open copy of the *Daily Mail*, which either Ted had provided for his customers or one of them had left behind, was another picture dating back to the time of Suzy's marriage to Rick Hendry. The pair of them, in suitably glamorous garb, had been snapped going into the Odeon Leicester Square for the preview of some long-forgotten film.

Suzy wouldn't have thanked the *Daily Mail* for the caption. 'Rick Hendry with ex-wife, former beauty Suzy Longthorne'. For someone whose entire career had been predicated on glamour, to be called a *former* beauty must, Jude estimated, be pretty hurtful.

But even more striking than the caption was the headline. 'TV'S MR NASTY DENIES UNDERAGE SEX ALLEGATIONS'.

Avidly Jude read what followed.

Yesterday, Rick Hendry, the Hannibal Lecter of Pop, angrily rejected the suggestion that he had taken advantage of young girls auditioning for ITV's successful *Pop Crop* series. The girls, who are too young to be named, claimed the ageing rocker "touched them up" in their dressing rooms before they sang for the judges in Norwich. Rick, busy in Brighton with more auditions for the new series, was unavailable for comment, but a statement issued by his agent said, 'These claims are totally false. The world is full of publicity seeking teenagers, who want their thirty seconds of fame. It's one of the downsides of celebrity that anyone can make allegations like this and get away with it. If any more of this nonsense is put about, Mr Hendry's lawyers are more than ready to prove his innocence in court.'

Jude took the paper across to show Carole, who read it and said rather sniffily, 'Huh. Can't get away from your friend Suzy, can we?'

When Jude got back to Woodside Cottage, there was a message on the answering machine. A male voice asked her to ring him back and gave a mobile number.

Intrigued, she replayed the message and tried to analyse the voice. Very laid-back, slightly mid-Atlantic, slightly arrogant, but with an undertow of charm. The voice of a man who was used to getting his own way. And distantly familiar.

She rang the number. The same voice answered straight away, with a cautious 'Hi.'

'My name's Jude. You left a message.'

'Oh, Jude, right. Thanks for getting back to me.' There was a silence, as if he was selecting an approach for the next stage of his conversation. 'Listen, my name's Rick Hendry.'

He left a pause for her to react. He was used to being recognized. Jude had known who he was as soon as he answered the phone, but she wasn't going to give him the satisfaction of sounding impressed.

'Yes, we met when you were married to Suzy.'

'Right.' He didn't sound as though he remembered. He had always been media- and celebrity-obsessed, so meeting one of his wife's friends who had no national profile wouldn't have registered in his long-term memory.

'It's about Suzy I was ringing,' he went on. 'And about what happened at the hotel last Tuesday.'

'Do you mean the death of that solicitor?'

'Right.' Again he seemed to consider his options for a moment. 'Listen, Suze told me you were around the place that night.'

'I didn't know you two were still in touch.'

'Sure, sure,' he said soothingly. 'We never lost touch. Very civilized divorce.'

Not in the version Suzy gave me, thought Jude. But then again, she didn't know of a single parted couple where both participants would give the same account of their split. So she let Rick Hendry go on.

'Suze is worried.'

'About what?'

'About you, to be honest.'

Jude was angry. 'Then why doesn't she tell me herself? We're friends. If she's got something to say to me, she can say it direct.'

'Hey, cool it, cool it,' he said. His voice had a caressing quality, which he clearly thought was sexy. And, although she was annoyed, Jude was not totally immune to its charms. Rick Hendry had a way with women. 'Yes, OK, Suze could say it to you direct, but I don't think she will. She feels bad about getting at you because, like you said, you're her friend. It's not that she's set me up to do this. I just know she's worried, and she wants you to back off.'

'Back off from what?' asked Jude, deliberately obtuse.

'From what you're doing. Snooping around. I know Suze would feel a lot happier if you . . . let sleeping solicitors lie. Listen, the guy committed suicide. That's what the police think. That's what everyone else thinks. So can you just leave it at that?'

'I'm not sure I can. I want to know what really happened.'

'Why?'

The direct question was hard to answer. The only formula of words Jude could come up with sounded impossibly righteous – phrases about truth and justice and resolution, which, if she voiced them, would only have sounded priggish. So she kept silent.

'Listen, Jude.' Rick Hendry let his voice deepen, as he focused the full beam of his charm on her. 'I still care about Suze. She's built that hotel up from nothing. She's done it all, it's her baby, and the whole set-up's pretty dodgy at the moment, from the financial point of view. Bad publicity she doesn't need. I'm not asking this for myself, Jude. I'm asking it for Suze. And I'm asking you, as her friend, just to let this thing rest – OK? Now, Jude, will you promise me you'll do that?'

'I'll think about it.'

She thought about a lot after she had put the phone

down, but not about giving up her quest to find Nigel Ackford's murderer. If anything, the call to Rick Hendry had strengthened her resolve.

The list of people who wanted to cover up the truth of that night at Hopwicke House was getting longer by the minute. And why was Rick Hendry suddenly so solicitous for the ex-wife from whom he'd parted with such acrimony? He said Suzy hadn't needed bad publicity, but he needed it even less – particularly at a time when the *Daily Mail* was running damaging stories about him. What was Rick Hendry's connection with Hopwicke Country House Hotel? Or with the young man who had died there?

The fact that she'd had the call from Rick so soon after reading about him neither troubled Jude nor surprised her. She had never had a problem believing in synchronicity.

Chapter Nineteen

The call came through to High Tor in the middle of the Tuesday morning. 'It's all right. I'm calling from the office.'

Which meant that Barry was out of earshot of the threatening Pomme, so why did he still have to whisper?

'It was very lovely to see you at lunchtime yesterday.'

Carole couldn't bring herself to reciprocate the sentiment, but she did manage to thank him for the meal.

'And I'm sorry you didn't feel ready to *come and see the new office with me.*' He made the words sound like a euphemism for something really disgusting.

'It wasn't a matter of "feeling ready" or not; it was a matter of not wanting to,' she snapped. Jude would disapprove of her threatening the continuance of Barry Stilwell as a contact within the Pillars of Sussex, but Carole had had enough of his sly insinuations, and she thought she'd probably exhausted his stock of relevant information anyway.

He seemed impervious to her put-downs. 'Don't worry, Carole, I'm prepared to wait for as long as it takes.' How about till hell freezes over and they hold the Winter Olympics there? 'You'll come round,' Barry went on. 'You know there's something between us.'

Loathing, on my side, thought Carole. Whatever Jude's views, the situation could not be tolerated much longer. The moment was fast coming when Barry Stilwell must be given a massive, unequivocal brush-off.

But he didn't let her get to that moment. 'There was one thing I thought I ought to make clear, Carole darling' – *Darling* – yeuch! 'about yesterday. I may have given you the wrong impression . . .'

No, I think the impression you gave me was exactly the one you intended to. The wrong impression was the one you seemed to take away of my reactions to your advances.

'It was my own fault. None of us are entirely responsible in our cups.'

'Oh, come on, you didn't have that much to drink.'

'I wasn't talking about yesterday. I was talking about the week before, after the Pillars of Sussex dinner at Hopwicke House.'

'Ah.'

'As I say, it's my own fault. I like whisky, but it doesn't like me. And I'm afraid it was the whisky that rather blurred my recollections of the end of the evening . . .' He paused, but Carole didn't give him any help. 'The fact is, I think I told you that I was up in Bob Hartson's room drinking whisky, and there were just the two of us.'

'That's what you said, yes.'

'Well, the point is, I'd completely forgotten . . . but his daughter was with us too . . . stepdaughter, that is. Kerry. Don't know if you know her?'

'I saw her briefly when I went to the hotel.'

'Right. Well, she was there – that night – so it was the three of us drinking whisky.'

'I see. And who finished first?'

'Sorry?'

'Who was the first one to stop drinking whisky and go back to their own room?'

'Oh. Kerry. Yes. Kerry's not much of a whisky drinker. She just had a small one and tootled off to her bed. And then, a bit later, I rolled off to mine.' He chuckled at the folly of his alcoholic excess. 'Had a bit of a head in the morning, I can tell you.'

'Hm. And on the way back to your bed in the middle of the night . . .'

'Yes?'

'You didn't happen to see Nigel Ackford, did you?'

'No, good heavens, no. Of course I didn't.' Having expressed his shock at the mere idea, Barry moved back into seductive mode. 'Do you know something, Carole?'

Yes, she thought. I know Bob Hartson has been on the phone, giving you a three-line whip to toe the party line.

Jude knew she ought to talk to Suzy directly; they had been friends for long enough. In the past there had never been any subjects that were off-limits between them, but suddenly there were. In their last two

161

conversations, Suzy had clammed up on her. And now the ex-husband was putting in his two penn'orth as well. Neither of them wanted any further investigation into the death of Nigel Ackford.

The Pillars of Sussex seemed equally against the idea. Nor did the police apparently have any trouble with the suicide verdict.

Jude might by this stage have started to think she was over-reacting. There was a lot of logic against the idea of Nigel Ackford having been murdered, and she might reluctantly have come round to the majority view. But two recent events made her more convinced than ever that something strange had happened that night at Hopwicke House. The conversation she had had with Rick Hendry was one of them. Why on earth should he suddenly be concerning himself with the affairs of the hotel?

The other anomaly had arisen from Carole's phone conversation with Barry Stilwell, which she had, needless to say, reported verbatim to Jude. The clumsiness with which the solicitor had supported Bob Hartson's alibi left no doubt that somebody was lying.

So, on one side, Suzy and Rick; on the other, the Pillars of Sussex . . . and possibly Kerry. Both groups had something to cover up. Or – unlikely though it might seem – were they working together to cover up the same thing?

Jude decided, before another direct confrontation with Suzy, she should try a more oblique approach. Someone else had been around Hopwicke Country House Hotel on the night of Nigel Ackford's death; and so far as Jude knew, he hadn't yet been a part of any cover-up. She had his mobile number; he'd given it to her once when there had been a crisis about a potential double booking in the restaurant. Jude rang Max Townley.

She decided there'd be no harm in a direct approach. It was as likely to work as any other. 'Wondered if we could just meet for a chat? Wanted to talk about that night at the hotel, when Nigel Ackford died.'

'Oh yeah. And I got a bit too deep into the vodka, because of what had happened with that bloody production company. I thought my television prospects were totally buggered.'

'That's right. Well, I've been, sort of, putting two and two together about things, and there are just a couple of ideas I'd like to run by you.'

Max sounded surprisingly enthusiastic. 'Sure, I'd be game for that.'

He was currently at the hotel, doing the morning preparations. He'd finish those round one, then be off duty until he came back about five-thirty to ready himself for the evening's dinners. His home was in Worthing – chef's hours necessitated living either on the premises or very near by – and he'd be happy to meet up with Jude for a cup of coffee.

As she ended the call, Jude asked herself about one of the great mysteries of the catering business. What do chefs do in the afternoon? Her own experience couldn't really provide an answer. When she had run a cafe, it had been a very ad hoc affair, with her doing most of the work and her various helpers mucking in as and when. Her life had not followed the rhythms of a proper restaurant chef. Given the fact that many of them worked late hours and were in early in the mornings to check the day's orders and start their preparations, she assumed a lot of chefs dedicated their afternoons to sleeping. Maybe some used the time to conduct elaborate love lives, to pursue academic study, or to go fishing. Perhaps, considering how little all but the top celebrity chefs were paid, some of them spent their afternoons as minicab drivers. It was a question to which Jude had never before directed her attention.

She had arranged to meet Max in the same coffee shop where she had talked to Wendy Fullerton. As she waited, she wondered what was going on in the mind of the girl who was presumably at work in the building society opposite. Was Wendy managing to maintain her detachment from Nigel Ackford's death, or were tears constantly threatening to break through the veneer of her make-up?

Jude had a feeling she probably needed to talk to Wendy Fullerton again. There were other questions to which Wendy might provide useful answers, answers which might provide direction for Jude's investigation. At the moment it felt rudderless, drifting in a sea which contained too many suspects and too little information.

When Max Townley arrived, Jude realized how little she actually knew him. She had met him a few times in the hotel kitchen; she had seen him posturing and bitching, presenting his persona of the temperamental culinary genius; but she had no idea what he was like beneath the surface. If he hadn't said that throw-away line about liking women, she would even have had doubts about his sexual orientation. A certain high campness was an essential ingredient of the image he presented to the world.

What became obvious as soon as he spoke that afternoon was how incredibly self-centred he was. Jude had wondered why he had so readily agreed to meet her, but it instantly became clear he thought her interest was in him rather than in Nigel Ackford, or indeed anything else in the world.

'I assume you know why I was upset, why I hit the vodka that night.'

'No, I'm afraid I don't.'

'I thought that was what you wanted to talk about.' Jude looked at him curiously, as he explained. 'The bad news I'd had that afternoon.'

'I remember you mentioning bad news, but you didn't tell me exactly what it was.'

'Oh.' Max looked flummoxed and slightly petulant. He was wearing grey jeans and a black Ted Baker T-shirt. He looked the smart off-duty professional who wouldn't need to change if filming was suddenly required. 'I'd heard that afternoon about the television pilot,' he went on, as though Jude should be familiar with all the details.

'The pilot you did as a TV chef?' she pieced together.

'Yes.' His lower lip jutted in childish petulance, as he continued, 'It was all set up. The producers told me it'd be a shoo-in. I'll show you the video one day. The format's a great idea – not just me cooking, but bringing in, like, these other unknown chefs, just people I've met at restaurants or pubs I've been to. So it's different from what anyone else is doing . . . though of course it's still me at the centre of the whole thing. No, you must see the video. I mean, it wasn't done with full production values, but, you know, it gives a very good idea of how the format would work. I'm bloody good in it – got a bloody sight more personality than Gary Rhodes or Jamie Oliver.' He sneered at the names. 'And I'm a bloody sight better cook. Oh, no, *I* wasn't the reason why the BBC turned the idea down.'

'Then what was the reason?'

'Went with the wrong production company, didn't I? Should have taken my talents direct to the BBC, rather than going through an independent. OK, the company I went with have got a good track record of getting programmes made, but it's all been with ITV.'

'Ah. Of course,' said Jude, as though this made everything clear.

'So the Beeb's going to be pretty resistant to anything they offer, isn't it?'

'I thought these days independent production companies sold across the channels.'

'No way. Well, some of the big ones do. I'm sure, if your production company's got a big hit and is flavour of the month, you can sell anything to anyone, but that's not the general rule.' Max had justified the reasons for his rejection, and he wasn't going to let mere details like facts get in the way. 'Some are always selling to ITV, some to the BBC. I should have realized, but I'm a bit naive when it comes to that kind of stuff. I mean, I haven't got a media background like you.'

Like me? She let it pass.

'But the trouble is, I'm really buggered now. Because I've been offered to the BBC, and been rejected – for the wrong reasons, but nobody's going to know that – it's like I can't be offered there again.'

'Couldn't you be offered to ITV?'

He grimaced. 'Not such a track record there with cookery programmes. They haven't really developed their own line in celebrity chefs. I suppose Channel 4's a possibility . . . unless you've got any other ideas?'

'Me?'

'Yes. Presumably that's why you wanted to meet.'

Jude couldn't quite believe the direction the conversation was taking. 'I'm sorry?'

'You said you'd been putting two and two together.'

'Yes.'

'And there were a couple of ideas you wanted to run by me.'

'But I said ideas about the night Nigel Ackford died,' Jude pointed out.

'Yes. And that was the day I'd heard about being rejected by the BBC. I thought you had some ideas about my future as a celebrity chef.'

His self-centredness was quite astonishing. He seemed unaware of any world outside his own. At that moment Jude knew rumours of Suzy having an affair with Max must be nonsense. Suzy would never link herself to such a blinkered egotist.

'Max,' Jude said gently, 'I didn't ask to see you to talk about your career.'

'Oh.' The disappointment was undisguised. 'But I thought you, with your media background . . .'

'Let's get this straight. I don't *have* a media background.'

'You said you and Suzy—'

'I met Suzy in my late teens when we were both models. We stayed friends, but I very quickly gave up the catwalk and went into theatre.'

'And television?'

'I did a little bit of television, yes.'

'Then you must still have useful contacts who could help me . . .'

She was surprised at the desperation of his naivety. She'd have expected him to be more streetwise. He'd rubbed shoulders with celebrities; he should have known better how the media world worked, and how short memories were there.

'Max, I ceased to have any contact with the world of television in the early seventies. Any people I knew who might have had any influence in the medium are long retired, probably dead. I'm afraid I can't help you at all in that way.'

His desolation was almost comical, and Jude realized once again how potent was the dream of television fame. Max nursed the fantasy of being taken up as a media darling, of having his face spread across the nation's screens and magazines, of lucrative deals for supermarket ads, of recipe books piling up at the top of the best-sellers' lists. That was his escape route, his way out of the daily grind of preparing unappreciated food for the guests at Hopwicke House. Television fame could get him out of his flat in Worthing, and into the glamorous metropolitan world which he reckoned was his rightful milieu. He could buy an even more expensive motorbike.

Max came back to life, his desolation replaced by a resentful curiosity. 'Then why did you ask to meet, if it wasn't about helping me to get on television?'

'I wanted to talk to you about what happened that night at the hotel.'

Max Townley looked puzzled. 'We have talked about it. I've told you. I was pissed off about being rejected by the Beeb, so I drowned my sorrows in vodka.'

'Something else happened.'

For a moment he genuinely did not remember anything else happening. Then he said, 'Oh yes, of course, that solicitor topped himself.'

'Yes. I wondered what thoughts you had about that?'

He shrugged. 'Not many. One solicitor more or less in the world – doesn't make a lot of difference, does it? Some people might even think it was a good thing.'

'But you didn't see or hear anything odd that night?'

He didn't like the new direction of her questioning. 'You've asked me this stuff before. And last time you even insinuated I might have been having it off with Kerry, which I didn't take to very kindly.'

'I'm sorry. But you are quite friendly with Kerry.'

'I'm friendly with lots of people – doesn't mean I shag them!'

'No. Incidentally, a friend of mine saw you on Saturday giving Kerry a ride on your bike.'

'What is this? Under bloody surveillance, am I?'

'It's just you saying you haven't got a relationship with Kerry and—'

'I haven't! I was just giving the kid a lift to some audition she wanted to go to in Brighton – all right?'

'Audition for what?'

'I haven't the faintest idea.'

His stock of goodwill was rapidly diminishing. Jude became more conciliatory. 'I'm not getting at you, Max. I'm just convinced that there was something funny about that young man's death at the hotel.'

'Funny?'

'Like it not being suicide.'

'But—'

'Like it being murder.'

'Ah.' Max considered this idea for a moment, but then decided it didn't concern him. 'Maybe. I wouldn't know. Like I said, I was dead to the world.'

'You didn't get up at all during the night? Or hear anything?'

'I've told you – no.' It sounded genuine. 'I did wake up at one point, and considered going to see Rick Hendry and throwing myself on his mercy. But then I guess I just went back to sleep again.'

'Rick Hendry?'

'Yes. Surely you know he owns Korfilia Productions. It was named after that overblown album he

170

did with his band – can't remember what they were called . . .'

'Zedrach-Kona.'

'Bloody hell, yes. Knew it was something poncy.'

'Max, you said you thought of going to throw yourself on Rick Hendry's mercy?'

'Yes. Well, after the success they've had with *Pop Crop*, Korfilia Productions could sell anything to any of the networks, so I thought maybe I might get him to back me as a celebrity chef. He knows how well I've done at Hopwicke House, so I thought if Korfilia Productions backed me, then the BBC would have to listen and—'

'No, I'm sorry. Stop.' Jude held up her hand. 'Why did you think of throwing yourself on Rick Hendry's mercy in the middle of the night at Hopwicke House?'

'Because he was *there*.'

'That night?'

'Yes. He was staying with Suzy.'

Chapter Twenty

'Hello. This is David.'

'Oh. David.'

'Remember?'

'Yes. Of course I remember,' said Carole. Though she'd tried to put all thoughts of their failed marriage behind her, she still recognized his voice.

'I was ringing about Stephen . . . and, erm . . . Gaby.'

Instantly she recalled how irritating she had found that little 'erm . . .', a mannerism her ex-husband contrived to get into almost every sentence he spoke.

'Oh yes. It is excellent news, isn't it? About them getting married,' said Carole conventionally.

'Very good. She's a . . . erm . . . sweet girl, don't you think? Stephen's done very well for himself there.'

Carole was forced to admit she had yet to meet their son's paragon of a fiancée. 'I'm having lunch with them this Sunday down here . . . well, near here.'

'Yes, of course. They told me. I was getting my . . . erm . . . getting my weekends mixed up. They're house-hunting, aren't they?'

'There was talk of looking at some properties, yes.' Carole was amazed at how stilted she sounded. They hadn't spoken for at least two years, but were instantly back to full awkwardness.

'Erm . . . Carole . . .'

'Yes?'

'I was ringing about our wills.'

'Oh?'

'I know you changed your will . . . erm . . . after we got divorced.'

'Yes,' she agreed with some asperity. 'It was one of the first things I did.'

'Yes, erm . . . I didn't, actually.'

'Didn't what?'

'Change my will.'

'Good heavens!' So if, during all the years she'd been in Fethering, David Seddon had stepped under a bus or met some other fatal accident, Carole would have inherited.

'David, why on earth didn't you?'

'I just . . . erm . . . didn't get round to it. I was, sort of, very cut up after . . . erm . . . after what happened, and I didn't really want to think about anything to do with it, so . . . I . . . erm . . . I knew anything I left would go eventually to Stephen through you.'

'You didn't know that. I could have left it to anyone.'

'Yes, you could have done. But I knew you wouldn't.'

She was dispirited to realize that he was right.

'I suppose, Carole, I thought if I met someone else, if I remarried, then obviously I would change my will in favour of . . . erm . . . but there hasn't been anyone to

173

change it in favour of.' Then, without much optimism, he added, 'Yet.'

'Well, I'm amazed.'

'Yes. I . . . erm . . . I knew you would be.'

'But you are going to change your will now?'

'Oh yes. Yes, absolutely. I am. And that's the point. I thought I ought to tell you.'

'There was no need. Since it never occurred to me that I might still be a beneficiary—'

'No . . . erm . . . it's the way I'm going to change it that is the point.'

'Ah?'

'I'm going to skip a generation.'

'Sorry? You'll have to explain.'

'Well . . . erm . . . the way I see it, Stephen is very well set up for himself, with his work.' Whatever that may be, thought Carole, yes. 'And he's obviously going to be much better set up when he's married Gaby.' Another indicator that her future daughter-in-law came from moneyed stock. 'Two incomes.' Or at least was well paid for what she did. 'So I'm going to . . . erm . . . change my will to leave everything to their children.'

'But they haven't got any children.'

'Yet. And, all right, they may never have any. The terms of my will take that into account. If they don't have any children, then everything'll go straight to Stephen and Gaby. But if they *do* . . . erm . . . it'll be divided among them . . . the children.'

'Right.'

'I thought that would be the prudent course to take. Avoid two sets of Inheritance Tax.'

'Yes, well . . . Very prudent. If Stephen and Gaby are happy with the arrangement . . .'

'They are. I've discussed it with them, of course.'

'Of course.'

'So I was wondering, Carole, if . . . erm . . . you might be thinking of doing the same.'

'Leaving my money to these . . . erm . . . conjectural grandchildren?' Oh God, she was doing it now.

'Yes. Exactly that.'

'Well, I hadn't really thought about it, David, but . . . well, it's certainly something to consider.'

'It is. Is there a solicitor who you deal with at the moment?'

Carole almost found herself giggling. But she didn't think her ex-husband was yet ready to hear about the oleaginous advances of Barry Stilwell.

'Because I . . . erm . . . I made my will through Humphrey – you know . . .?'

'Yes.' Their former mutual solicitor, who had represented David in the divorce. Carole certainly wasn't going to deal with him. Humphrey was symbolic of a period in her life she wished to blank out completely.

'But perhaps you wouldn't want to . . . erm . . .?'

'No, I wouldn't,' Carole agreed hastily. 'No, if I decide to go ahead with the change, I'll use someone down here.' And it wouldn't be Barry Stilwell. The thought of his having a professional reason to lure her into his new office was not to be contemplated.

'Right. Well . . . erm . . . good to hear your voice.'

'Yes.' She couldn't in all honesty reciprocate. Hearing David's voice had set all kinds of unwelcome

175

thoughts running through her head and would, she knew, disturb her sleep that night.

'And . . . erm . . . if not before . . . see you on September the fourteenth.'

'September the fourteenth?' came the baffled echo.

'The wedding, Carole.'

'Oh yes, of course. The wedding.'

Jude had called Inspector Goodchild, mobile to mobile, as soon as Max Townley left the coffee-shop, but he was actually in his office at the Worthing Police Station. A short walk. Yes, why didn't she come round straight away?

The fastidiousness and slight condescension in his voice were so familiar she felt she had met him many more times than their one previous encounter. His office was small and institutional, but somehow contrived to look soigné. A couple of well-tended pot-plants and a photograph – not, predictably, of family, but of a Scottish beach – added to the distinction given by his almost foppish charcoal suit. The image resolutely denied that Inspector Goodchild was a standard-issue, insensitive copper.

Jude refused the offer of tea or coffee. He gave her an avuncular look and linked his hands on the desk in front of him. 'So, Jude, what have you got to tell me? Something new, I hope?'

'Yes. Well, new to me, anyway.'

He chuckled, and she realized this had been the wrong thing to say. Of course, Goodchild's look seemed to imply, we in the police have rather more information to hand than a mere amateur could possibly accumulate. Jude's words had put her on the back foot right from the start of the interview.

'So, what breakthrough do you wish to confide in me, Jude?'

'Just that the Pillars of Sussex were not the only people staying on the Hopwicke House site on the night of Nigel Ackford's death.'

The Inspector gave her a shrewd look, as though she had told him something he hadn't been expecting, but then let his face relax into a smile. 'So who are we talking about here?' he asked blandly, before siphoning all the wind out of her sails. 'Miss Longthorne's ex-husband. "Television's Mr Nasty"? Rick Hendry?'

'Yes,' Jude was forced to admit.

Inspector Goodchild steepled his hands together and pressed them against his lips, almost as though he were suppressing a laugh. 'I'm sorry, Jude. We do rather have the advantage of you, you know. You see, appealing and charming though the concept of the amateur detective may be, investigation is actually our job. When we in the force make enquiries, generally speaking people tell the truth. So, though at the time of their stay none of the Pillars of Sussex may have had any idea that they were so close to Mr Hendry, Miss Longthorne told me he had been there as soon as I asked her whether any other people were staying on the premises.'

'I suppose she would have done,' Jude mumbled in her humiliation.

'Yes. She's a very honest woman.'

Not to me she hasn't been. But the thought only made Jude more aware of the gulf between her own amateurism and the police's professional information-gathering resources.

'But congratulations,' Inspector Goodchild went on, with a smile of condescension. 'Well done for working that out.' He stopped as a thought struck him. 'Why, may I ask, did you think Mr Hendry's presence so important? You weren't about to suggest that he murdered Mr Ackford, were you?'

'No,' Jude growled disconsolately.

'Good.' Then, with a new hardness in his voice, he continued, 'Because I would really discourage you from throwing around accusations of murder. That's the point where your little games cease to be harmless. You might find yourself in court on charges of defamation.' The moment of censure was allowed to register before the Inspector's mocking smile returned. 'So, any other information – or indeed suspicions – you want to share with me?'

Jude decided she might as well press on. She couldn't make Goodchild's estimation of her any lower than it already was. Contrary to popular advice, in some holes you might as well keep digging.

'All right. What about Bob Hartson's chauffeur, Geoff?'

'What about him?' The smile played infuriatingly about his lips. 'Are you about to drop the bombshell that he was also at Hopwicke House that night?'

'Well, yes, I . . .'

'This is so kind of you, Jude – to have gone to so

much trouble. Yes, we do know that Mr Hartson's chauffeur was there. He slept in the staff quarters . . . the converted stable block.'

'But—'

'And his movements can be vouched for all the time he spent on the premises.'

'By whom?'

'Mr Hartson himself, and his daughter Kerry.'

'Ah well, you'd expect them to—'

'And Miss Longthorne herself,' the Inspector concluded implacably.

Jude felt like a schoolgirl hauled up in front of the head teacher. And with no defence. She had done what she was being accused of.

And Goodchild gave her a full, head-teacherly dressing-down for her breach of the rules. Drawing to a close, he said, 'It is deeply irresponsible to make random accusations. After a death, people are, not unexpectedly, hurt and confused. They need to grieve, not to have their pain compounded by the insensitive probings of amateurs. So I would ask very firmly, Jude, that you and your friend immediately cease any further investigation into this unfortunate young man's death.'

Jude still had just enough defiance left in her to demand, 'So that you can get your nice safe suicide verdict at the inquest?'

'The inquest has already happened,' he coldly informed her. 'As I anticipated, it was adjourned to give us time to gather together our evidence. When that is presented at the reconvened inquest, the coroner will form his own opinion as to the cause of Mr Ackford's death.'

He didn't say it out loud, but Jude knew Inspector Goodchild would have bet his pension on a verdict of suicide.

The shingle of Fethering beach crunched beneath their feet. The sea gargled against the sand. Gulliver, quixotically determined to rid the world of seaweed, traced eccentric circles around the two women. The April sun was paling now, but earlier in the afternoon it had held the promise of summer.

The decision to walk on the beach had been vindicated. Jude, furious after the humiliation of her encounter with Inspector Goodchild, had suggested going straight to the Crown and Anchor for a drink, but Carole's inbuilt Calvinist streak demanded a walk first. Then they would have earned a drink. Rather as her grandmother would make her have a slice of plain bread and butter before she was allowed one with jam on.

'I think I'm going to have to confront Suzy,' Jude announced grumpily. 'Now I know Rick Hendry was there that night. I bet it was him who called her on her mobile.'

Carole sniffed. She was still feeling raw and exposed after the call from David. Her pale blue eyes blinked behind their rimless glasses. 'I can see that it's interesting, the fact that he was there, but I don't see how it can possibly have anything to do with the death of Nigel Ackford.'

'If it doesn't, why would Suzy want to keep it quiet?'

'That doesn't take much working out. If she's as paranoid about publicity as you say, the last thing she wants is the tabloids knowing her ex-husband had been there. Particularly at a time when they're already sniffing around him over this underage sex thing.'

'True. So you reckon it's just a coincidence he was at Hopwicke House the night of the death?'

'I haven't got enough information to reckon anything,' Carole replied rather tartly. 'But I find it pretty unlikely that someone like Rick Hendry would have any dealings with the Pillars of Sussex.'

'Yes, it's hard to see an obvious connection.'

'Jude, it's hard to see even an extremely obscure connection. The two worlds couldn't be further apart.'

'And yet they did come together that night at Hopwicke House – at least, geographically.' Jude stopped walking and her brown eyes thoughtfully scanned the waters of the English Channel. 'I'll ring Suzy when I get home. We've got to sort this out.'

'Yes.' Carole looked a little wistful. 'And I can't really come with you when you confront her.'

'No. We're old friends. The meeting has got to be handled with great delicacy and sensitivity.'

The minute she'd said the words, Jude knew they were the wrong ones. Carole, already bristling, bristled further. 'And of course I haven't got anything in the way of delicacy or —'

'I didn't mean that. Just . . . Suzy and I go back a long way, if she's going to talk to anyone, she'll talk to me.'

'And probably lie to you again.'

'Maybe. We'll see.'

'Huh.' Carole's feathers hadn't yet been satisfactorily smoothed down. 'I wish there was something useful I could do.'

'But there is. You can get more information on the Pillars of Sussex.'

'How?'

'Come on, Carole. Your ex-husband advised you to consult a solicitor about your will.'

'Yes, but if you think I'm going to get into a professional relationship with Barry Stilwell, you can—'

'Who said anything about Barry Stilwell? There's another solicitor, very conveniently also based in Worthing, who's a past president of the Pillars.'

A smile sweetened Carole's sour face. 'Yes, of course. Donald Chew.'

'All right, Jude,' Suzy agreed with surprising readiness when her friend rang. 'Let's talk. Do you fancy lunch in London?'

'When?'

'Tomorrow. I've got to go up for a couple of meetings, and a bit of body maintenance.'

'What do you mean?'

'Hair, facial, nails, massage. Staving off the ravages of time.'

'You still look great, Suzy.'

'Maybe.' As an acknowledged beauty for as long as she could remember, Suzy had never been winsome about accepting compliments. 'But looking great takes a little bit longer every day.'

'Tell me about it,' said Jude automatically, though the line wasn't really appropriate for her. She didn't work hard on her appearance. She was overweight and, in her layers of floaty garments, at times looked down-right scruffy. But it didn't bother her. She wasn't terribly interested in people who let that kind of detail put them off. 'OK, where shall we meet?'

Suzy named an exclusive women's club in Mayfair.

'Renton and Chew.' The voice was very carefully modu-lated, its natural vowels corralled into middle-class receptionist-speak.

'Good morning. My name is Carole Seddon, and I wanted to talk to someone about making a change to my will.'

'Certainly. And who have you dealt with before, Mrs Seddon?'

'No one. This is my first contact with your firm.'

'Right. And could you tell us, Mrs Seddon, how you came to hear about Renton and Chew? Was it through seeing an advertisement, personal recommendation, or just random selection from the *Yellow Pages* or similar listings directory?'

God, thought Carole, is there anywhere left in the world where you can avoid questionnaires? 'It was through personal recommendation.'

'Excellent, Mrs Seddon. That means we must be doing something right.' But the words didn't sound spontaneous. The receptionist was still sticking to her script. 'Well, Mrs Seddon, perhaps I could put you through to Donna Highstone, who is very experienced in matters of wills and—'

'The personal recommendation I had was to Donald Chew.'

'Ah. Yes, well, Mr Chew himself is very busy at the moment with—'

'The recommendation came from someone connected with the Pillars of Sussex.'

Having worked out the lies she was going to tell, Carole was not about to deviate from her chosen course. What she said did have the desired effect. There was an impressed 'Oh' from the other end of the line. 'Perhaps I should have a word with Mr Chew then. May I ask, Mrs Seddon, the name of the person from the Pillars of Sussex who gave you the recommendation?'

'Nigel Ackford,' Carole announced, exactly according to plan.

'Ah. Um, well, er . . .' The receptionist's script was now out of the window. So was her assumed accent, as she floundered on. 'Um. Tell you what, Mrs Seddon, I'll speak to Mr Chew. And maybe you've got a number what I can call you back on?'

Chapter Twenty-One

The exterior of Suzy Longthorne's club looked like an eighteenth-century private house. But, given its Mayfair location, very few British private citizens could have afforded to live there, even if the property didn't include a swimming pool in the basement, first-floor gym suite, second-floor beauty salon and top-floor restaurant with a panoramic view across the roofs of London.

Nor indeed could many private citizens have afforded the annual subscription, which, as it happened, Suzy didn't pay. When the premises opened in the late eighties, she and various other famous faces had been offered life membership to enhance the club's image and ensure celebrity-studded press coverage for the launch. Few of the other honorary members had continued to use the facilities, but Suzy, as ever recognizing a bargain when she saw one, was a regular visitor. Her trips to London were essential breaks from the pressures of running Hopwicke Country House Hotel, and a necessary part of what she had described as her 'body maintenance'.

Suzy had already put in an hour's swimming and an

hour in the gym by the time Jude arrived for lunch. She had also been massaged and had her facial. The glowing skin, with her hair swept back in a bandana, showed off the natural beauty of her cheekbones. Then a couple of quick meetings and she would be back in time to spread the largesse of her loveliness over the evening's diners at Hopwicke House.

Though the club's membership was exclusively female, men were allowed in as guests, and so the top-floor dinning room looked just like any other expensive restaurant. The chef had, in fact, been recently poached from one of London's most fashionable eateries, and the menu proffered to Jude was both lavish and exciting. In spite of all the equipment on the lower floors, the club had no pretensions to be a health farm. Its *raison d'être* was the pampering of its members. Those who got pleasure from depriving themselves were at liberty to pursue that course; those who enjoyed self-indulgence were equally free to follow their desires.

Suzy chose not to drink alcohol. 'I'll wait for the one I grant myself at the end of the day. Never tastes so good if I've had one earlier. But don't let me stop you.'

Jude didn't. She consulted the wine list for half-bottles, but Suzy said it'd be simpler to order a bottle, and there was no demur from her guest. Jude didn't have anything to do in the afternoon except return to Fethering, and a mild alcoholic haze was the best condition in which to ignore the third world discomforts of southbound trains from Victoria Station. She was slightly nervous about the forthcoming conversation, and thought a couple of glasses of the excellent New Zealand Sauvignon Blanc Suzy had ordered might relax her.

She was also encouraged by her hostess to use the menu to the full, so again she did, ordering a smoked duck's breast salad, to be followed by monkfish with spinach and ginger. Suzy limited herself to a rare steak and green salad. She had never gone to the anorexic lengths of some models, but always ate sensibly. And Jude had known her far too long to feel any guilt about eating larger meals in her presence. Suzy Longthorne's looks remained her fortune and her business equipment, so a proper diet was just another element in her 'body maintenance'.

When they were both settled with a drink, the hazel eyes focused on Jude, and it became clear that Suzy had thought through exactly what she was going to say.

'First, I owe you an apology. I've been less than honest with you, which I shouldn't have been, because you've been my friend for a long time. I value your friendship, and I don't want to do anything that threatens it. But there are other things I value too. I don't have much choice about valuing the hotel; that's my living, all my savings are tied up in it, and I can't put it at risk.'

Jude might have said something at this point, but the pace of Suzy's narrative did not allow her to. 'But I gather, from things you've said, you believe there was something sinister about that young solicitor's death. Can I ask what your basis is for thinking that?'

Jude realized this was the first time they had really

discussed the events of that Tuesday night. Previously, Suzy had cut the conversation short; now she was prepared to listen.

'All right. My thinking Nigel Ackford might have been murdered is based on things he said to me when I found him drunk and put him to bed. He was very optimistic, he seemed to think he'd turned a corner, both professionally and personally. He told me he was going to ask his girlfriend to marry him. And, all right, I know you're about to say that he had a history of depression and that his mood swings were—'

'Jude, I wasn't about to say anything. I know nothing about him. He was simply a young man called Nigel Ackford who was inconsiderate enough to die in my hotel.'

'Didn't any of the Pillars of Sussex say anything to you about him?'

'No. Nothing personal. They just agreed with me that his timing and choice of location couldn't have been more unfortunate.'

'And did they ask you to cover up?'

'They didn't have to ask, Jude. Every instinct within me wanted to cover up.'

'So you'd be happy to cover up a murder?'

Jude stopped, as her duck breast salad was delivered by an impassively handsome young waiter.

After he'd gone, Suzy giggled, reminding Jude how much she loved her. 'You've got a great sense of timing. Now he's overheard that, I'll probably be asked to leave the club.'

'Sorry, Suzy.' Jude too giggled at the notion.

The ice had been broken. Jude felt closer to Suzy than she had since the death had come between them. 'Look, you know I want Hopwicke House to succeed for you. I'm not trying to do anything that'll threaten your business.'

'I know, Jude, but regardless of whether or not it's your intention, what you're doing could threaten my business.' Suzy sighed. She wasn't enjoying holding out on her friend. 'Apart from anything else, logic is not on your side. All you're basing your suspicions on is some drunken rambling from a young man who – you now tell me – had a history of depression and mood swings. If that's all the evidence there is to support a murder verdict, I'm not surprised the police were happy with suicide.'

'There is something else. You must remember.'

But the puzzlement with which Suzy shook her head suggested that she didn't.

'The letter. The death threat.'

She remembered it now. And her expression suggested she'd rather she hadn't.

'I know you told the police it didn't exist, but you can't say that to me. You and I saw it. And Kerry saw the letter too – she was the one who found it.'

Reluctantly, Suzy acknowledged this.

'I haven't talked to Kerry about it yet, but—'

'*Yet?* Jude, what is all this "yet"? Are you telling me you are going to continue investigating this death?'

'Yes. I'm afraid I am.'

Her friend sighed exhaustedly, and looked out over the vista of London. Though the roofs gleamed with

April sunshine, to her everything looked bleak. 'All right. I can't stop you. I've known you long enough to know nobody can stop you when you've got a bee in your bonnet.' The will to resist had gone out of her. 'What do you want to ask me?'

'Which room did Kerry find that note in?'

The answer came in a long exhalation of despair. 'The four-poster room.'

'And, in retrospect, Suzy, don't you think that's significant?'

'Yes. It probably is.'

'A note's left in a room telling someone they're not going to wake up the next morning, and the next morning the occupant of the room is dead . . . I think there's more than a 'probably' in that.'

'If you say so.'

'Suzy – ' Jude's brown eyes locked on to the famous hazel ones ' – do you know what actually happened that night? Do you know how Nigel Ackford died?'

An impatient shake of the head. 'No, I don't.'

'Well, I'm more convinced than ever that he was murdered.'

The waiter's timing was immaculate. He just caught Jude's words as he swept away her salad plate. The conversation in the kitchen must be fun, she thought.

'If he was, I can guarantee you one thing, Jude. His death had nothing to do with anyone working at the hotel. He brought his trouble with him. He must have offended one of the Pillars of Sussex.'

'So you're admitting it's possible he was murdered?'

'Possible?' Suzy Longthorne didn't seem to have a lot of respect for the word. 'Anything's possible. It's possible that Elvis Presley's still alive. It's possible that somewhere Lord Lucan is riding Shergar off into the sunset. Possible. But unlikely.'

'If you just entertain the possibility, Suzy, then you can help me.'

There was a defeated shrug from the shapely shoulders. 'All right, Jude. Against my better judgment. All I really want to do is let sleeping solicitors lie, but—'

'Funny. That's exactly the expression Rick used.'

'Rick?' Suddenly Suzy was alive again. And worried.

'Rick Hendry. Your ex-husband.'

'You've been in touch with Rick?'

'He rang me.'

'Why?'

'Basically, to tell me what you've been trying to get me to do for the last week – lay off the investigation.'

'Oh, God.' Suzy sank back in her chair.

'I know he was at Hopwicke House that night,' said Jude softly.

'Oh, God. Oh, God,' Suzy repeated. Then, with a vanquished look at her friend, she asked, 'How much else do you know?'

Chapter Twenty-Two

The receptionist at Renton and Chew was the one Carole had spoken to on the phone, but her vowels had been reconstituted for their face-to-face encounter. She had rung back very quickly the previous day and fixed an appointment for Carole with Donald Chew for eleven o'clock on the Wednesday morning. Carole had brought with her a copy of the post-divorce will, which left everything to Stephen. Even if she didn't get any information about the Pillars of Sussex or Nigel Ackford's death, she did still have legitimate business to discharge.

The offices were smart, in a neat Georgian house in a neat Georgian square near the Worthing seafront. Though extensively modernized, they retained certain quasi-Dickensian features. Windows bulging with asymmetrical panels of glass, narrow creaking stair-cases, porcelain fingerplates and door handles, an old-fashioned intercom on Donald Chew's desk, all dated the office's image, contradicting the evidence of the thin-screened computers, fax machines and photo-copiers. Yes, we've got all the latest technology, the message read, but basically we're still an old-fashioned family firm. Your secrets will be safe with us. We know the world is full of distasteful inevitabilities – like death, divorce and house purchase – but here we will deal with them as discreetly as an embalmer titivating a corpse. We at Renton and Chew exist – as we have for generations – to help you cope with the little nastinesses of life.

Donald Chew himself reinforced that image. Carole had never met him before, but he was dressed more or less exactly as he had been when Jude saw him asleep in the bar of Hopwicke House. It was a different pin-striped suit, but only Donald himself or his tailor would have known that. Though the nearly regimental tie was not identical to the one he'd worn at the hotel, it was very much of the same school. And the reassuring gold watch-chain looped across his waistcoat was an original. Carole was reminded of surgeons she had met, who dressed in a way that was almost a parody of how a surgeon should look. Donald Chew's appearance was part of an act, and Carole believed everyone who put on an act had something to hide.

Beneath the hairless dome of his head, Donald Chew's rubicund face wore an understanding smile. Again, the reference point was Dickens. Here was the solicitor who, at the end of the book, would make all well, restore the riches to the rightful heir and reveal that there was no legal bar to the young lovers marrying. In Dickens he would have been called something like Mr Cheerybumble.

'My dear Mrs Seddon, how very nice to see you,' he

said, all bustling bonhomie. 'Now do please take a seat. Can I offer you a cup of coffee or tea or something?'

She asked for coffee, which was ordered over the quaint intercom system, and waited to see what happened next. Carole had worked out her plan of campaign and intended to stick to it. The speed with which the senior partner had suddenly become available for their meeting suggested he had an agenda, arising from her mention of the Pillars of Sussex and Nigel Ackford. At some point he was bound to bring the subject back to that, so all she had to do was pursue the legal enquiry which was the pretext for her presence.

Pleasantries about the good April weather and winter really being over and the nice view of the sea from his office took them as far as the delivery of the coffee – and some iced biscuits, which Carole refused. The girl from reception acted as waitress. When she was gone, Donald Chew beamed magnanimously and asked, 'So, Mrs Seddon . . . how can I help you?'

She described the circumstances of her son announcing his engagement – 'Oh, how delightful, what splendid news for you' – and the thought of changing her will to benefit her potential grandchildren rather than Stephen himself. She didn't give the idea its proper attribution to David, but since Donald Chew neither knew nor was ever likely to meet her ex-husband, this did not seem unreasonable.

'Well, that is an increasingly popular course for people to take, Mrs Seddon – and a very practical one. None of us wants to pay two sets of Inheritance Tax, do we? And given the value of property these days, many more people are becoming liable for Inheritance Tax. The only caution I would offer is that it's important that all parties know what's going on. There could be unfortunate reactions if, say, your son was unaware of your plans and had been counting on a personal legacy at such a time as – unfortunately, but inevitably – you should reach the end of your natural span.'

'You mean when I die?'

With the very tiniest wince at her indelicacy, the solicitor acknowledged this was indeed what he meant.

'Well, don't worry about that, Mr Chew. I would certainly not consider taking such a step without discussing it with my son. In fact, I'm meeting him and his fiancée – ' she still didn't feel natural with the word – 'for lunch this Sunday, so that will give me the perfect opportunity to raise the matter with him.'

'Excellent, excellent. I'm sorry, but I did have to mention the point, to avoid any misunderstanding.'

'There won't be any.'

'Good. Fine. And am I to understand, Mrs Seddon, that you have already made a will?'

She confirmed that she had and slid the copy across the desk. Donald Chew quickly scanned the text. 'Well, all seems very straightforward. And that's the only change you wish to make – to nominate your son's children as the sole beneficiaries rather than your son – er . . . Stephen – himself?'

'That's right.'

'Then I think—'

He was interrupted by a buzz from the intercom. 'Please excuse me, Mrs Seddon. Yes?'

The receptionist's crackly voice said, 'Another call from Mr Floyd at the *Fethering Observer*, Mr Chew.'

'You know I'm in a meeting.'

'He's very insistent,' the voice crackled back.

'Say I'll definitely fix a time to meet him next week. I'll call back in the next half-hour.' He switched off the intercom and switched on his professional smile. 'So sorry, Mrs Seddon. Now where were we? Ah yes . . . nominating your son's children, right. There are no other personal legacies you wish to make at this point?'

For a brief, insane moment, Carole wanted to leave something to Jude. Nothing big, just a kind of keepsake, to show how much her friendship had been appreciated. But, as soon as she'd had the idea, it felt inappropriate and sentimental. Carole Seddon didn't do things like that. If Jude wanted to remember her, well and good. There was no need for emotional blackmail.

'No. No personal legacies,' she replied.

'Well, the change will be very straightforward,' Donald Chew announced, prompting the knee-jerk thought in Carole: straightforward, yes, but it'll still involve me coming back for another meeting and a considerable number of solicitor's working hours added to your bill.

'What I propose is that I should work out an appropriate form of words and produce a new will document which, maybe if you were to make another appointment for a couple of days' time, you could come in and check over? It goes without saying we could get the will witnessed by members of my staff – unless you wish to have friends do that service for you?'

'No, no. Your staff'd be fine.'

'Good.' He patted his watch-chain with satisfaction and chuckled. 'Well, that is, as I believe the young people these days say – "sorted". If only all of the clients who came into this office had such simple problems to sort out.'

'Thank you very much, Mr Chew.' Carole drained her coffee cup. 'Should I make an appointment with your receptionist?' She rose as if to leave, confident that he wouldn't let her go quite so easily.

He didn't. 'No need to rush away, Mrs Seddon. I always like to get to know a bit about my clients. Not nosiness, you understand – just so that one feels a personal closeness to the people one is representing in a professional capacity.'

'Right.' Carole sank back into her chair, waiting to see what would come next.

'Well, you're divorced, we've established that, and you live in . . .?'

'Fethering.'

'Charming spot, charming spot. And still working?'

Carole gave a brief history of her employment at the Home Office. She knew the solicitor was just playing for time and was interested to see how he'd get round to what he really wanted to talk about.

Not very subtly was the answer. 'My receptionist said you had a connection with the Pillars of Sussex, Mrs Seddon.'

'Not a direct connection. Through a friend.'

'Ah. And that was why you contacted our firm?'

'It was the first time I'd needed a solicitor since I moved down here. Someone in London dealt with the conveyancing and what-have-you on the Fethering house. I asked for advice from my friend and got a recommendation for Renton and Chew.'

'Good, good.' But he still didn't know enough. 'And this friend of yours is a member of the Pillars of Sussex, is that right? If so, he must be someone I know.'

'No, not a member. It's a she.'

He let out a patronizing chuckle. 'Oh, then she certainly wouldn't be. So is she married to a Pillar perhaps?'

'No, no, she just met this young man, called Nigel Ackford – ' the name sent a flicker of paleness across the claret face in front of her ' – and he said he worked for a solicitor and if she ever needed one, she should get in touch with Renton and Chew.'

'Very gratifying.' But Donald Chew didn't sound gratified. He looked suddenly less urbane than he had for the rest of their meeting, even perhaps a little confused. Carole could see him evaluating his next move. He had an agenda, she had a feeling it was an agenda which he had been given by someone else. And one of the items on it, she felt sure, was finding out how much she knew.

Carole decided to toss something his way. 'My friend said that Nigel Ackford was a great friend of somebody called . . . Bob Hartson?'

'Yes. I'm not sure that "great friend" is quite appropriate, but they knew each other, certainly. Mr Hartson is another client of this firm.'

'Oh, so you deal with the legal side of all his property deals?'

'I suppose that is a way of putting it, yes.'

Carole pushed a bit harder. Retaining a tone of naivety, she continued, 'My friend says the Pillars of Sussex is an organization devoted to professional backscratching.'

The description pained Donald Chew. 'I think that's a rather cynical view. The primary purpose of the Pillars is a charitable one. We've raised an enormous amount of money in the Sussex area. Recently we've been working for a children's cancer ward at Queen Anne's Hospital. We've raised over a hundred thousand for that – be handing over the cheque at a ceremony next week. If you saw an event like that, you'd perhaps have a more generous view of the Pillars.'

But Carole was not to be won round so easily. 'I am afraid I'm always a bit cynical about male-only organizations.'

'Well, you shouldn't be. Yes, all right, some of the Pillars' activities are strictly men-only.' He let out a bluff, masculine laugh. 'And we probably do drink more than we should at our dinners. But our womenfolk are involved too.'

'Oh?' Carole didn't like the concept of 'womenfolk', with its implication that the females belonged to a different tribe.

'The November dinner,' Donald Chew went on, 'is always a ladies' night, for wives, girlfriends and – ' he chuckled ' – other women in relationships we don't delve into too deeply. And some of the fund-raising events are organized by the womenfolk. My wife Brenda's very active for the Pillars. You should talk to her. That'd change your image of the society.'

'Perhaps I should.'

'You could actually help her too. Right now she's organizing an auction of promises for the Pillars. Happening Saturday week. Brenda's taken too much on herself, as usual, so she's in need of willing helpers.'

'But don't the willing helpers all have to be wives of Pillars of Sussex members?'

He pooh-poohed the idea. 'Good heavens, no. As long as they don't mind a bit of hard work – that's all that matters.' So while for the men, membership of the Pillars of Sussex was an essential passport to their rituals, 'womenfolk' didn't have to pass any tests to be entitled to do the boring bits.

'As I say, have a word with Brenda. We're in the book. Only three Chews in the local directory, and we're the East Preston ones.'

'Perhaps I will.'

'She'll put you right. Whatever image we may have locally, there's nothing sinister about the Pillars of Sussex.'

'But don't you think any society that's secretive is bound to get that sort of reputation?'

The solicitor shrugged. 'Maybe. Like the Masons, I suppose. They've had their share of bad press. But there's no basis for those kind of allegations about the Pillars of Sussex.'

'So it's not true that a lot of deals get made at the society's dinners?'

'Certainly not. The dinners are social functions – just opportunities for like-minded people to get together and relax over good food and good wine.' He was now positively Pickwickian in his innocence.

'I see,' said Carole, apparently retreating. 'My friend must've got the wrong end of the stick.'

'Yes, I'm rather afraid she has.'

'Oh, well. Perhaps I'd better be off.'

Again she made as if to leave, but again the solicitor detained her. Whatever information he had been delegated to extract, he hadn't got it yet.

'Mrs Seddon,' he began, with an attempt at casualness, 'You said your friend knew of some connection between Nigel Ackford and the Pillars of Sussex?'

'Well, yes. He told her he was going to some Pillars of Sussex dinner, so he must have been a member and—'

'No, no, Mrs. Seddon. He was a guest, not a member.'

She shrugged, deliberately provocative. 'Same difference, isn't it?'

'Certainly not.' He was, as she had intended him to be, affronted. Edging a little closer to what he wanted to find out, Donald Chew went on, 'Did you actually meet Nigel Ackford?'

'No,' she replied, honestly.

'Mm . . . the fact is – this is rather awkward, Mrs Seddon. You haven't heard anything recently about Nigel Ackford, have you?'

'No,' she replied, dishonestly.

'Well, I'm afraid I have rather bad news about the poor young man. He is no longer with us.'

'I'm sorry?'

'He's dead, Mrs Seddon.'

'Oh dear. He was very young.'

'Not even thirty.'

'Poor boy. And may I ask, Mr Chew, how did he die?'

The solicitor smiled a smile of avuncular solicitude. 'I'm afraid I don't know, Mrs Seddon. But I'm sure we'll hear in time. Maybe at the funeral, which, of course, as his employer, I will attend.' Donald Chew sighed at the unfairness of life. 'It's very sad. Why should someone so young suddenly die?'

Why indeed? thought Carole.

Chapter Twenty-Three

After her lavish lunch with Suzy Longthorne, the last thing Jude really felt like was fish pie, but she didn't want to offend the cook in Carole, so she did her best with her piled plateful. The new bottle of Chardonnay helped maintain the comforting haze which had been engendered by the lunchtime's Sauvignon Blanc. She was excited too, and although Carole wanted to talk about her meeting with Donald Chew, Jude was full of what she had learned from Suzy.

'Rick Hendry was actually staying at the hotel that night! Well, not at the hotel – in Suzy's barn conversion behind the hotel.'

'Why? Surely they're not back together again?'

'No. It was just Rick living up to his image as the meanest man in rock. He'd been in Brighton doing auditions for his *Pop Crop* show, and he wanted to save on accommodation costs, so a free bed at his ex-wife's place sounded like a good idea. But at least that explains it, doesn't it?'

'Explains what?' asked Carole a little testily. She was miffed that Jude's news had taken priority over hers.

'Explains the way Suzy's clammed up over what happened. A death in the hotel would be bad enough publicity, but if it got out that Rick Hendry was on the premises at the time, the tabloids'd be all over her. I can see the headlines now – "TV's Mr Nasty in Death Riddle at Ex-wife's Hotel." '

Carole tapped her chin thoughtfully. 'You said the chef told you he was there?'

'That's right. Max.'

'I wonder who else knew.'

'What are you thinking?'

'Just that you said the girl Kerry was terribly keen on the idea of a career as a pop singer – or whatever they call themselves nowadays. And Rick Hendry's television show is very influential in launching young singers' careers.'

'I see. Yes.' Jude nodded. 'Bit of a coincidence. If Kerry did know he was there, she wouldn't have missed the opportunity to introduce herself. She's not lacking in self-confidence, that kid. And, actually,' she remembered, 'Max said something about taking her to an audition in Brighton.'

'Maybe you should ask her about it.'

'Don't worry. I will.' Jude forked the remainder of her fish pie to the side of her plate. She really had tried, but after that lunch . . . She avoided Carole's reproachful eye, as she went on, 'Still, it makes me feel better about Suzy.'

'What does? I'm sorry. What do you mean?'

'Well, as you know, she's one of my oldest friends' – Carole nodded curt acknowledgment of this fact – 'and

I hated the idea she was lying to me, or holding out on me, so Rick's presence does at least explain her behaviour.' The lines around the brown eyes tightened with frustration. 'But I've thought it through from every angle, and I still can't see how Rick being there can have had any connection to Nigel Ackford's death.'

'No, of course it can't. That's to do with the Pillars of Sussex. Some internal feud or argument there.'

'I'm afraid you're right.' Jude looked wistful. 'We're never going to find a connection between Rick Hendry and those wretched Pillars.'

'No.'

Jude shook herself out of introspection and looked her friend straight in the eye. 'So tell me about your meeting with Donald Chew.'

Which Carole did. And Jude heard how the Pillars of Sussex were now even covering up the fact that Nigel had died by suicide. Let alone murder.

'Well, they can't keep that up for ever. The adjourned inquest will happen at some point. The press're going to get hold of the story then.' The pile of blonded hair shook gloomily. 'Unless of course the coroner is a Pillar of Sussex, or the local newspaper proprietor is, and he's given his reporters instructions to stay away.'

'I don't think that'd be possible,' said Carole, with the authority of her Home Office experience.

'Hm. I like the idea of a conspiracy theory better.'

'Well, according to Donald Chew, you shouldn't entertain any such thoughts. He kept insisting that there's nothing sinister about the Pillars of Sussex. Just a charitable organization with purely philanthropic intentions.' Carole chuckled at the idea as she said, 'He was even trying to get me to help his wife with some fund-raiser they're doing.'

Jude started at her friend. 'Well?'

'Well what?'

'Carole, what are you waiting for?'

Brenda Chew's voice wasn't quite the genuine article, but it had been strained through a filter of gentility. 'Mrs Seddon. Yes, of course. How lovely to hear from you. Donald said you might be in touch.'

Which Carole thought was a little odd. The solicitor's suggestion had been vague, and she had said nothing about acting on it. An instinct for caution came to her. Did Donald Chew know that her insistence on meeting him meant that she was suspicious about the death at Hopwicke House? Had he anticipated her contacting his wife as a continuation of that investigation?

She didn't let these thoughts show in her voice, as she went on, 'He said you might be glad of some help with this auction of promises you're arranging for the Pillars of Sussex.'

'Always glad of help,' Brenda Chew agreed. 'I'm the last to complain about that kind of thing, but it is remarkable how often I'm the one who ends up making all the arrangements. Lots of people volunteer at the start, but as time goes by, and the real work starts, it's amazing how many of them find they have other commitments or dates they can't do or . . . Though, as I say, I'm not complaining. One is just so pleased to be able to do something to help such a good cause.'

'Yes. Your husband didn't actually say what the cause was for this particular event.'

'Didn't he? Typical Donald. Dear oh dear, the male of the species never have the command of detail that we do, do they? The auction of promises is to help build a cancer patient day centre at Queen Anne's Hospital.'

'Oh. Donald did mention you'd raised money for a children's cancer ward there.'

'Queen Anne's is one of the Pillars' favourite charities,' said Brenda Chew primly, 'but it's by no means the only one we support. There are a lot of institutions across Sussex which have had cause to be grateful to us over the years.'

'Admirable.'

'Yes. But we do most of it very quietly. A big presentation like the hundred thousand for the cancer ward will of course get publicity, but a lot of the Pillars' charity work is – ' she lowered her voice piously ' – invisible philanthropy. We don't usually court public recognition.'

'Oh well, you can rely on my discretion.'

'That's very good to hear, Mrs Seddon.'

'Please call me Carole.'

'Yes, of course. And call me Brenda. Now, Donald said you aren't actually the wife of a Pillar, are you?'

'No.'

'So are you married, Carole?'

'Divorced.'

'Oh.' It was a long time since Carole had heard so much disapproval of her marital status.

'And you would have time to help us in our efforts for the auction of promises? I only ask because, as I say, people do have a tendency to drop out after a short while.'

'Yes, I've got plenty of time —' She stopped herself from saying 'on my hands'. That somehow sounded pathetic. 'I'm retired.'

'Oh, good. Well, if you don't mind leaping in straight away, my ladies are coming round here for coffee tomorrow morning for a meeting about the auction. Eleven o'clock. Would you be free?'

Carole assured Brenda Chew that she would be, and confirmed she knew the address from the phone book. As she put the phone down, the feeling of caution came back to her. Her entrée to the world of Pillars of Sussex womenfolk had been so smoothly achieved, she wondered whether they were as keen to find out about her as she was about them.

Chapter Twenty-Four

'Jude?'

'Yes.'

She had instantly recognized the voice at the end of the line, but made him go through the process of identifying himself. 'Rick Hendry.'

'Two calls so close from a major celebrity. How exciting.'

He ignored her sardonic tone. 'Listen, I know you had lunch with Suze.'

'Impossible to have secrets these days, isn't it?'

'Well, I like to think it is.' Once again he deepened his voice to concentrate his charm; once again, to her annoyance, a part of her responded. 'That's really what I'd like to talk to you about, Jude.'

'Talk away.'

'No, not on the phone. I'd like us to meet.'

'Why?'

'Because I think we have mutual interests.'

'Suzy?'

'Suzy's one of them. And Suzy not getting hurt is another.'

'Keep going.'

'The rest can wait until we meet. Tomorrow morning all right for you?'

'Possibly.'

He ignored the wariness in her response and gave her the address of a hotel conference suite in Brighton. 'Eleven o'clock. Ask for me.'

Jude was annoyed she'd let herself be steam-rollered, but pleased the meeting had been set up. Rick Hendry had known she'd say yes, partly because she was in the course of an investigation, but also because women rarely said no to him. His arrogance about his magnetism had some justification, and that annoyed Jude even more.

The Chews' home in East Preston was a bungalow. The purchase had been prudent, as had everything else in the life of Donald and Brenda Chew. The mortgage had been long paid off, and its accompanying endowment bonus shrewdly invested. Those dividends, together with the extensive pension schemes Donald had set up – not to mention his continuing income from the practice – ensured that the couple lived in considerable splendour.

Though splendour, of course, was not the same thing as taste – or, at least, not the same thing as Carole's taste. After only a few moments in the bungalow, she found she was challenging herself to find anything in the living room to which she would have given house room. No expert, and fully aware that her own decorative style was minimalist to the point of austerity, Carole still winced at everything that caught her eye.

None of it was cheap. A great deal of money, and quite possibly the services of an interior designer, had been lavished on the room, but there wasn't a single item Carole would have bought – or even have put on display if it had been given to her by her dearest friend. Carole had never liked windowpanes with swirling designs of lilies on them, or pink curtains ruched like the petticoats of a Toulouse-Lautrec dancing girl. She'd always had an aversion to gold Dralon three-piece suites, and never been that mad on rough brown stone fireplaces with beaten brass surrounds. She disliked porcelain figurines of small children with tears welling from their eyes, had a positive aversion to floppy clowns splaying winsomely out of baskets. And she really hated tasselled velvet picture frames holding photographs textured to look like oil paintings.

Carole knew that in time the challenge to find something in the house that she might have bought herself would become obsessive. She found herself taking against the door handles and the window-catches. Even the window sills were spoiled by curli-cues of gold, and the light switches were tarted up with brass and onyx surrounds.

Competition to this decorative nightmare was offered by her hostess's dress sense. Brenda Chew was tiny-boned and delicate; mere survival without being crushed by her large husband must be one of the achievements of their marriage. She was wearing a skirt, blouse and cardigan of pastel fluffiness, whose every available edge was beaded with gold braid. Diamond-patterned white tights did little for her thin legs, and her patent-leather shoes had large pink bows on them. The impression she gave was of being gift-wrapped rather than dressed.

But any image of fluffy femininity was dispelled as soon as Brenda Chew spoke. Her voice on the phone had expressed only the imposed gentility, not the steel that lay beneath. 'Carole, do let me introduce you to some of our other ladies. All towers of strength, without whom I could not begin to achieve all that I do.'

The other ladies, a half dozen of them seated around the room, were mostly about Brenda's age, sexagenarians on the verge of becoming septuagenarians. They were expensively dressed and cosseted, their faces lined in spite of the large volume of designer creams that had been rubbed into them over the years. Carole got the feeling that few of these ladies had worked for their living. They were of the generation that had played golf, tanned themselves in Spanish villas, brought up children with the help of au pairs, and cooked cordon bleu meals with the bacon their husbands had so satisfactorily brought home.

She took in the names as they were introduced, but there was only one who really interested her. She was the youngest woman in the room, in her early forties, ten years younger even than Carole. Expensively dressed, but with more taste than the rest of them: grey knitted silk top, well-cut white jeans, black boots with high heels. Short blonde hair and a family likeness so strong Carole had identified her before being told that her name was Sandra Hartson.

Her shape and posture shadowed her daughter's, though Kerry carried herself with more attitude, a stroppier jutting of the hips than her mother. Sandra Hartson had probably looked more like Kerry when Bob had married her, but now she was altogether more tentative, even self-effacing, as though her fragile personality had been crushed between the egos of her daughter and her second husband.

Carole felt a little glow of triumph. She would talk to the woman, get to know her, and through her find out more about Bob Hartson. The thought made Carole feel empowered. Up to this point, Jude, because of her connection with Hopwicke Country House Hotel and Suzy Longthorne, had been the dominant partner in their investigation. Contact with Sandra Hartson offered Carole a more equal role in the proceedings.

But she couldn't start her probing straight away. Particularly because no one else was allowed to take the initiative in any room which contained Brenda Chew.

'You haven't missed much, Carole. I was just bringing the ladies up to date with what's been achieved so far. As you know, the auction of promises is being held on Saturday week at Hopwicke Country House Hotel.'

Carole nodded knowingly, though the information was new to her.

'Members of the Pillars of Sussex will be filling up tables with their guests, and remember, ladies, we don't want any empty seats. Sixty is the dining room's capacity, so we want sixty paying bottoms on those seats. Tickets are only a hundred and fifty pounds a head, and for that the guests will not only be able to enjoy the auction of promises, but also an excellent gourmet dinner cooked by the resident chef at Hopwicke House, Max Townley. I'm sure most of us have already tasted his cuisine and know what a treat we have in store.'

A murmur of pampered agreement ran around the room.

'We're only up to thirty-two definite acceptances at the moment, so I really do urge you to use all your feminine wiles' – a little giggle greeted this daring proposition – 'to get those seats filled. Of course, I will be doing a ring-round of some of those who're dragging their feet, but I can't do it all on my own, so, ladies, I am relying on you as well.'

'I'm quite optimistic of getting four from the bridge club,' one elderly lady volunteered.

'Very good, Betty.'

'And I'm sure Bob can be relied on for half a dozen,' said Sandra Hartson, 'if he pulls in a few favours.'

This was greeted by an appreciative chuckle. The womenfolk all knew about Bob Hartson pulling in favours. But his wife hadn't spoken with any pride in her husband's power. She had simply said what was required of her, and retreated back into her shell.

'Thank you, Sandra. So lots of effort from all of you, please. I want to be in a position of actually turning people away. Use any means at your disposal – not forgetting those feminine wiles.'

If something had been worth giggling at the first time, it proved worth giggling at again.

'Another thing I wanted to mention was our auctioneer. Now we all remember that James Baxter did the job for us last year. And, though we're very grateful for all the hard work he put into the job, the fact remains that he wasn't really very good. It makes so much difference to these kinds of occasions if you can get an auctioneer with a bit of personality, a bit of charisma. A celebrity, of course, would be an enormous bonus. James has volunteered to do the job again this year and since I haven't actually said no, we do have him there as a long stop – but, if we could get someone else . . . So, ladies, think of all the celebrity friends you have.'

There was a silence. The womenfolk didn't seem to have many celebrity friends.

With a sigh at the poor quality of the people she had to work with, Brenda Chew continued. 'Oh well, there we go. Now, can we move on to the promises themselves? I've made a superhuman effort of persuasion, and the list is beginning to look quite impressive, but we still need more. We've had some examples of magnificent generosity – like Bob and Sandra's offer of a week in their villa near Malaga.' She nodded graciously to the donor, before making an implied criticism, 'All the successful bidders will have to pay for is the cost of the flights.

'And Suzy Longthorne has been kind enough to

offer a luxury weekend at Hopwicke House. Then we've got parachute jumps and days in speedboats and a hospitality box at Goodwood and lots of dinners for two. But we do need more – particularly in the services area. You know, last time the bidding went quite high for the complete bodyscrub, and the golf lesson with the Worthing professional, and the week's loan of a cleaning lady. So that's the kind of thing we want to be thinking of, ladies. Things that people will bid over the odds for.'

For a moment, Carole tried to work out the economics of the auction of promises. She had got the firm impression that there was a three-line whip for attendance among the Pillars of Sussex. If they all brought their womenfolk two-thirds of the seats in the hotel dining room would be filled, so the people who were doing the bidding would be the same people who had donated the promises. Being a Pillar of Sussex was evidently an expensive business.

She was dragged out of her sums by the realization that Brenda Chew was addressing her. ' . . . and we were wondering whether you, Carole, as a newcomer to our little group might have any ideas?'

'Ideas for promises?'

'Yes. Particularly, as I say, for services. Any thoughts?'

Carole didn't have any. Or, rather, the ones she had were so pathetic that she didn't dare voice them. She was sure she could persuade Ted Crisp to donate a bar meal for two at the Crown and Anchor. She herself could offer to walk people's dogs on Fethering beach.

Maybe Jude would agree to do a couple of hour's healing? None of them seemed to have quite the gloss the Pillars of Sussex womenfolk would require.

'Sorry, I can't think of any ideas off the top of my head. Give me a couple of days and maybe I'll come up with something.'

Brenda Chew let out a long-suffering sigh, the schoolmistress whose charge had once again failed to produce her homework. 'Don't worry, I'm sure I'll think of something else. Not having children or grand-children to distract me, of course I know I have lots more time on my hands than you other ladies.' Her voice was heavy with sarcasm. 'And, as ever, if you want a job done – better to do it yourself.'

Carole suspected she had identified Brenda Chew's type when they first spoke on the phone, but now she had no doubt about it. Her hostess was one of those women who went round in a perpetual aura of mar-tyrdom, who never let anyone forget how hard she was working and how little she complained of the fact. From her experience in the Home Office, Carole knew exactly how impossible such people were to work with.

The meeting continued. Brenda Chew delegated various tasks to individual ladies, but with a kind of patient defeatism, as if she knew they'd get their com-missions wrong and she'd have to end up doing everything herself. She asked Sandra Hartson to co-ordinate any new offers of promises, but again with the air of someone who knew she'd have to come in and pick up the pieces.

At twelve-thirty sharp Brenda signalled the end of

the session, and the ladies dispersed variously to golf clubs, hairdressers or lunch parties. As she left the bungalow, Carole noticed its nameplate. 'Innisfree' had been pokered out of a plaster piece of driftwood, over which three brightly coloured pixies coyly peeped. No, there really was nothing round the Chews' home that she would have given house room to.

She found herself beside Sandra Hartson as they walked to their cars, and saw an opportunity to maintain contact. Carole tried to think what Jude would have said in the circumstances. Jude never had any problem easing into a conversation; it was a skill Carole didn't have, and envied.

'I believe I've met your daughter,' she announced, more brusquely than she'd intended.

Sandra Hartson stopped, slightly alarmed. 'Kerry?'

'Yes. I was looking round Hopwicke Country House Hotel and she was introduced to me. I gather she works up there.'

'Work experience. She's learning the rudiments of the hotel business. At least, she is for the time being.'

'Thinking of moving on?'

Sandra Hartson looked rueful. 'Kerry has ambitions to be a pop singer. Like every other girl her age.'

'Do you think she has the talent to make it?'

The woman shrugged. 'I'm not sure it's a matter of talent these days. Not sure it ever has been. It's promotion and packaging – and investment. Maybe Kerry'll make it. She certainly will if her stepfather has anything to do with the matter.'

Carole was surprised at how much edge had been

put into the last words. And also, was it usual for a wife to refer to her husband as her daughter's stepfather? Carole wanted to talk more to Sandra Hartson.

But the woman had already clicked the remote to unlock her Mercedes. Now wasn't the moment for further conversation. So, in an atypically effusive manner, Carole said, 'It's been such a pleasure to meet you, Sandra. Do hope we meet again. Let's exchange addresses and phone numbers.'

Sandra Hartson looked slightly bewildered by this sudden chumminess, so Carole quickly pointed out that, according to Brenda Chew's schedule, Sandra was meant to be the collection point for offers of new promises. With contacts duly scribbled down, they parted.

And Carole Seddon felt a little glow of achievement. Jude would be proud of her.

Chapter Twenty-Five

Rick Hendry had aged since Jude last saw him in the flesh, but he had aged sensibly. The long permed hair had been abandoned as soon as Zedrach-Kona split up in the early eighties, and he'd opted for a short crop, which had become more fashionable over the years and still looked smart now the blackness was dusted with grey. His wardrobe had changed as well. Gone were the romantic frilled shirts, the heavy brocades and velvets that would not have been out of place in an upholstery catalogue. In their place came a lot of grey: shirts in stone and slate, charcoal jackets and trousers. The only remaining concession to the dandy was his pair of trademark black cowboy boots.

Rick had dealt with advancing years more gracefully than many of his contemporaries; no straggly pony tails or white-flecked stubble for him. Whenever re-forming Zedrach-Kona for a final bank raid of a tour was mooted – as it frequently was – people asked Rick Hendry whether he would grow his hair long again to recapture the band's former glamour. He never gave a straight answer to the question, though he had long ago decided he would have wigs made. Nor, in spite of pleas from other band members, would he commit himself to when the group would re-form. His former colleagues had been less shrewd with their money; for them a revival tour was a necessity; for Rick, with his canny investments and his reinvention as a television person- ality and producer, it was a pension, waiting to be taken when he decided that the time was right.

Rick Hendry had no sagging jowls or beer-gut either. He'd taken care of his body and was still as thin as a whip. Though the rock publicity machine had blown up the mandatory debaucheries of Zedrach-Kona, Rick himself had only dabbled lightly with drugs and alcohol. A control freak by nature, he disliked any- thing that limited his command of himself or his circumstances. So, all the time he was encouraging the press to run stories about cocaine-fuelled post-concert orgies and the other excesses necessary for a rock star image, he had kept himself almost entirely clean.

Rick Hendry was a businessman. He would have made a fortune in whatever industry he'd chosen. But, as a young man, he'd seen rock music as his most promising opening.

He smiled when Jude was ushered into the office. His was a big smile, much caricatured in the music press. The teeth had always been too bulky for his mouth and expensive cosmetic dentistry had ensured that their makeover was exactly like the original – though now with an unnatural whiteness. The famous smile deepened the grooves of his facial muscles.

'Long time no see. Take a seat.'

She knew that was all he would offer. No peck on

the cheek, certainly no refreshment. Other men might have conducted this interview over lunch, or at least a cup of coffee, but Rick Hendry lived up to his legendary parsimony. The room chosen for the meeting was anonymous, just another conference suite in a town whose main business was conferences.

Why hadn't he made more effort, Jude thought with annoyance. He'd initiated the meeting, and she'd made her way there on the train from Fethering at a time that fitted in with his schedule. But he was the supplicant. He was the one who wanted something. (Well, actually, Jude wanted something too, but he wasn't to know that.) Rick had known she would turn up, exactly when and where he specified. The infuriating thing was that his confidence had proved justified. There she was.

'Great to see you, Jude.'

'And you, Rick. What brings you to Brighton?'

'Work, of course. It's always work. The way the *Pop Crop* thing has taken off is just out of this world. Broadcaster wants a new series almost before the last one's finished. So I'm here auditioning the young hopefuls.'

'Female young hopefuls or male young hopefuls?'

He gave her a sharp look, suspicious she was referring to the tabloid allegations. Jude kept the stare of her brown eyes steady, and he backed off. 'Both. I make and break boy bands and girl bands indiscriminately. Have you seen the show, by the way, Jude?'

She shook her head. 'Not for me, I'm afraid. Unlike most of the viewing public, I've never confused humiliation with entertainment.'

He didn't take the criticism personally, just smiled one of his big smiles. 'You're right, of course. I'm constantly amazed that "ordinary people" still put themselves up for this garbage. They should have seen enough of the programmes to know that everyone who's on them ends up getting stuffed. Any television producer with half a brain in an editing channel can make a "member of the public" look stupid. But still they turn up – each one presumably convinced they can break the sequence, that their natural personality will shine through, that they'll become stars. They're wrong – ' another big smile ' – but don't tell them. I'm making a lot of money out of them being wrong.'

'But some of the ones who've been through *Pop Crop* must've had talent. I read somewhere they've had number-one records.'

A cynical laugh. 'Talent and number ones don't have a lot to do with each other. The *Pop Crop* kids have done well just because of the promotion and coverage they've got. Give the same amount of airtime to a choir of donkeys with sore throats and they'll go to the top of the charts.'

Jude couldn't help admiring his candour. With a journalist, he'd have been extolling his programme's encouragement of new talent, its achievements in giving young people hope and aspirations, its contribution to the nation's cultural heritage. With her, he cut the bullshit.

There was a tap on the door; it opened. A purple-haired girl in T-shirt and jeans pointed to her watch. Rick Hendry nodded. The door closed.

Jude got in first. 'Better move on to what you wanted to say.'

'Yeah. It's still about that night you talked to Suze about.'

'Tuesday last week.'

'Right. Gather you know I was there.'

'Max Townley the chef told me.'

Rick gave a little nod, as if that confirmed his conjecture. 'Listen, Jude, it's very important no one else knows about that.'

'Why? There doesn't seem to have been any publicity about that solicitor's death. So you can't use your previous line about protecting Suzy and the hotel.'

'I'm not so sure that—'

'So is it maybe you who needs protection, Rick?'

'Not protection. I just don't need publicity at the minute.'

'Because of these allegations about you and underage girls?'

He was angry, but contained himself. 'That was a load of baseless tabloid garbage!'

'Anyway, how does Suzy have anything to do with that? She's hardly an underage girl. In fact, I'd have thought the news that you'd spent a night under the same roof as your ex-wife could do your image a lot of good at the moment.'

'Jude, just take my word for it – my presence at the hotel has to be kept a secret.'

'OK, I'm not about to rush to the press with the news. That's not the sort of thing I do.'

'And you're not about to rush to the press with news about that boy's death?'

'No, of course I'm not.'

'And you're going to stop snooping round trying to find out how he died?'

He'd gone too far there. Firmly, Jude shook her head. 'I'm going to find out everything I can about that.'

'But you mustn't! You can't!' For the first time in their conversation Rick Hendry lost his cool.

'I don't see why you're so worried,' said Jude evenly. 'You didn't have anything to do with it, did you?'

'Of course I didn't. I never even met the guy. Or any of the other Pillocks of Sussex or whatever they're called.' It was the same name Max Townley had used for them. Jude wondered whether it was more than coincidence. 'Except Bob Hartson, of course.'

'Oh, you know Bob Hartson?'

'Not know well. I've met him at the odd charity do.'

'I see.' So at least there was some connection between the worlds of the pop impresario and the Pillars of Sussex. 'You still haven't told me, Rick, why what I'm doing frightens you so much.'

'I'm not frightened.' But he sounded at least anxious. 'I just know how out of hand publicity can get. News of a murder at a hotel owned by Suzy Longthorne would get all those scavengers licking their chops. Then, if they found out that I'd actually been on the premises when it happened.'

There was another tap at the door. 'I'm bloody coming!' he screamed. The door didn't open.

'You used the word "murder", Rick,' said Jude coolly. 'I thought there was general agreement that Nigel Ackford committed suicide.'

'I used the word "murder" because that's what you seem to think it was. And if you go on snooping around, other people will start using it. Which will be extraordinarily bad news for Suze and for me.'

'You still haven't given me a good reason to stop "snooping", as you call it. In fact, the more you go on about it, the more I get the feeling you have something to hide.'

He shrugged, and sighed. The anger was back under control. 'I'm not going to convince you, am I, Jude?'

'Not unless you give me a reason, no, Rick.'

'If I said for the sake of your friendship to Suzy?'

'You've already said that. My friendship with Suzy is fine, even though I know she's holding out on me just as much as you are.'

He stood up, apparently defeated. 'I'm going to have to get back.'

Jude rose too. 'It's been good to see you. Though I don't know why you bothered to drag me over here. This conversation doesn't seem to have advanced much from the ones we had on the phone.'

'No.' He gave her the big, toothy smile again. All friends, it seemed to say. 'Incidentally, Jude, I gather from Suze that you first thought the boy had been murdered because of something he said to you the night he died.'

'That's right.'

'And, since then, have you found out anything else that has confirmed your suspicions?'

Jude was forced to admit that she hadn't much more corroboration. 'Only the fact that everyone involved in the case seems desperate to hush it up.'

Her answer apparently relieved him. 'Yeah. Well, like I say, nobody likes bad publicity.' He paused for a moment, then turned the beam of his smiling charm on her. 'Nothing I can do to make you lay off, is there, Jude?'

'What do you mean?'

He made a wide, slack gesture with his hands. 'Might be something you need. Few people have got everything they need these days, have they?'

Jude couldn't believe what she was hearing. 'Are you trying to bribe me, Rick? Are you offering me money?'

'Needn't be money.' He shrugged. 'I'm lucky enough to be able to organize most things people might want.'

'Like what?' asked Jude, still incredulous. 'An appearance in the starting line-up for *Pop Crop*?'

The speed and violence of his reaction amazed her. Suddenly he was close to her, his hand on the scarf around her neck. Then he seemed to remind himself of who he was, where he was, and what he was doing. He relaxed his grip and stepped backwards, manufacturing a little laugh. 'No, *Pop Crop*'s all above board. No cheating or unfair influence allowed there. The auditions are sacrosanct.' Still trying to lighten the atmosphere, he went on, 'Besides, we haven't quite got to your generation of singers yet.'

A very tentative tap on the door sounded. 'This time I must go.' He opened the door. 'See you, Jude.' And he was gone.

Leaving her with more questions than answers.

The biggest question being – why had he asked her to meet him? As she walked back through the anonymous carpeted corridors to the hotel's main reception, Jude went through their conversation in detail. And the question that seemed most important to her was Rick's asking whether she had any new evidence to support the theory that Nigel Ackford had been murdered.

She could be wrong, but Jude got the feeling he'd been trying to find out how much she knew.

Chapter Twenty-Six

They certainly did a good Sunday lunch at Hopwicke Country House Hotel. Like everything Suzy Longthorne arranged on the premises, the meal was traditional, but with a few extras that distinguished it from the run-of-the-mill. So, yes, it was roast beef with Yorkshire pudding, roast potatoes and vegetables, but each component was special. The meat had been selected from one particular farm in Scotland. The pudding batter contained a couple of secret ingredients known only to Max Townley. The roast potatoes were crisped to perfection, animated with the occasional surprise of a few sweet potatoes. The range of vegetables, and the way their tastes complemented each other, provided their own private gastronomic experience. The gravy was rich and thick, and the Hopwicke House home-made mustard (available in jars for purchase at reception) was to die for.

Stephen had ordered a wonderfully robust St Emilion to accompany the food and, in his practised perusal of the wine list, had shown an expertise which his mother would never have suspected. Carole wondered if he had always had an interest in fine wines, or whether this was a new skill born of his relationship with Gaby. And, once again, she felt guilty for not knowing the answer. Was it her fault she and Stephen seemed so far apart?

In physical appearance there was no doubt about their being related. Stephen had inherited his mother's angularity, and had the same pale blue eyes. Like her, he had needed glasses from an early age and, after a flirtation with contact lenses in his twenties, had now reverted to them. That he sported rimless ones was a point of fashion rather than a homage to her own, but Carole could see how much they increased the likeness between them. And the fact that Stephen's hair was prematurely greying only accentuated it.

Whether he was similar in personality, Carole realized with a shock, was another important detail she didn't really know. Wouldn't it be shaming to have to ask his fiancée what her son was really like?

Because there was no doubt that Gaby seemed to know Stephen really well. Carole had had no idea what to expect from her potential daughter-in-law, and had been seriously anxious about the encounter. Indeed, she'd woken at three and stayed awake for a couple of hours that morning, something that had rarely happened since the worst stage of her break-up with David.

If forced to put a face to Gaby before they met, Carole would probably have opted for an older version of Kerry. All she knew of her son's choice was the implication of money – the parents' spending summers in the South of France, the casual booking into Hopwicke House. The image that had formed in Carole

Seddon's prejudiced mind was of a spoilt trust-fund baby, someone who worked more for social convenience than financial necessity.

She certainly wasn't expecting the plumpish, bubble-haired blonde with the comfortable body and broad smile who greeted her in the Hopwicke House bar. Nor was she expecting to be greeted with a warm hug. The embrace took her by surprise, and she responded like a stick insect.

The first good news, though, was that Gaby was undoubtedly English. Carole tried, without success, to stop herself from feeling a politically incorrect glee at this discovery.

She had expected the young couple would be drinking deterrently fashionable cocktails, but they were both on white wine, so she ordered the same. While Stephen went to the counter to get her drink, Gaby gestured to their elegant surroundings. 'Fabulous place, isn't it? Wonderful to see how the other half lives. I told Stephen it was daft to spend this much on a weekend, but you know what he's like.'

And again Carole didn't.

What became clear during their conversation in the bar, and later in the dining room, was that Gaby didn't have private money. In fact, the rich one in the partnership was Stephen. Carole had known he was doing well at whatever it was he did, but she hadn't realized quite how well. In a couple of hours, his fiancée told her more about her son's current life than she had ever known. Or perhaps had ever thought to ask.

Carole was also comforted to discover that Gaby

was bored to tears when Stephen talked about his work. So it wasn't just her. Even better, Gaby didn't understand what he did either. Carole realized her image of her son had been coloured by this. Since there were so many subjects off-limits in their occasional conversations – subjects like David, Stephen's childhood, Carole's banal daily life in Fethering – she had allowed her son to go on about his work in exhaustive detail. At least the subject was a safe one. But by making him talk about other things, Gaby revealed a whole new side to her fiancé, a side hitherto unknown to his mother.

To Carole's amazement, she discovered her son could actually be quite funny. He had a disposition towards pomposity which she had always accepted as part of his personality, but Gaby constantly punctured that self-importance. And Stephen took it from her, with good humour, even relish.

The proscription on talking about his work also revealed that Stephen Seddon had a whole repertoire of other topics for conversation, most of which – to his mother's total surprise – were related to the arts. This was down to Gaby's influence. The 'agency' she worked for, which Carole had assumed to be something to do with the world of finance, turned out to be a theatrical one. She represented actors, of both genders. (She explained to Carole, amid some giggling, that the word 'actress' had become very démodé in these politically correct times. Now there were male actors and female actors.) As a result, most of Gaby's evenings were spent crossing the country to see clients or potential clients in theatres and ever more unlikely fringe venues. Whenever possible, Stephen accompanied her.

This was Carole's biggest surprise in a day of surprises. Apart from a couple of early attempts on her part to take him to pantomimes, her son had never shown even the mildest interest in the theatre. He was marginally more likely to go to a cinema, but even that hadn't happened very often. So to hear him discussing the latest offerings from the National Theatre and the Royal Shakespeare Company was, for Carole, like being introduced to someone she had never met before.

Apart from the theatre, there was of course another topic of conversation. The wedding. Needless to say, Gaby did most of the talking on the subject, but Carole had been unprepared for the enthusiasm with which Stephen contributed his own views. She was also surprised to discover how little advanced the plans for September the fourteenth were. The young couple hadn't even got a venue sorted yet.

'But won't you be getting married from your parents' house?' asked Carole, who knew the conventions in these matters.

Gaby grimaced. 'Wouldn't work. They've only just moved to this little flat in Harlow.'

Harlow. *Essex*, thought Carole, with all the prejudice a middle-class person in West Sussex automatically feels at the mention of that county, reckoned by everyone – except those who live there – to be the 'commonest' in England.

So what was all this about Gaby's parents spending their summers in the South of France? Even as the question came into Carole's mind, her potential daughter-in-law answered it for her. 'Also, Mum'd flap terribly about organizing a wedding. She and Dad always go to France in August, which is when the arrangements would be busiest. It's my gran, you see. *Grandmère*. Mum's mum. She's in a home out there, bit gaga, but they always go and visit.'

Oh. So Gaby wasn't completely English. Carole comforted herself with the thought that, on first meeting her, nobody would ever know it.

'Where are you thinking of getting married then? Somewhere in London?'

Gaby gave a large expressive shrug which, now Carole knew her provenance, looked distinctly Gallic. 'Don't know.'

'But we've got to sort it out quickly,' said Stephen.

'I know that, darling. But it's difficult, isn't it, Carole, when you don't have any faith? I mean, I totally lost it with Catholicism in my teens, and Stephen's told me he was brought up without anything in the way of religion.'

Carole was a bit miffed. Was that the impression her son had given? Though Carole herself had never since her teens believed in any kind of god, she still put 'Church of England' in the box marked 'Religion' on forms. Stephen had been christened, and he'd had to undergo school assemblies with prayers and hymns. The way Gaby described it made Stephen's upbringing sound godless.

But Carole suppressed such thoughts and asked, 'So what are you going to do?'

Another – very definitely Gallic – shrug. 'Find somewhere we like, set up the wedding there.'

'What about here?' Rather daringly, Carole gestured round the dining room.

Her son looked puzzled.

'They do weddings here, I know. Suzy Longthorne told me.'

'Is she the dishy one?'

'That's right. She owns the place.'

'And seems to be doing most of the work.'

Carole had been too preoccupied with her lunching companions to notice before, but Stephen was right. Suzy Longthorne was doing everything in the dining room, with the help of only two waitresses. All the tables were full, and the various courses were arriving on time, but at the cost of a lot of hard work. Perspiration shone through Suzy's perfect make-up as she scuttled back and forth to the kitchen.

Idly, Carole wondered what had happened to Kerry. The Sunday before, she remembered, Jude had said the girl was to have lunch with her parents. Maybe the relaxed terms of employment her stepfather had organized for her gave her every Sunday off.

And if Kerry was unavailable, why hadn't another emergency call gone out to Jude to come in and help with the waitressing?

Carole tuned back in to the conversation between her son and his fiancée about the possible merits of Hopwicke House as a wedding venue. They seemed surprisingly keen on the idea, and Carole began to question her wisdom in suggesting it. If the wedding

235

was right on her doorstep, she'd be bound to get involved in local arrangements. Better somewhere distant, anonymous, where she would have independence, where she could just turn up for the ceremony and leave as soon as she wanted to. But she couldn't deny that the thought of her son's wedding being at Hopwicke House did give her a little buzz of excitement.

At the end of the lunch, after lingering over their coffee, Carole insisted that it was her treat. Stephen demurred, saying the suggestion had been his and everything would go on the one bill, but his mother stood her ground. She was so delighted to have met Gaby, she would like to buy them lunch as an early engagement present. On his own, Stephen would have dug his toes in, but Gaby's presence rendered him gracious. With a shrug and a smile, he accepted Carole's largesse.

They said goodbye in the hall. Stephen and Gaby announced they were going to have a walk and would collect coats from their room. But the eye contact between them suggested that was not at all what they intended to do when they got back to the four-poster. Carole realized she wasn't at all embarrassed by the blatant lust she saw in the young couple's eyes; she found it heart-warming.

After they had gone upstairs, she settled the bill with Suzy Longthorne at the reception desk. Carole had never in her life paid half as much for a meal for three, but she didn't mind. Such gestures were rare, not because she was ungenerous, but because she didn't feel at ease with the flamboyance generosity usually required. Paying for this lunch, though, made her feel good, even gracious.

Suzy Longthorne presented her customary polished exterior, but she looked absolutely exhausted.

'That was a terrific lunch,' said Carole. 'You were a bit short-staffed, weren't you?'

The hotelier did not take this as a criticism. She just grimaced and said, 'Couple of people let me down at the last moment.'

'Surprised you didn't ask my friend Jude.'

'Oh, I did, but she couldn't make it.'

'Ah.' Carole took the proffered credit card slip and, enjoying her new mastery of the grand gesture, added a tip that would have covered a meal for three at the Crown and Anchor.

Carole Seddon drove the Renault back to Fethering in a haze of well-being. The most remarkable thing had happened. She found that she actually *liked* her son's fiancée.

And, through Gaby, she saw the prospect of getting to know – and like – Stephen.

On her arrival back at High Tor, Carole was surprised to see Jude pottering around in her front garden. She had assumed her neighbour had some other commitment which had prevented her from answering Suzy Longthorne's SOS. Carole was even more surprised to hear that Jude had received no summons to help out at the hotel.

It had indeed been a day of surprises.

Chapter Twenty-Seven

'I don't suppose,' said Carole, as she served coffee to Jude on Monday morning, 'that you can think of any promises?'

'Promises? Sorry, you've lost me.'

'For this auction of promises thing. I want to get back in touch with Sandra Hartson – you know, Kerry's mother – and I feel I need an excuse. If I had a promise to offer her, she wouldn't be suspicious.'

'What kind of promises are they?'

'Weeks at Spanish villas, weekends at hotels, dinners for two – all the kind of stuff the well-heeled middle classes value.'

'Forget it. Unless someone fancies an afternoon for one at Woodside Cottage.'

'Oh, and services.'

'Like what?'

'Facials, hairdos – usual stuff.'

'Hm.' Unconsciously Jude's plump hand played with a hanging tendril of blonde hair. 'I suppose I could offer a balancing session.'

'Balancing session?' Carole was constantly surprised by her neighbour's new skills. Had Jude spent some time working in a garage? 'What, for the wheels of their cars, because most of them have got these huge big off-road vehicles with—'

'No, Carole, no. Balancing their bodies, their personalities.'

'Oh.' The voice went frosty. This sounded like more of Jude's New Age healing nonsense.

'You'd be surprised how much take-up you'd get for it. Particularly from the women.'

'But these are women who spend all their time tanning themselves and playing geriatric golf. I suppose they might want to get balanced to improve their swings, but that's the only—'

'Well, if you don't like the balancing idea, I could offer kinesiology.'

Carole looked blank.

'Kinesiology is a natural health care system, based on muscle testing . . .'

'Ah.'

' . . . to analyse minor functional imbalances.'

'Right.'

'It's a holistic system which uses massage, nutrition and contact points to balance the whole person.'

Carole nodded, but her face remained blank. 'And you say the "womenfolk",' Caroline winced at the word, 'of the Pillars of Sussex will go for it?'

'I'm sure they will.'

'Well . . .' Carole wasn't convinced, but at least she had something to offer Sandra Hartson as an excuse for getting in touch with her.

'Why do you want to talk to Sandra, anyway?' asked

Jude. 'Have you got some new line on the investigation you're not sharing with me?'

'Of course not.' Though making a breakthrough on her own did have an undeniable appeal. 'I've just a feeling that if we're going to find out more about that night at the hotel, using any contacts we've got with the Pillars of Sussex is going to be a good idea.'

'I agree.'

'And the wives – or should I say "womenfolk" – are part of that communication system. Brenda Chew, Sandra Hartson – Bob Hartson is a very powerful man.'

'Oh yes.'

'I'm sure if anything odd has been going on in the Pillars of Sussex, he'd know about it.'

'And Kerry knows more about that night than she's letting on. I'm going to get back in touch with her.'

'Through the hotel?'

'No, directly.' Jude remembered something and tapped her fingers on her chin. 'Mind you, I am going to talk to Suzy. Find out why the hell she lied about calling me yesterday morning. She really is behaving very strangely.'

Their plans for the next stage of the investigation were just about in place when the phone rang. Carole answered it.

'It's all right,' a conspiratorial voice whispered. 'I'm calling on my mobile from the garden shed.'

She'd completely forgotten the existence of Barry Stilwell.

*

'I'm sorry, Jude. I wasn't deliberately lying.'

'Yes, you were, Suzy. You told Carole you'd rung me, and you hadn't.'

'OK, I lied, but it wasn't important. I just wanted to get her off my case.'

'As you want to get me off your case?'

'Yes, Jude.'

'But when we met in London, you were fine about things. What's made you change your—'

'Please. This is just for the time being. I'll be in touch when this has all blown over.'

'When what has all blown over?'

'Oh, the financial crisis at the hotel. The press interest in Rick.'

'You know I've seen him?'

'Yes, he said.'

'For a couple who had such a bitter divorce, you seem to be constantly in touch.'

'You don't know the situation.'

'I know what you feel about him. God, I listened to enough of it just after the split-up happened.'

'Yes, and I'm very grateful to you, Jude.'

'So why are you once again living in each other's pockets?'

'Time heals.'

'Not that much, Suzy. I think you're so closely in touch because you share a secret. Something you both want to hide.'

There was a silence. Then Suzy Longthorne announced coldly, 'You asked if I wanted you off my case, Jude. The answer is yes.' The coldness gave way to desperation. 'Please, Jude.' The emotion in Suzy's voice was the real thing. 'I'll give you a call in a month. Then we'll get together and I'll explain everything. I will. Trust me.'

'The number of times you've lied, Suzy,' said Jude implacably, 'you haven't given me much reason to trust you.'

'No.' Another silence.

'OK.' The moment had passed. Jude's tone was lighter now. 'By the way, is Kerry there? I wanted to have a word with her about—'

'Kerry doesn't work here any more,' said Suzy, firmly ending the conversation.

'I was ringing, Sandra, about a new promise.'

'Yes?' the woman at the other end of the line sounded bewildered and a little deterrent, as though a 'promise' were possibly some kind of double glazing system.

'It's Carole. Carole Seddon.'

'You said.' Still no recognition.

'We met at Brenda Chew's.'

'Oh, yes.' Now she knew, and everything in her middle-class upbringing was activated to cover the lapse. 'Of course. How lovely to hear from you, Carole. Sorry, I was preoccupied with . . . Anyway, so good to hear you. The Pillars of Sussex Auction, yes. So what promise have you managed to get?'

'A session of kinesiology . . .?' said Carole tentatively.

She needn't have worried about its reception. 'That would be wonderful,' Sandra Hartson cooed, sounding more animated than she had at any time during their acquaintance. 'Do you really know someone qualified to do that?'

'My next-door neighbour's a trained kinesiologist,' said Carole, with the casual mastery of being well connected.

'And she's really prepared to give the service free?'

'I've managed to persuade her,' confided the omnipotent Carole.

'Does she know the Pillars of Sussex?'

'She's heard about them. Knows about the good work they do.'

'That's excellent. Kinesiology.'

Carole had not expected Sandra Hartson to be into alternative therapies. 'Have you tried it?'

'Oh yes.'

'And it worked?'

'For a while. I don't know why I stopped going, really. I suppose it was when I moved on to reiki. Or maybe it was round the time I had the colonic irrigation . . .'

Carole was beginning to get a clearer image of Sandra Hartson's personality. An alternative therapy junkie, constantly in search of a quick fix for all her problems. Carole wondered what pressures put Sandra in such permanent need of help, and whether being married to Bob Hartson was one of them.

'Anyway, Carole, well done. That's a terrific

promise. I'll certainly bid for the kinesiology session myself.'

Carole was struck again by an anomaly in the system of charity giving. Sandra Hartson must have been rich enough to buy as many kinesiology sessions as she wanted to at the going market rates, and yet she was prepared to pay way over the odds in the context of an auction of promises. Surely not just to show off to her friends? The Pillars of Sussex and their women-folk must already have seen enough evidence of the Hartson wealth. Odd.

Still, Carole's opening gambit had worked well. Time to use that platform to advance her investigation. 'Incidentally, Sandra, you know you said your daughter Kerry probably wouldn't be staying long at the hotel . . .'

'Sorry?' Their recent encounter seemed to have made little impression on Sandra Hartson.

'Yes. When we were going to the car.'

'Right.' But she still didn't sound as though she remembered.

'Anyway, I heard through a friend of mine who works up at Hopwicke House that Kerry has left.'

'Seemed a bit pointless for her to stay on in the circumstances.'

'What circumstances?'

'Well, I can't see Kerry ever going back into the hotel business after what's happened.'

'I'm sorry? I'm a bit behind you, Sandra. What has happened?'

The mother's voice took on a note of awestruck pride. 'Kerry's ambitions look as though they may be realized. She's passed the audition. She's going to be on *Pop Crop*.'

Chapter Twenty-Eight

'I rang to say congratulations.'

'What for?' Kerry Hartson sounded suspicious. Why was Jude, whom she only knew vaguely, ringing her again?

'Congratulations on getting the *Pop Crop* audition.'

'Oh, yeah, well, thanks. It's a big opportunity for me, and I'm determined to do my absolute best. I'm really going for it.'

Instantly the girl had dropped into interview mode. Jude could picture her, sitting in her flat in Brighton, looking at the sea and indulging the fantasy of the television crew around her, the fawning presenter asking about her next single. She could even imagine Kerry tidying up her sitting room, in case the interviewers arrived unannounced. The prospect of fame could have a wonderful effect on the domestic habits of teenagers.

'You heard from Suzy, I suppose?' the girl went on.

Jude saw no reason to contradict her. 'She said you were going to stop working at the hotel.'

'Yeah, well, that was like only work experience, but I don't reckon I'm going to end up in hotels. Obviously, now *Pop Crop*'s come up, well, I've got to, like, really go for it, haven't I?'

Still in interview mode. Jude wondered whether Kerry would repeat herself as much in a real interview, and decided the answer was probably yes.

Time for a change of tack. Time to find out where Kerry really was on the night of Nigel Ackford's death. When last asked the question, she had claimed to be drinking whisky in her father's room. Bob Hartson had supported that, and had claimed Barry Stilwell as a witness. Somebody had been lying, though, and, determined to find out who, Jude spelled out to Kerry the inadequacy of her alibi.

The girl was thrown. 'Look, why're you on about this again? I'll have to tell Dad you've been asking.'

If that was meant to be a threat, the words had no effect on Jude. 'Fine. But you answer me first.'

'I don't have to.' Archetypal adolescent defiance.

'No, you don't have to, but if you don't, I will know for definite that you have something to hide.'

There was a silence while Kerry took in the logic of this. Then she asserted, 'I haven't got anything to hide. I did go up to Dad's room, like I said, and drank a bit of whisky with him—'

'Just the two of you?'

'No,' she snapped. 'There was someone else there.'

'Barry Stilwell says he was there, but he says you weren't.'

'Well, I wasn't there all the time. I just had a drink and left them to it.'

'So where did you go then?'

'I went to bed.'

'You weren't in your room when I turned in round three.'

'No, I was— It was later than that when I left Dad's room.'

'Your father said you left about two.'

'Yes, well . . .' She was really floundering now. 'Dad's never got a good sense of time, and when he's been at the booze . . .'

'That doesn't sound very convincing to me, Kerry.'

'It's the truth. Ask that solicitor.'

'Barry Stilwell? The one who first of all said he was with your dad, but you weren't there, and then changed his tune and suddenly remembered you *had* been there? I don't think he's a very reliable witness. In fact, I've a feeling Barry Stilwell will say anything your father tells him to say.'

Kerry Hartson might have been expected to pick up on this criticism of her precious father, but she didn't. Instead, she spoke as if new light had come flooding into her life. 'Of course, I've got it. The reason we're getting all mixed up over this.'

'Oh?' asked Jude cynically. 'And what is that?'

'It's Dad.' The girl chuckled. 'He's always had this dreadful thing with names – mixes people up. He said the solicitor was with us, right?'

'Yes. Barry Stilwell.'

'But that's it, you see, it wasn't Barry Stilwell in the room with us while we were drinking the whisky.'

'Then who was it?'

'Dad's own solicitor. Mr Chew.'

'Donald Chew?'

'That's right. Yes.'

Jude reckoned a long time had passed since she had heard quite such a preposterous lie, but she let it pass, thanked the girl for clearing the matter up, and moved on. 'Going back to the *Pop Crop* thing.'

'Yeah. Exciting, isn't it?' And then, as if the words hadn't been said enough, 'I'm really going to go for it.'

'Good for you. And you got it by doing an audition in Brighton?'

'Sure. There were a lot of people, but I thought if I, like, gave it my best shot – really went for it – well . . . And it turned out OK.'

'And you were auditioned by Rick Hendry?'

'Right.' A note of caution had come into the girl's voice.

'Was that the first time you'd met him?'

'What do you mean?'

'I mean, was the audition the first time you met Rick Hendry? Or had you met him before up at the hotel?'

'No,' said Kerry Hartson. 'First time I met him was at the audition.'

But she sounded as guilty as hell. Jude wondered how soon after putting the phone down on their call, Kerry would be ringing her stepfather.

'Carole Seddon?'

'Yes?'

'It's Brenda Chew.'

'Oh, good afternoon.'

'I heard from Sandra Hartson about the promise you'd secured for the auction. This session of . . . canasta . . .?'

'Kinesiology,' said Carole, as though she had been familiar with the word from birth.

'Yes. Well, I'm very grateful to you, but I thought I'd better check the details.'

'I gave all the details to Sandra.'

'But I just wanted to double-check.'

Recognizing Brenda Chew's inability to delegate, Carole said rather tartly, 'The details are all exactly as I gave them to Sandra. My next-door neighbour, who is a trained kinesiologist, is offering a free two-hour session for the auction of promises at the Hopwicke Country House Hotel next Saturday.'

'Yes. That's exactly what Sandra Hartson said.'

'Of course it is. It's exactly what I told her.'

'Hm. So what is your friend's name?'

'Jude.'

'Jude what?'

'Most people just call her Jude.'

'Oh dear. I'm not sure that that will look quite right in the catalogue though I suppose, in the world of alternative therapies, you might expect people to be a bit odd. Still, I'll discuss it with her.'

'What?'

'I'm going to telephone her. Could you give me the number?'

Carole did so, and then asked, 'Are you just going to ring her to say thank you for the offer?'

'Yes, yes, that's right.' A moment's pause. 'Well, and just to double-check all the details.'

With difficulty Carole managed not to grind her teeth.

'Oh, and there's another very good bit of news, Carole.'

'What's that?'

'You know I was saying at our meeting how useful it would be to our cause if we could get a celebrity auctioneer . . .?'

'Yes.'

'Well, I've got one.'

'Who?'

Brenda Chew's voice was full of smug pride as she announced, 'That man from the television. Rick Hendry.' She went into a very bad impersonation of his catch-phrase. 'I wish I'd been born deaf!'

'What! Who on earth fixed that?'

'Oh, I did. As I may have said before, if you want a job done properly, do it yourself.'

Chapter Twenty-Nine

Carole's second appointment with Donald Chew was the following afternoon, but before revising her will she went for coffee at Woodside Cottage, and she and Jade pooled their new information.

'What seems to be happening,' said Jude, 'is that the divergent elements of the case are drawing together. For a long time we couldn't find a single connection between the world of Rick Hendry and the world of the Pillars of Sussex, but now we're spoilt for choice.'

'Yes. I can't imagine what pressure was put on him to take on this auctioneering job.'

'From what I know of Rick, it must have been pretty strong. He's never been known for his charity works. Having long pockets is part of the image he's so carefully built up. He deliberately refused to take part in the Live Aid recording, regularly refuses to have anything to do with Children in Need, Red Nose Day and all those other telethons. So the idea of him turning out for the Pillars of Sussex . . . somebody's twisted his arm pretty hard.'

'Suzy?'

'I doubt it.'

'Well, maybe you could ask her?'

Jude grimaced. 'She's trying to freeze me out at the moment. Doesn't want to talk to me.'

'Is that permanent?'

The narrow thread of jealousy in Carole's nature meant she couldn't help hoping the answer would be yes, but Jude shrugged off the suggestion. 'No We've been friends for too long for anything like that to be permanent.'

'Oh,' said Carole.

'Anyway, you will talk to Donald Chew about the alibi he's supposed to be providing for Kerry?'

'I don't quite know how easy it'll be to bring the conversation round to that.'

'Won't be a problem, Carole. He'll probably volunteer the information. I'm sure the Pillars of Sussex grapevine has been busy overnight. Bob Hartson will know that his daughter's changed her story, and the damage limitation work will be well under way.'

'All right. I'll do my best.'

'Meanwhile I'm going to recontact Wendy Fullerton – you know, Nigel Ackford's on-off girlfriend. There may be something else she can tell me about his background.'

'Might be useful, yes.' But Carole didn't sound very convinced. What we really still need is a timetable of the movements of everyone in the hotel that night.'

'And in Suzy's house as well.'

'And don't let's forget the stable block – the staff quarters. How many potential murderers have we got in there?'

'Me?' Jude suggested. 'Kerry – Max – Ooh, and of course, Bob Hartson's driver, Geoff.'

'Is he in the frame then?'

'Wish he was,' said Jude wistfully. 'But Inspector Goodchild seemed to rule him out. Anyway, Geoff wouldn't have had a key to the hotel and, according to Max, he was snoring away in his bedroom after the kitchen door was locked.'

'Which was before Nigel Ackford was killed.'

'Yes.'

'Max could have been lying,' Carole suggested.

'He could have been. He's lied about plenty of other things. But we don't know for sure, do we? Frustrating business, solving murder mysteries, isn't it?'

'Mm.' Carole picked up her handbag in a determined fashion. 'Well, let's see what I can find out this afternoon from my friendly local solicitor.'

As soon as her neighbour had left, Jude did an hour of yoga. Her mind was filled with permutations of the suspects at Hopwicke Country House Hotel and of how Nigel Ackford might have died and the yoga, she knew, would empty and cleanse her, leaving a more effective brain in a more relaxed body.

She went through the comforting movements which were by now almost instinctive, and which left no spare concentration available for niggling thought. In the privacy of her bedroom her plump body posed and balanced with surprising grace, and at the end of the session she felt, as she had known she would, completely recharged.

Jude was just rolling up her mat when the phone rang. It was Max Townley. He sounded ill at ease; he wanted to talk. Jude suggested lunch at the Crown and Anchor.

'Your death's made it to the *Fethering Observer*,' said Ted Crisp.

'What?' said Jude, spluttering in to her Chilean Chardonnay. 'But I haven't even been ill.'

'Listen, I do the jokes. Actually, I was talking about that solicitor you mentioned up at Hopwicke House.'

'Really?'

'Look.' The landlord thrust over the counter a copy of the local paper, folded to an inside page. There, amid two-inch reports of thefts from cars in Littlehampton car parks, monies raised by a sponsored cycle ride, and the appointment of a new primary school head, was a snippet that read:

HOTEL DEATH

Worthing solicitor Nigel Ackford was found dead in his room at a local hotel. The cause of death is as yet unknown. Ackford's employer, Donald Chew, senior partner of the long-established firm Renton and Chew said, 'Nigel Ackford was a very promising young man. He will be sorely missed.'

'How do they do it?' asked Jude in disbelief.

'Do what?'

'Keep all the facts out. Look, no mention of the Hopwicke Country House Hotel. No mention of the Pillars of Sussex.'

255

'I think your last four words have answered your own question, Jude. The Pillars of Sussex have got fingers in most of the local pies. If they want to control what gets printed, I'm sure they can lean on someone at the *Fethering Observer*.'

'But that's illegal, isn't it?' Jude protested. 'Leaning on people?'

'Good heavens, no.' Ted Crisp adopted a mock-posh accent as he went on, 'The Pillars of Sussex only lean in the most elegant and discreet way. They don't send round the heavies with nail-studded baseball bats, nothing crude like that. Oh no. But they might offer someone fast-track entry to the exclusive local golf club, or smooth the granting of planning permission for a new extension, or issue an invitation for an all-expenses-paid week in a Spanish villa. None of it's actually illegal, it's just the way business has always been conducted in this country. And to think all that's continuing under a so-called Labour government . . .' Ted Crisp's beard shook with fury. 'Don't get me started.'

'No,' said Jude hastily. 'No, I don't want to.'

'I mean, the thing is' – apparently he hadn't heard her – 'the thing is, the Labour Party was founded to look after the working people of this country, to challenge the kind of unfair system of privilege by which a tiny percentage of the people controlled a huge percentage of . . .'

Jude was quite relieved that Max Townley chose that moment to enter the pub. He was in his black leathers – no doubt the precious Ducati was parked outside – and he looked distinctly nervous.

Jude introduced him to Ted, whose flow he had so mercifully interrupted. 'What would you like to drink?'

'No, I should do this, Jude.'

'Come on.'

'All right. Don't normally drink at lunchtime, but I'll have a half of Guinness.'

'I'm going to eat something. What about you?'

'Well . . .'

'It's only pub food, but—'

She knew she'd said the wrong thing as soon as the words were out. 'Only pub food?' Ted Crisp repeated. 'Only pub food? What is this?'

'I'm sorry, it's just that . . .' this was going to make things sound even worse, 'Max is a chef.'

Framed by beard, the landlord's mouth opened and closed in soundless affront. Fortunately, before he could say anything, Max eased the situation. 'Yes, I'm a chef, but I've served my time working in pubs, and that's where I've come across some of the best food I've ever encountered.'

'Too right,' said Ted Crisp, somewhat mollified.

'So what do you recommend today?' asked Max, continuing the fence-mending.

'You won't go wrong with the pork chops Normandie.'

'Done with apple, calvados and cream in the sauce?'

'Exactly.'

Max nodded. 'I'll go for that.'

Ted Crisp grinned with satisfaction and looked at Jude. 'And for madam?'

'I suppose I'd better go for the same.' But she was bewildered. 'Doesn't sound like your usual menu, Ted. I was expecting fisherman's pie and sausage and mash.'

'New chef,' the landlord confided with a conspiratorial wink. 'At catering college in Chichester, but moonlighting here a couple of days a week.'

Max approved. 'That's the time to get them. I did some of my best stuff while I was training. I'll look forward to my pork chops Normandie. Wish the chef luck from Max Townley. Ooh, and let me pay for the food.'

This assertion of his own fame and the chat with Ted Crisp seemed to have relaxed Max, but once he was seated in a booth opposite Jude, his nervousness returned. 'Suzy sent her love,' he said.

'Oh. So she knew you were meeting me?'

He shrugged. 'I just mentioned it.'

Jude had a feeling a lot of things were being 'just mentioned' on the grapevine between Hopwicke House and the Pillars of Sussex.

'I haven't had my usual emergency calls from Suzy to go and help out.'

'No, well, we just haven't been busy.'

Jude knew from Carole that the dining room had been crammed full for Sunday lunch. So Max was lying about that. How much else would he lie about?

He took a sip from his Guinness and became more serious. 'Listen, I owe you an explanation, Jude.'

'Oh?'

'When we last talked . . . you know, in that coffee place . . .'

'Yes?'

'I wasn't entirely truthful in what I said.'

She didn't respond, just waited for him to continue.

'I said I hit the vodka and just passed out for the night.'

'Yes. So you didn't see anything of what other people in the hotel were doing.'

'That's right. That's what I said, but . . .' He ran his fingers through his short black hair, this wasn't coming easily to him. 'In fact, I did see some people that night.'

Jude let the silence expand between them.

'The thing is . . . I told you about Rick Hendry being there, at Suzy's place and I said that I'd thought of going to talk to him . . . you know, about my possibilities in television, through Korfilia Productions . . .'

'You mentioned that, yes.'

'Well . . . In fact, I did. I didn't just think about going to see Rick. I did go to talk to him. I mean, knowing he was there so close. I was just in the staff quarters, he was at Suzy's. When would I get a better opportunity? And I was in such a bad state, having heard that afternoon about the failure of my other television pitch, and, yes, I was a bit pissed, so I thought I'd really go for it.'

Just like Kerry, thought Jude. Clearly the recipe for television success was to 'really go for it'.

'So you went and asked Rick Hendry whether he would help launch your career as a television chef?'

'Yes.'

Max's confession was interrupted by the arrival of their pork chops Normandie. He sniffed the sauce appraisingly and poked at the dish of vegetables to assess their texture.

'Sorry, Jude. Occupational hazard.'

'Can't you ever forget your work and just enjoy a meal?'

'Oh, sure. I eat all kinds of rubbish and don't notice. But when I'm sitting down to a meal where I know the chef's *trying . . .'*

'And this one is?'

'You bet.' He dabbed his knife into the sauce and tasted it off the point. 'He's succeeding too, I'd say.'

They started eating the food, which was indeed excellent, and Jude waited. This time she knew she wouldn't need to prompt Max. They were working to his agenda; sooner or later he'd get back into his confession.

Sooner, as it turned out. 'So, anyway, that night I did go to see Rick at Suzy's place.'

'And?'

'And what?'

'And did he say he'd take you on, get Korfilia Productions to nurture your television career?'

He seemed surprised by the question. 'No, he said it wasn't really their kind of show. But he was OK about it. Generous. You know, he listened to me while we had a few drinks.'

'What time was this?'

'I suppose I went over about quarter past twelve.'

Jude did the calculations. At that time the Pillars of Sussex had still been carousing in the bar.

'And I stayed till Suzy came back from the hotel.'

Half-past two, quarter to three.

'So that was it? You didn't see anyone else, apart from Suzy and Rick?'

Max cut off a small cube of pork, put it in his mouth and chewed. When he'd finished, he looked Jude straight in the eyes. 'Yes, I did see some other people.'

'Who?'

He dabbed at his mouth with a paper napkin. 'I went back to my room, full of Rick's vodka – well, Suzy's vodka – but I didn't pass out straight away. I was quite wakeful, actually, so I thought, to put me off to sleep, I'd— You know that thing, when you've been drinking a lot, you want just one more drink, the final nightcap?'

Jude nodded.

'That's how it was with me. So I went back into the hotel to raid the bar.'

'What time was this?'

'Quarter past three, I suppose. Something like that.'

'I was already in bed by then. I'd locked the kitchen door.'

'I wondered who'd done that. But' – he produced a big bunch on a chain from his pocket – 'I have my own keys. So I let myself in and, while I was in the bar, I heard some people coming downstairs. It was Kerry, and her stepfather, and that old guy – you know, one of the Pillocks – bald, red-faced – the one who arrived early to check the details for the dinner.'

'Donald Chew?'

'That's right. Anyway, they were chatting – sounded like they'd had a few drinks themselves – and

I heard them saying goodnight to Kerry, and she went out through the kitchen to her room. Then I came out of the bar, and the old bloke was just going up the stairs to bed, but Kerry's dad saw me, and he asked if I could find him a bottle of Scotch and put it on his bill. So I did. He went upstairs to bed, and I went back out through the kitchen to my room, locking the door behind me.'

Max finished on a note of barely disguised triumph. He had told her everything he had to tell her.

Jude didn't believe a word of it.

His duty discharged, as soon as he'd mopped up the last of his Normandie sauce with a piece of bread, Max announced he had to get back to the hotel. There was a special lobster dish that needed preparing for that night's dinner.

Before he left, he asked permission from Ted Crisp and went through to have a quick word with the chef. When he returned, he took Jude's hand in his, focused his blue eyes on her brown ones and said, 'I'm sorry about all the confusion, Jude, but I really do feel better for having made a clean breast of it. Better late than never, eh?'

And Max Townley was gone.

As she quietly sipped her way through another glass of Chardonnay, Jude sorted out the implications of what Max had told her. Rick Hendry and Suzy Longthorne now seemed to be in the clear. Max had been with Rick for the first hours, and presumably Suzy could vouch for him for the rest of the night.

And, assuming there hadn't been a conspiracy

between Bob Hartson, his stepdaughter and Donald Chew, no suspicion could attach to Kerry. She'd been drinking with her father and his solicitor until Max had seen her leave the hotel for the stable block. The kitchen door had subsequently been locked and, though the chef possessed keys, Kerry didn't. So she couldn't have had anything to do with the murder.

There were many reasons why Jude felt sure Max had been lying to her: he had betrayed himself by the suddenness of his approach; by the command he'd shown over details of timing; and by the unnecessary production of his hotel keys as a visual aid. Everything was too convenient, too pat, to be spontaneous.

That being the case, the question then arose: who had set him up? Who had wanted him to lie, and what inducements had they used to persuade him to do so?

Jude analysed the benefits of the new set of circumstances, as detailed by Max to various individuals, and soon decided the significant figure in the scenario was Kerry. At the time of Nigel Ackford's death, the girl was safely outside the hotel, actually locked outside it. But very little suspicion had ever been attached to Kerry. The spelling-out of her movements was not to clear her of implication in the murder. It must have been for another reason.

Suddenly Jude understood. Max had not been leant on by Bob Hartson. Indeed, his new version of events did not help Bob Hartson at all. It left Kerry's father and Donald Chew both on the loose in the hotel at the relevant time. They had no alibis.

One detail was needed to confirm she was right.

With a hurried explanation to the bewildered Ted Crisp, Jude went into the pub kitchen. There she confronted the equally bewildered and very young student chef responsible for their excellent pork chops Normandie.

Yes, he'd been well pleased that Max Townley had liked his cooking. Of course he'd heard of the chef up at Hopwicke House. And yes, Max Townley had asked him for his contact numbers.

'Why?' asked Jude.

'Because there's a good chance he's going to be doing a telly series. Going to be a different format from all the other TV cookery programmes – include lots of new young chefs.' The young man beamed. 'That's why Max Townley was interested in me. He's going to make a pilot programme soon, and he's looking for young chefs for that.'

Jude had been right. The incentive for Max to lie had been the backing of Korfilia Productions in the realization of his television dreams. And the offer had been made by Rick Hendry.

And the important part of the lie was that it established Kerry was still with her stepfather when Suzy returned to join her ex-husband. In other words, there was no time at which Rick Hendry and Kerry Hartson could have been alone together.

Which, for a television personality being hounded by the tabloids over his interest in young girls, could be a very significant point of self-protection.

Chapter Thirty

The revised will was on Donald Chew's desk when Carole was ushered into his office. She reflected rather sourly that the document could have been on his desk by the end of their previous meeting. A few sentences added to a standard form and the job was done. The inventions of word-processing, faxes and email must have reduced the workload of solicitors enormously. But respect for 'the law's delay' was one of the foundations of their professional principles – and certainly of their fee structure. So, in a provincial practice like Renton and Chew, everything had to take a long time, and all communications be sent by post.

After another bonhomous Dickensian welcome and an accepted offer of coffee, Donald Chew asked her to 'run her eye' over the will and check it was now in the form she wished. (If it wasn't, the document would no doubt be removed for the lengthy changing of a couple of words and another appointment be made for a further meeting.)

Having scrutinized the insertions and then, as a double-check, read through the whole will, Carole agreed that the changes had been made according to her instructions. Since that was the moment her coffee arrived, Donald Chew suggested that, if she were happy about the arrangement, Carole's signature could be witnessed straight away by himself and his receptionist.

Their business was done. Carole could think of no pretext on which she could extend the encounter, but she did not need to. Donald Chew seemed happy – even keen – to talk further. This could have been part of his usual professional manner, but she had a feeling he had an agenda to elicit information from her, or to impart some to her. So she was content to let his pleasantries unroll.

'Delighted you got in touch with Brenda,' he began. 'She's always so pleased to have extra helpers' – he chuckled – 'though often she has to end up doing a lot of things herself.' Decades of marriage had taught Donald Chew the party line on his wife's perpetual martyrdom.

'Well, anything I can do to help. It's in a good cause.'

'Oh yes. And Brenda was very grateful for the promise you organized. What was it . . . callanetics?'

'Kinesiology.'

'Ah,' he said with a masculine chuckle. 'Something for the ladies, anyway.'

'No. In fact, kinesiology is a highly respected natural health care system.' What on earth was happening? Carole Seddon defending alternative therapies?

'I'm sure. Anyway, very grateful to you for organizing it. And will you be at the auction of promises itself, Mrs Seddon?'

Carole hadn't entirely decided about this, but she thought she probably should be. A hundred and fifty pounds was a huge amount to shell out for what would most likely be an uncongenial evening, but contact with Hopwicke Country House Hotel remained important. And if, as it seemed, Jude was temporarily *persona non grata* there . . .

'Yes, I would like to. The trouble is, I don't know anyone—'

'Nonsense. You know Brenda. Have a word with her. She'll see you're put on our table.' He decided this was perhaps more than he could promise on his wife's behalf. 'Or at least on a table with a nice bunch of people.'

'I'll give her a call about it.'

'Good. Good.' He looked out at the sea through his office window. 'Never tire of that view, you know. Lovely, isn't it? The sea. Never still, always changing.'

This moment of poetry from the solicitor was unexpected, until Carole realized he was just playing for time. Donald Chew was tense. There was something he needed to say to her, and he was having difficulty getting round to it.

She agreed the view was lovely, and waited.

'You remember last time you were here, Mrs Seddon . . . we discussed the young man who used to work here. Nigel Ackford, you know, who was up at the hotel.'

'Oh yes,' Carole recalled, as if she hadn't heard the name since Donald Chew last mentioned it.

'There was an announcement of his death in the *Fethering Observer.*'

'Really? I haven't seen it yet.'

'No mention of the cause of death.'

'Presumably there'll be an inquest?'

'There has been a preliminary one; adjourned until there's more evidence,' said the solicitor, confirming what Jude had heard from Inspector Goodchild. 'Post-mortems, that kind of thing I suppose.'

'Yes.'

Donald Chew sighed wearily. 'I feel rather bad about it.'

'Why?'

'Well, because I was actually at the hotel the night he died. You know, you always have the feeling perhaps there was something you could have done. Probably not true, but . . . And those Pillars of Sussex dinners can get a bit rowdy and I'm afraid too much gets drunk and . . . I don't know. Always a tendency to feel guilty after someone's died. I'm sure I'll get over it.'

Carole felt certain he had not yet unburdened himself of everything he needed to, and sure enough, after a silence, Donald Chew continued, his eyes still fixed on the sea. 'I suppose I feel guilty because I'd drunk more than I intended that evening. In fact, I'd intended to drink virtually nothing, but . . . the road to hell and all that.'

Carole let him run on. 'I even went on drinking after we'd left the bar. Bob Hartson offered to share a bottle of whisky with me up in his room, and I'm afraid I succumbed to that temptation too. Must have been up there for an hour, drinking with Bob – and his daughter Kerry. Goodness, for a child of her age, can she put the drink away?' He chuckled, but still hadn't finished what he had to say. 'So, do you know, it was about quarter past three by the time I actually fell into my bed. Bob and I staggered downstairs to say goodnight to Kerry. She had a room in the stable block out the back, staff quarters, same place the chef and Bob's chauffeur spent the night. And then I tottered off to bed.'

He shook his head; his eyes were full of self-loathing. 'Dear oh dear. Don't we ever learn? Why is alcohol so seductive while we're drinking the stuff, and why does it make us feel so – *uncomfortable* afterwards.' He had nearly let out a stronger adjective, but bowdlerized for Carole's benefit.

From that point the conversation moved away from Nigel Ackford. Donald Chew talked further about the auction of promises. Carole said how much she was looking forward to it. Their meeting ended with great apparent cordiality.

And it left Carole feeling exactly as Jude had felt after her conversation with Max Townley in the Crown and Anchor. Someone was very deliberately orchestrating the alibis of the people present at Hopwicke House on the night Nigel Ackford died.

That afternoon Carole and Jude went for a stroll on Fethering beach. It was such a beautiful day – April coyly demonstrating how lovely an English spring can be – that Gulliver got the bonus of a second walk among the infinitely intriguing smells of seaweed, salt and tar.

'Rick Hendry's got to be behind it,' Jude announced. 'He's the only one who benefits from this new scenario that's been spoon-fed to us. And the alibis he's set up have nothing to do with the murder. They're just to cover any time he might possibly have been alone with Kerry.'

'Suggesting that he did spend some time alone with Kerry that night?'

'I'd say almost definitely, yes. And if news of that got out, with the current interest in Rick and underage girls, the tabloids'd go into a feeding frenzy.'

'Yes, Jude, but what if Kerry herself talks?'

'She's been very effectively bribed to maintain her silence. Coincidence of timing, don't you think, that she suddenly passes an audition to be on *Pop Crop*?'

'Rick Hendry using his media power?'

'Exactly. Just as he did with Max Townley. Amazing what people will do for the promise of television fame.'

'But how did he persuade Donald Chew to fall in line?'

'No idea, but he did somehow. The coincidence is too great for it to be above board. Just think of the unnecessary detail Donald gave you. He was fulfilling his part of an agreement to back up what Max told me.'

Carole nodded and looked thoughtfully out over the sea. 'Yes, it all makes sense. But I'm sure Bob Hartson's involved somewhere.'

'Not in this alibi business. Rick, Suzy, Kerry and

Max are in the clear, but Bob Hartson – and Donald Chew – are left wandering around the hotel just at the time when Nigel Ackford was most likely killed. Neither one of them has any alibi at all.'

Chapter Thirty-One

Jude had just parted from Carole and entered Woodside Cottage when her mobile rang. 'It's Wendy Fullerton.'

'Oh, hello. How are you?'

'Fine,' the girl said shortly. She didn't want to dwell on how she was. 'Listen, you know you asked me to ring if anything else came up about Nigel.'

'Yes?'

'Well, there is something. I don't know whether it's important or not, but it's . . . odd. I don't know if you remember, but I was using Nigel's mobile.'

Jude had forgotten, but said, 'Yes.'

'His latest bill arrived yesterday. He must've given a change of address to the phone company when he moved in with me, and then forgotten to say he'd moved out, and then of course . . .'

The sentence died away, and Jude was aware of the tension in the girl's manner. 'So what's odd about it, Wendy? Presumably you opened the bill?'

'Yes. Like I said, I'd been using the phone, so a lot of the calls – particularly the later ones – were mine, but it was the ones before that seemed odd.'

She ran out of steam again. 'How, odd?' Jude prompted.

'In the itemized listing there were some numbers I recognized. A lot of calls to me obviously, and some to Renton and Chew and . . .'

'Yes?'

Wendy Fullerton took the bull by the horns. 'There were also a lot to a number I didn't recognize.'

'A local number?'

'Yes. 01903 prefix. I just—' She was getting quite emotional now. 'It's not a number I know and—'

'You haven't rung it, have you, Wendy?'

'No, I kind of want to, but . . .'

Jude understood completely. Wendy Fullerton had taken comfort in the news that Nigel Ackford had wanted to marry her. Maybe the knowledge was helping her cope with the complexities of bereavement. Now she was faced with the evidence, from his telephone bill, that Nigel had been ringing someone else a lot in the last weeks of his life. Wendy's comforting image was threatened. Maybe she wasn't the woman he had loved.

'What you're asking,' said Jude softly, 'is whether I'll call the number for you and find out who all the calls were to?'

'Yes.' The girl's relief was almost palpable. 'If you wouldn't mind?'

'Of course I wouldn't. Give me the number' Jude wrote it down on the back of a shopping receipt. 'And I'd better take your mobile number too. That is, presumably you do want me to let you know who it is?'

There was a pained silence from the other end. 'Even if the news, from your point of view, is bad?'

Wendy Fullerton summoned up her courage. 'Yes. Whoever it is, let me know.'

Jude would have made the call straight away, had the sound of a car stopping not drawn her to the front window. A smart new BMW Mini had parked outside Woodside Cottage, and out of it, elegant in burgundy silk shirt and white jeans, stepped Suzy Longthorne.

The hug enveloped Jude in a perfume far too exclusive for her to be able to name, let alone afford. 'I'm sorry,' said Suzy. 'I've hated holding out on you. I felt so guilty, I thought I'd just come straight round and talk.'

'Bless you.' Jude grinned in surprise. 'Almost time for a drink. I could stretch a point. How about you? Or are you waiting for the one glass after you've tidied up dinner.'

'No,' Suzy replied. 'I'll have one with you. No one booked in tonight.'

Another lie from Max, thought Jude as she fetched a bottle of white Bordeaux from the kitchen fridge. He hadn't had to rush off from the Crown and Anchor to prepare a lobster dish for that evening's diners. But she didn't say anything, as she handed her friend a glass.

'Thanks. Listen, Jude, I don't know everything Rick's been up to, but I gather he's been messing you about.'

'I'm not sure he's been messing me about. He's certainly been ring-fencing himself in alibis, so he's covered for every minute of that Tuesday night he spent at your place.'

Suzy Longthorne smiled ruefully as she sank into one of Jude's much-draped armchairs. 'Rick is just so paranoid about publicity.'

'Isn't that a bit of a pot and kettle situation? You've had your moments too.'

'Yeah, OK. But I've never been as bad as Rick. As soon as he heard about that solicitor dying, he went into complete damage-limitation overdrive. I wasn't to breathe a word to anyone. I must let him know the minute anyone asked about what'd happened, the minute anyone showed any signs of suspicion.'

'So all your early holding out on me – were you just following orders from Rick?'

'Not entirely. Things've been dodgy at the hotel for a while. The death was just the last straw, and if I could do anything to keep it quiet, then I was damn well going to try.'

'That's why you didn't tell the police about the threatening note?'

'That's why I tried not to tell anyone about any-thing. And that included you. I'm sorry.' Suzy reached across and squeezed her friend's hand. 'Forgive me?'

'Nothing to forgive,' said Jude lightly. 'But what's changed? Why're you no longer clamming up on me?'

'I think the threat of bad publicity has blown over.'

'What makes you think that?'

Suzy shrugged. 'The young man's death has been reported in the newspaper. That hasn't prompted any further enquiries. I like to think the danger's passed.'

'Yes, I saw that in the *Fethering Observer*.' Jude looked shrewdly at her friend. 'Very minimal reporting. Not even the name of the hotel mentioned. Do you have any explanation for that?'

'Just got lucky.' Suzy looked as though she believed the explanation. But over the years, under a lot of different circumstances, Jude had seen the same innocence in the famous hazel eyes. So she reserved her judgment, and changed the subject.

'When did Rick arrive at your place that evening?'

'Seven o'clock, eight o'clock. I went across and said hello to him just before we started serving the dinner.'

'You were expecting him?'

'Oh yes. He'd rung to say he was going to be working in Brighton and could he stay? I didn't particularly want to see him, but I didn't want to make a big deal of saying no.'

'And do you know what he did during the evening while you were looking after the Pillars of Sussex?'

Suzy shrugged at the unimportance of the question. 'I've no idea. He cooked himself something – and left the dirty plates, as usual. Maybe he watched television, fixed a few deals on his mobile phone. Quite honestly, I'm no longer interested in what he does.'

'Was he still up when you finished at the hotel?'

'Yes. Rick always did keep late hours. Required part of the rock and roll lifestyle, I suppose.'

'And was Max with him when you got back to the barn?'

'Max?' Suzy was incredulous. 'No. Why on earth should he have been?'

Jude mentally ticked off another lie told by the chef. And probably engineered by Rick Hendry. 'So did you and Rick talk before you went to bed?'

'A bit. We rarely see each other face to face, and there's always financial stuff lingering on that we have to sort out.'

'So how long did you talk?'

'I don't know, Jude. A quarter of an hour, maybe, twenty minutes – I was beat, so we went to bed.'

'Separately?'

Suzy gave her friend a look of long-suffering, as if the question didn't need an answer. But she still gave one. 'Yes. Separately. The break between Rick and me was so total, and so painful, that there's no danger of anything like that being rekindled – on either side.'

'Just asking.'

Suzy smiled a weary forgiveness.

'And Rick didn't leave the house again during the night?'

'No. I'm certain he didn't. I'm a very light sleeper, and that barn's like a sounding box. You can hear when someone drops a sock, let alone opens the front door.'

'So you didn't hear anything during the night?'

'No. For the few hours I was allowed, I slept very deeply. And if I slept deeply, that means there was nothing to hear.'

Jude felt it was about time she said, 'I'm really sorry to be asking all this stuff.'

'Don't worry.' Suzy grinned wryly. 'You're still convinced that young man was murdered, aren't you, Jude?'

'Yes.'

'Huh. Always were a lover of the dramatic. He topped himself. That's all there is to it.'

'You're probably right.' It was worth one more try. 'But, Suzy, going back to that night . . .'

Suzy Longthorne rolled her eyes in mock-horror. 'Again? All right, what about that night?'

'The note. You're not going to deny we both saw that note.'

'I'm not denying it any more. The note existed.'

'And Kerry found it in the four-poster room before six o'clock that evening.'

'That's what she said.'

'So who put it there, Suzy?'

The famous face took on the expression which had crushed generations of tabloid journalists and paparazzi. 'I hope you're not looking at me.'

'No, I'm not. And, actually, I didn't put it there either.'

'Well, that doesn't leave many people who were around the hotel during the relevant period. The chambermaid had done the four-poster room about eleven that morning. She'd have told me if she found anything like that. So either Kerry was playing out one of her fantasies . . .'

'Or Max put it there – for reasons I can't imagine.'

'Or . . .' Suzy twisted her face in mock-concentration – and still managed to look beautiful. Then her expression changed. 'Just a minute. There is one other person who could have planted the note.'

'Who?'

'The old bald bloke. You know – the Pillar of Sussex who arrived early.'

'Donald Chew?'

'That was his name. He was asleep in the bar, wasn't he? But we don't know how long he'd been there. Technically he could have had time to put the note in the four-poster room.'

'And he was Nigel Ackford's boss, so there are definite connections between them.'

'Yes . . .' Suzy Longthorne took a thoughtful sip of wine, then shook away introspection. 'Still, I really don't want to think about the hotel. Actually, as I was driving over, I was – for no very good reason – thinking about that photographer who kept coming on to us – you know, back in the sixties. Czech I think he was. Kept saying – ' she assumed an exaggerated accent ' – "I want you both to come back to my studio, so that we can see what will develop." Always the same joke. He was dreadful. What was his name?'

And they were into half an hour of giggly nostalgia.

Then, her all-too-short moment of freedom at an end, Suzy had to return to Hopwicke House. She kissed Jude on both cheeks and asked plaintively, 'Friends?'

'Friends,' Jude confirmed.

Only when she was tidying up prior to bed did Jude come across the receipt on which she'd written down the number Wendy Fullerton had given her.

She looked at the large round watch, strapped to her wrist with ribbon. Ten past ten. A bit late for a social call, but . . .

She was answered after two or three rings. To her surprise, it wasn't a woman's voice. A young man's, quite educated, but tense and urgent. 'Hello?'

'Could you tell me who I'm speaking to, please?'

'Karl Floyd. Who're you?'

'My name's Jude.'

'What's this about?'

'I believe you knew a young man called Nigel Ackford . . .'

'So?'

'He died recently.'

'I know that.'

'And in the weeks before his death he was on the phone a lot to you, so—'

'That's enough!' said the young man with sudden vehemence. 'Why's everyone always on to me about Nigel? I'm not going to talk about him. And I'm going to chuck this mobile and get a new one.'

The line went dead.

Chapter Thirty-Two

Carole Seddon really resented having paid out a hundred and fifty pounds to attend the Pillars of Sussex Auction of Promises. At that price, she thought bitterly, I hope I at least find something that's relevant to the investigation. As it turned out, she got rather more than she had bargained for.

None of the attendees at the auction would be staying overnight at the hotel. Not that the Pillars of Sussex intended to drink any less than was their custom, but on this occasion they had their womenfolk with them. And, among that class and that generation, one of the marriage vows taken by wives was to drink less than their menfolk at social events, and to drive them home.

Brenda Chew had asked her 'little group of helpers' to arrive at six, though the pre-dinner drinks were not scheduled to start until seven-thirty. The early call was avowedly 'so we can double-check everything's all right', though, in fact, it was so that Brenda could reiterate to her helpers how much hard work she'd put into organizing the event, but how she didn't mind at all, she was used to it.

She was also very concerned with the stage management of her bouquet – at exactly what point in the evening it should be presented to her, and who would say the few words about 'the infinitely dependable Brenda Chew, who has worked far beyond the call of duty to make this event such a success, and without whom nothing on the fund-raising side of the Pillars of Sussex's work would ever happen.'

Since, however, the presentation was meant to be a surprise about which she knew nothing, getting her anxiety across with regard to the bouquet was quite a challenge, but a challenge Brenda Chew met with consummate skill born of long practice. Indeed, the finesse with which she managed to make her points without actually mentioning the word 'bouquet' might well form the basis for a long-running Radio 4 panel game.

In spite of their rapprochement, Suzy had not called on Jude to help out with the event, but, working with waitress staff Carole had not seen before, the hotelier had yet again transformed the dining room into a magnificent venue. From a centrepiece on each table swirled a display of greenery intertwined with ribbons picking up the colours of the Pillars of Sussex tie. As well as a thick menu, at each place-setting stood a stout auction catalogue with the association's insignia embossed on the front. Beneath this crest, given appropriate star billing, was printed the name of the evening's auctioneer.

Carole flicked through and found the promise of 'A two-hour session of kinesiology given by a well-known professional practitioner.' So Brenda had decided that the attraction of the package would not be augmented by the addition of Jude's name.

By a quarter to seven, there was nothing left for Carole to do. All possible double-checking had been double-checked, and Brenda Chew was engaged in indicating to Sandra Hartson and some other helpers the best curtain behind which her bouquet should be hidden. As soon as the week for two in the Hartson's Spanish villa had been knocked down by the auctioneer, that would be the ideal cue for the flowers to be produced. If Rick Hendry could be persuaded to make the presentation himself, that would also be ideal. Since Brenda was still abiding by the rule of not mentioning the word 'bouquet', explaining all this was a complicated procedure.

Carole drifted through to the bar, to find Donald Chew, dressed in a dinner jacket that knew his contours well, sitting there with a glass of whisky in his hand. No surprise, really. Daft to bring two cars and, since Brenda had to be there at six, her husband would have had to tag along. Donald could always be relied on to kill a bit of time with a glass in his hand.

The way he greeted Carole suggested the drink wasn't his first of the day. He rose unsteadily and enveloped her in a whisky-hazed hug. 'My dear Mrs Seddon, wasn't expecting to see you here, though now I come to think of it, entirely logical you should be since you've been helping Brenda on the . . . Amazing how much she gets done, Brenda, isn't it?' Long habit still did not allow him to mention his wife without an accolade to her remarkable industry, but the words sounded less than heartfelt.

Carole sat down, and Donald subsided with relief back into his chair. 'Will you have something to drink? Only have to ask the lovely Suzy and . . .'

'No, thank you. I'm sure there'll be plenty of drinking later on.' Carole was very good about alcohol when she was driving. (She had actually been very good about alcohol when she wasn't driving – until she met Jude.) Like the rest of the womenfolk, she would be restricting her intake that evening.

Still, she had a perfect opportunity to start getting her hundred and fifty pounds' worth. Jude had filled her in on the truncated conversation with Karl Floyd, which raised some potentially interesting speculations about Nigel Ackford's private life. And here was Carole fortuitously sitting next to the young man's boss.

'Mr Chew . . .'

'Oh, please, call me Donald,' he said expansively. 'Out of the office. This is a social meeting, not a professional one.'

'Very well. Then you'd better call me Carole.'

'I would be honoured to, Carole.' Still very much the conventional gentleman of the old school. And yet there was something else in Donald Chew, something else beneath his bonhomous exterior. Carole had been aware of it on their other meetings, but never so strongly. The drink seemed to have weakened his facade, and what showed through looked very much like pain. Carole found herself wondering what life was really like inside the Chews' marriage. Why had they not had children? Why was Brenda so obsessively busy all the time? Why was she constantly seeking approval? And, come to that, why did her husband drink so much?

As if prompted by her thought, the suspicious face of Brenda Chew suddenly poked round the dining-room door. 'Donald, I'm not going to warn you again. If you're drunk tonight, I don't want you with me.'

The face vanished as quickly as it had appeared. Donald Chew's jaw fell and into the embarrassed vacuum Carole easily dropped a change of subject. 'Donald, I'd like to talk a bit more about Nigel Ackford.'

But it wasn't the right subject. The claret-coloured face clouded instantly. 'There's not much purpose in that, Carole. Nigel's death was very sad, a tragedy for one so young, but I don't really think we should dwell on it. Time to move on. Apart from anything else, I seem to remember you saying you'd never met him.'

'That's true, but my friend did.'

Donald Chew sighed ingenuously. 'I don't honestly think I have anything more to say about Nigel Ackford.'

Carole took a risk. 'You wouldn't by any chance know about a note that was found in his room at the hotel?'

The solicitor looked very alarmed. 'What do you mean?'

His reaction was sufficient for her to persevere. 'A note was found in the four-poster room early on the evening of the dinner. It read:

ENJOY THIS EVENING.
IF YOU'RE NOT SENSIBLE,
IT'LL BE YOUR LAST.

Rather than cranking up his anxiety, to Carole's surprise, this seemed to relax Donald Chew. 'Oh yes.' he smiled. 'I left that for him.'

'But why?'

'To wish him luck for the evening.'

His response sounded innocent, but Carole had to say, 'It doesn't sound like a good-luck wish.'

He sighed. 'Nigel and I had argued about a lot of things – professional things – he had all kinds of misplaced scruples about our work. He didn't seem to understand how necessary solicitors are for the smooth-running of life and society, he didn't realize how much good we do. I tried to persuade him, and engineered his introduction to the Pillars of Sussex. It was a terrific opportunity for someone his age. So I left him the note. He knew what it meant. Enjoy yourself, join in, don't get on your high horse about ethics. If you don't do as I suggest, I said – then this is the last Pillars of Sussex evening you'll ever attend.'

'Oh.' Carole was utterly deflated. The explanation sounded all too credible. Had Jude over-dramatized once again?

'Did you tell the police about the note, Donald?'

'Of course I didn't. Given the way the night ended, I wasn't going to volunteer the fact that I'd been up to his room.'

'The room must've been locked. How did you get the letter in?'

'Pushed it under the door. I was only wishing him luck, for heaven's sake. There was nothing sinister about it.'

'Did you know it was Kerry Hartson who found the note?'

'No, I didn't.'

'Or that later that night it disappeared?'

'No.'

The openness of his reply suggested that Donald Chew was probably telling the truth. Time to move on. 'I was wondering,' she said, 'about Nigel Ackford's private life.'

The solicitor spread his hands wide. 'Who can say? These young people, they don't get married early like my generation did. Goodness knows what they get up to.'

'But do you happen to know what Nigel himself got up to?'

A shake of the head. 'Not really. Some talk of a girlfriend at some stage.' His words were slurring badly now. As his wife had feared, Donald Chew was already very drunk. 'W-working in a building society or something – I never met her.'

'But, Donald, you knew him well.'

'Just in the way a boss knows an employee.'

'Did you ever hear any suggestion – or get any impression that Nigel Ackford might have been gay?'

'Gay?' The word went through him like an electric shock.

'Yes. Homosexual.'

'Why would I know about that?' he asked in a state of panic.

'Because you worked with him.'

'No. I don't think . . . No, there was nothing of that. You've got the wrong end of the stick.' He lumbered to his feet. 'Excuse me, I must – sorry. Call of nature.'

And he stumbled out of the bar.

When the Pillars of Sussex assembled with their womenfolk, Carole was struck, not for the first time, at how much easier men have it on formal occasions. For them, 'black tie' on an invitation is a very simple directive. And, though some try to tart up the basic image with frilly shirts, rainbow ties, cummerbunds and amusing braces, at bottom they all know that they'll look fine in a simple, unadorned dinner suit.

Whereas for women, the potential choices are infinite. Even within the description of a 'little black dress'. Carole was aware that the all-purpose one she was wearing (and had worn for every formal event since her retirement) too obviously trumpeted its Marks and Spencer's origins. Those of the Pillars' womenfolk who had also opted for black were wearing much more expensive designer labels, but without the aplomb with which such garments were modelled in fashion magazines.

And the women who had ventured beyond black provided a wonderful demonstration of the old truism that money does not necessarily imply taste. There must be a way of dressing the older woman elegantly for a formal evening, but British designers appeared not to have found it. The basic sartorial rule among the Pillars' wives seemed to be that all their dresses should be made of two contrasting fabrics, divided at the waist. (Since most of the guests were of an age when waists become ill-defined, this was a bad idea.) Whether the top half was in heavy velvet and the bottom in something silky and diaphanous, or vice versa, did not seem to matter. Colours were either too garish or too subdued, and accessories gold and fussy. The womenfolk would have looked better if they'd simply worn the price tickets. In that way, they could have made the main point – how much they'd paid for the dresses – without looking dreadful in them.

As if to provide a shaming benchmark for their lack of taste, among the womenfolk floated Suzy Longthorne, stunning in the simplest of long sleeveless dresses in burgundy silk. Carole felt grateful for the anonymity of her own Marks & Spencer's black.

Suzy recognized her and flashed a quick professional smile. 'Did I gather you were one of the people in charge?'

'A mere helper. You'll find the one who gives the orders is Brenda Chew. Over there in the gold brocade skirt with the green bolero jacket.'

'Right.' Suzy Longthorne looked anxiously at her Piaget watch. 'I want to get them through to the dining room soon. Otherwise I'll have a grumpy chef on my hands. The first course is a soufflé.'

'Sounds great.' If the hotelier thought she was one of the organizers, Carole might as well take advantage of the fact. 'Is it you we have to thank for persuading your ex-husband to be our auctioneer tonight?'

'Nothing to do with me,' Suzy replied, with considerable asperity. Another look at the Piaget. 'He hasn't arrived yet. Always leaves everything to the last minute.'

'Do you think he'll come?'

'If Rick says he's going to do something, he'll do it. He's always true to his word.' A wry grin came to the famous lips. 'Well, professionally at least. Not perhaps if you're married to him. I'll go and have a word with Mrs Chew. Mrs Chew, would you like me to start telling your guests to move through?'

Suzy wafted away, and Carole was joined by James Baxter who, as current president of the Pillars of Sussex, felt it his duty to meet everyone. He introduced himself and, with some puzzlement, asked who she was with. He thought he knew all the members' wives and girlfriends; the idea that someone had brought along a new specimen of womanfolk apparently caused him considerable excitement.

'No, I'm on my own. I've been helping Brenda out with the arrangements.'

'Ah. Right.' He was glad he had placed her. 'Well, let me introduce you to some people.' James Baxter turned to a couple who had just come in from the hall. 'Evening, Barry. Evening, Pomme. I'd like to introduce you to Carole . . . er, Seddon, wasn't it?'

The expression on Barry Stilwell's face was one Carole would treasure forever. Indeed, in subsequent moments of low spirits she would often try to cheer herself up by recapturing the image.

He looked like a fox who'd mistakenly gatecrashed a Hunt Ball. His eyes bobbled like frogspawn in a jar and his thin lips trembled. 'Ah. Ah. Carole . . .'

'Good evening, Barry. And you must be Pomme.'

Anyone who described Barry Stilwell's second wife as 'statuesque' would have to be thinking, not so much of the Venus de Milo, as of the Statue of Liberty. The idea that she spent every Thursday evening line-dancing was mind-boggling. God had been very generous to her with all of His gifts except, from the expression on her face, a sense of humour.

'You know each other?' she asked in the manner of a matron summoning small boys to cold showers.

'Er . . . yes,' said her husband, in a voice as thin as his lips. 'We did meet once.' Then, with a ferociously pathetic flash of his eyes, he pleaded, 'Didn't we, Carole?'

She could see the relief flood his body as she confirmed that this was indeed the case. Carole had no intention of embarrassing Barry Stilwell further. The pleasure of watching him squirm was quite sufficient; she didn't need anything else. Since the attraction between them was all in his mind, she felt emotionally untouched by the encounter. But she was amused by the speed with which he left her and moved on to greet other Pillars and their womenfolk.

For Carole, the crowning glory of the moment was Pomme's dress. Its inspiration was vaguely Spanish. Under a tiny scarlet silk waistcoat, her huge body was

291

swathed in frills and swirls of a midnight-blue material, braided in red piping from which dangled fluffy red bobbles of wool. Yes, it was actually true. Pomme was wearing pom-poms.

Brenda Chew approached, with an anxious-looking Sandra Hartson in tow.

'I think we'd better go through to the dining room. I'll tell people. You'd have thought the hotel staff'd do that, but there doesn't seem to be anyone here.' This was characteristically unjust, since Carole had heard Suzy Longthorne offering the service.

'I don't know where Bob's got to,' said Sandra. 'He was bringing Kerry.' She looked at her watch. 'He should be here by now.'

'Don't know where Donald's got to either. He's drifted off somewhere.' But Brenda Chew didn't sound very concerned about her husband's whereabouts. She'd said she didn't want him around if he was drunk, so Donald Chew had made himself scarce.

Brenda started shepherding Pillars and womenfolk through to the dining room, so Carole followed Sandra out into the hall. 'Did you say your husband was picking Kerry up?'

'Yes, from her flat. Ridiculous, isn't it, a girl of her age having her own flat in Brighton?'

Interesting to hear this common first reaction being voiced by the girl's own mother. 'But presumably you're not far away?' suggested Carole. 'You can keep an eye on her.'

'Yes, one or other of us drops in most days. Well,

Bob more often than I do, I suppose . . .' Sandra Hartson seemed to lose her way.

'I'm surprised to hear Kerry's coming this evening.'

'Not her usual idea of entertainment, I agree. But we needed to make up the table, and Bob asked her. At first we got all the adolescent whingeing about how she'd be bored out of her skull, but when she heard that Rick Hendry was going to be here . . .'

As if cued by Sandra's words, at that moment her daughter came in through the hotel's front doors with her stepfather, whose arm was draped lightly round the girl's bare shoulders. Kerry's little black dress showed how much easier it was for a woman to look stunning at fifteen than when she reached the age of the Pillars' womenfolk.

Only a step behind father and stepdaughter came the unmistakably lanky figure of Rick Hendry. His evening dress was entirely conventional, except for the grey silk of his shirt.

'Where've you been?' asked Sandra Hartson tautly.

'It's all right,' her husband soothed. 'We got delayed. Geoff's parking the car now. We're fine, don't worry.'

'You've missed the reception.'

'But we're here in time for the dinner,' said Rick Hendry, with a laid-back open-palmed gesture, 'so no problem.'

Sandra gave the old rocker a small smile of acknowledgment. Clearly they'd met before.

'Yeah, don't get all uptight, Mum,' said Kerry. 'Stay cool.'

Her mother suddenly became aware of Carole's

presence and remembered her manners. 'Oh, this is Carole Seddon, who's been helping with the organization of the evening.'

Rick Hendry nodded an uninterested nod, but, as he shook her hand, Bob Hartson repeated her name, and gave her a piercing look. Then, with a hearty chuckle, he put his arm round his stepdaughter's waist, and followed Rick into the crowd.

For a nanosecond Sandra Hartson seemed to freeze, watching them. Then she too went through into the bar.

Carole looked around the comforting calm of the Hopwicke House hall, and wished that, rather than going through to the dining room, she could spend the whole evening there – or, even better, back at High Tor with Gulliver and the television. She wasn't looking forward to what lay ahead.

She took a deep breath and went through to join the Pillars of Sussex and their womenfolk.

Chapter Thirty-Three

To Carole's relief, Brenda Chew had not sat her at the same table as Barry and Pomme Stilwell. Throughout a whole dinner, the humour of his discomfiture might have palled.

Although she wasn't feeling at ease, Carole could recognize what a good dinner Max Townley had supplied. The Pillars of Sussex had conventional tastes, but, as with the Sunday lunch, the chef had worked subtle refinements on the traditional. Whether he had the personality to project himself on television Carole did not know, but his cooking skills were certainly up to the mark.

She had been put at the same table as the Chews, though only Brenda was in evidence. At the beginning of the meal, she had said, with what sounded like callous disregard, 'Oh, Donald has probably dozed off somewhere. Don't worry, he'll turn up.' And that was the last time he had been mentioned. Though his chair remained empty, no one else on the table thought this worthy of remark, and his wife hadn't time to worry about him. She was too occupied buzzing from table to table, 'double-checking' and demonstrating how much hard work she was putting into the evening.

The other couples at her table didn't do a lot for Carole. When introduced to the editor of the *Fethering Observer*, she was hopeful of his having fascinating 'stories behind the news' to share, but he proved an extremely dull dog, only interested in counting down the days to his imminent retirement and a life of uninterrupted sea fishing.

Then there were a Mr and Mrs Goodchild – Carole didn't catch their first names. He was a tall man, apparently a police officer, whose talk was all about golf.

Another couple were very excited about the preparations for their daughter's wedding, and, once she'd established that her son was also getting married, Carole managed a bit of conversation with them. But the incredibly detailed knowledge they could bring to the subject of their daughter's plans only made her realize again how marginalized she was in the lives of Stephen and Gaby.

One thing Carole had made a point of finding out was the timetable for the evening's proceedings. She had done her own bit of double-checking with Brenda Chew, and established that, when the coffee arrived, an announcement of a ten-minute 'comfort break' would be made and, at the end of that, the auction would begin.

Carole, who had a lifelong aversion to queuing for the Ladies', prudently decided to take the moment of finishing her dessert as a cue to leave the dining room and cross the hall. Which should ensure she reached the limited toilet facilities – only two cubicles in the Ladies' – before the rush.

So, as she put the last spoonful of Max's summer pudding (not exactly the right season, but an ambrosial taste) into her mouth, Carole looked around the room to see if anyone else had anticipated her plan.

Things looked good. Donald Chew's seat was still empty. So was Kerry's, but while his wife looked quietly on, Bob Hartson was regaling his table with some loud anecdote. All of the other Pillars' womenfolk were in their seats. Rick Hendry was out of the room, and so was Suzy, the latter no doubt directing operations in the kitchen.

The moment was right. Even if Kerry had gone to the Ladies', there would still be one empty cubicle. Carole dabbed at her mouth with her napkin, picked up her handbag and discreetly left the dining room.

The minute she was in the hall, she saw there was something different. The door opposite the bar, which she had never really noticed before, was open.

Carole moved across to the entrance, and looked down.

The cellar light had not been switched on, but enough illumination spilled from the hall chandelier to illuminate the steep steps.

At the bottom of them lay an inert body. The bald head identified it as that of Donald Chew.

Chapter Thirty-Four

Carole Seddon's upbringing did not allow her to make a habit of arriving unannounced on people's doorsteps at half-past ten at night. But this was an exceptional occasion. The lights were still on in Woodside Cottage. And Jude was her friend, for heaven's sake.

The white wine was open almost before she'd finished announcing Donald Chew's death.

'What happened, Carole? Was the word "murder" mentioned?'

'Certainly not. Nor suicide. Plenty of talk of a tragic accident, mind. There was a police inspector there. He took charge of things. Called Goodchild.'

'Tall man, rather smooth?'

'Yes,' agreed Carole, surprised.

'He was the one who investigated Nigel Ackford's death. Came and talked to me.' Jude looked thoughtful. 'So he actually is a Pillar of Sussex . . .'

'Don't know that for sure. He could have been someone's guest. All the members were being encouraged to drum up support from their friends.'

'But at least he's close to the Pillars of Sussex.'

'Yes. Everyone seems to be. The editor of the *Feth-*

ering Observer was at my table too, which might explain the minimal coverage the paper gave to Nigel Ackford's death.'

'I wouldn't be surprised if the same thing happens with Donald Chew.'

'Not so sure, Jude. He was a respected local figure, a pillar of the local community as well as a Pillar of Sussex. I should think there'd be a big spread about him.'

'Yes, but I wouldn't be surprised if the exact circumstances of his death were glossed over. "Following a tragic accident . . .", that kind of thing.'

'Probably.'

'Did Inspector Goodchild actually talk to you, Carole? Or to anyone else?'

'No. He called out the local police, and said that if further investigations were required, he'd be in touch with us. He had a copy of the guest list and contact numbers.'

'But he can't just leave it like that,' Jude protested. 'A suspicious death – the second suspicious death at Hopwicke House – can't just be shuffled under the carpet.'

'There wasn't any suggestion it would be. As I say, everyone was talking about an accident.'

'It couldn't have been an accident. That cellar door is always kept locked.'

Carole shook her head. 'Usually it is. But Suzy had left it open tonight. Because of the large party in the dining room she was expecting extra bottles might have to be brought up at some point.'

Jude looked disappointed. 'So, for those who go with the "tragic accident" scenario, what's supposed to have happened?'

'All right.' Carole spelled out the Pillars of Sussex's consensus. 'Donald Chew was very drunk. I can vouch for that. I talked to him in the bar before the reception and he was well away.'

'Did he say anything of interest – I mean anything useful to our investigation?'

'Well . . .' Carole's thin nose wrinkled as she tried to concentrate. Death had upstaged her memories of the conversation in the bar. 'Oh yes. He did explain the threatening note.' She repeated what Donald Chew had told her, concluding, with a rueful nod, 'And it all sounds quite feasible. So at least we know where that note appeared from.'

'Yes. But we don't know where it disappeared to.'

'What do you mean, Jude?'

'Remember, it vanished from Suzy's apron in the kitchen. Someone must've taken it.'

'Oh yes,' Carole agreed thoughtfully.

Jude moved on. 'Anyway, don't let's bother about that for the time being. You were saying Donald Chew was pretty drunk before the dinner?'

'Yes. His wife Brenda had spotted the signs and told him if he couldn't behave, she didn't want him around to spoil her big evening. Apparently her acting like that was not uncommon. The Pillars of Sussex seemed to find the spats in their marriage rather an amusing spectator sport. So the theory is that Donald, knowing how drunk he was and not wishing to provoke the wrath of Brenda, went off and fell asleep in the residents' lounge. Apparently he drops off to sleep quite easily, particularly when he's in his cups.

'Then, the theory goes, Donald wakes up and he's desperate for another drink. The dinner's in full swing, he knows better than to antagonize his wife, the bar can be seen from the dining room, so the only source of booze he can think of is the cellar. He finds the door open, starts down the steps, loses his footing in his inebriated state and lands head first on the stone floor. End of story – and end of solicitor.'

'And it was definitely the fall that killed him?'

Carole shrugged. 'Who knows for certain until his body's been examined by a police surgeon? But among the Pillars that was the general assumption.'

'So how did they react?'

'With remarkably little emotion, really. The only surprise seemed to be that something like that hadn't happened to Donald Chew before. They all knew he had a big drink problem.'

'Any individuals react strangely?'

Carole shook her head. 'No. Well, one or two seemed quite relieved that the evening had been broken up. They'd managed to eat their gourmet dinner, and weren't going to have to sit through the auction of promises.'

'Yes, I'm quite relieved that no one's going to take me up on my two-hour kinesiology session.'

'I thought you were properly qualified,' said Carole, affronted.

'I am. But it's a long time since I've practised. I'm a

bit rusty.' She smiled for a second, then turned serious. 'What about Brenda Chew? Was she devastated?'

'She was, yes.' Carole shook her head in disbelief. 'But not because her husband was dead. The way she reacted, you'd think Donald had engineered his death deliberately to scupper the auction of promises – on which she had worked so far beyond the call of duty. Strange . . . Probably it was a shock reaction, and she will mourn him in time – but this evening all that seemed to upset her was the fact that she wasn't going to be presented with her bouquet.'

'Huh.'

'Still, at least she will have another event to organize – where once again she can complain that nobody else pulls their weight.'

'What's that?'

'Donald's funeral.'

'Thanks, Carole. Very tasteful.'

Their glasses had mysteriously become empty. Jude refilled them in silence. Then she said, 'I'm assuming we don't accept the accident verdict?'

Carole was more cautious. 'Well, it is possible.'

'Come *on.*'

'Oh, very well. No, we don't.'

'And, putting the suicide verdict on one side for the moment – if it was murder, who could have done it?'

'You mean who wasn't in the dining room during the dinner?'

'Exactly.'

'Obviously the hotel staff were in and out. I hadn't seen any of the waitresses before.'

'Let's forget them then – concentrate on the people who were also in the hotel on the night of the first death.'

'All right. Well, your friend Suzy Longthorne was in and out of the dining room all evening, Max was presumably in the kitchen – Ooh, and I noticed when I left to go to the loo, just before I found the body, Rick Hendry wasn't in his seat either.'

'But Bob Hartson was?'

'Yes, definitely.' As Carole pictured the scene, another recollection came back to her. 'Though Kerry wasn't.'

'Any idea where she was?'

'No. Maybe she was in the Ladies', but I didn't see her come out. I mean, as soon as I'd looked down in the cellar and seen the body, I went and found Suzy in the kitchen. Then she told Inspector Goodchild. Quite honestly, from that point everything got chaotic. Kerry and Rick Hendry both reappeared, but I haven't a clue where they came from.'

Jude circled a thoughtful finger around the top of her wineglass. 'I'm sorry Bob Hartson isn't in the frame. I'd been moving towards casting him in the role of murderer.'

'He could have murdered Nigel Ackford. There's no way he had anything to do with Donald Chew.'

'Pity.'

'I suppose it's possible that the two deaths are unconnected?'

This tentative suggestion was immediately blown away. 'Do you really believe that?'

'No,' Carole admitted. 'They're connected.'

*

She was offered a rather surprising connection between the deaths the following morning.

Her phone rang and a voice of anguished embarrassment whispered, 'It's all right. Pomme's at her mother's.'

'Ah,' said Carole, then, mischievously, 'It was a great pleasure to meet her last night. Though unfortunate, of course, that the evening ended as it did.'

'A tragedy,' said Barry Stilwell. 'A terrible tragedy. Awful when anyone dies, but when it's a fellow solicitor . . .'

'Doubly awful,' suggested Carole, who was having serious difficulty in not giggling.

'I have to confess,' he said, with an audible gulp of nervousness, 'that I did find yesterday evening rather difficult.'

'I think being present when someone dies is always difficult.'

'I didn't mean that. I meant earlier in the evening – when I actually saw you and Pomme face to face.'

'Ah.'

'It did make me think a bit about . . . what we're doing.'

Speak for yourself, sunshine. I'm not doing anything.

'And I did rather think that . . . Well, Pomme is sometimes a— can be jealous at times, and she keeps getting it into her head that I might be . . . chatting up other women.' With justification, thought Carole. But she stayed silent and let him blunder on. 'So I thought we might cool it for a bit – if that's all right with you.'

Perfectly all right with me, since from my point of view no heat has ever been involved. 'Yes, fine, Barry. Do what you think's best.'

'Yes, well, er . . . Just for the time being.'

'Mm.'

'And then, in a little while, when Pomme has, as it were, calmed down we might be able to, er, pick up and – who knows?'

I do, thought Carole firmly. She wondered why he had rung. Nothing had happened the night before to prompt suspicion in the substantial bosom of Pomme. Unless she was one of those wives who is irrationally jealous of every woman her husband even looks at, Carole got the feeling Barry's call had another agenda. She was aware of him edging towards it.

'As I say, tragic about poor old Donald.'

'Tragic.'

'Terrible how these accidents happen . . . don't you agree?'

'Oh yes.' Carole now knew the direction in which Barry was worming his way. He had once again been set up by someone powerful in the Pillars of Sussex to check out what she and Jude were thinking, whether they had accepted the accidental explanation of Donald Chew's death. She waited.

'Erm . . . well . . .' Barry Stilwell wasn't finding his appointed task easy. Eventually, bluntly, he asked, 'You're convinced it was an accident, Donald's death, aren't you?'

'What's the alternative?' She wasn't going to make it any easier for him.

'Well, erm . . . Do I gather you *are* convinced it was an accident?'

'No,' said Carole. Let him sweat a bit.

'Ah. Right.' Her response seemed to have confirmed his worst fears. 'Take your point. I suppose there could be a view that it was suicide.'

'And why would Donald Chew want to commit suicide?'

'Well, being in the hotel again – it must have brought it all back to him.'

'Brought all what back to him?'

'Hopwicke House was where his young colleague, Nigel Ackford, died.'

'I'm well aware of that, Barry.'

'And, um, well . . . don't breathe a word of this to anyone, of course, but did you know about Donald?'

'Did I know what about Donald?'

'Well, that – I mean it wasn't much of a secret among the Pillars of Sussex. He – I know he was married but . . .' Barry Stilwell cleared his throat, 'Donald Chew was homosexual.'

'Oh,' said Carole, at one level unsurprised. There had always been something slightly unreal about the solicitor, as though he were playing a part, as though he had something to hide. What Barry had just said could explain that.

'Anyway,' he went on, 'there was a feeling around his office, I gather, that Donald was very attracted to the young man.'

'Was the attraction mutual?'

'That I wouldn't know. But the suggestion was that

Nigel Ackford's suicide might be in some way related to his relationship with his boss.'

'Really?'

'Yes. Apparently Donald Chew arrived at the hotel early that Tuesday evening, and there was some suggestion that he was hoping to . . . er, meet up with the young man before the dinner . . .'

Who was making all these suggestions? Carole wondered.

'And maybe Nigel resisted his advances, or said that their relationship had to end and maybe Donald was so upset that . . .'

The implication was left dangling in the air. Rather as Nigel Ackford had been.

'So the thinking is,' Barry Stilwell continued with new energy, 'that if Donald's death wasn't accidental – and of course it may well have been accidental – but, if it wasn't, that being back in the hotel affected him emotionally and . . .'

This time Carole helped him out. 'And Donald Chew committed suicide in remorse for having murdered Nigel Ackford?'

'Exactly.' Barry seemed enormously relieved that she had finally pieced the scenario together.

'And, for those of us who were suspicious of murder having been committed, all the loose ends are neatly tied up?'

'Yes.' He now sounded positively cheerful. 'End of story.'

Don't you believe it, thought Carole.

Having unburdened himself of his duty, Barry

Stilwell could now afford a moment of philosophy. 'Sad, to think what goes on inside human minds, stuff we never know about. We only see the surface of people, don't we? And we've no idea what they're really thinking. Awful. Nigel Ackford. Donald Chew. Two people dead, and what really lay behind it we'll never know.'

Oh yes, we will, thought Carole.

Chapter Thirty-Five

The task was not one Jude relished, but she knew she had to do it. And not on the phone; this had to be face to face.

At least she had an excuse. Her promise to contact Wendy Fullerton was overdue. She left a message on the girl's mobile, but got no reply on the Sunday. Wendy rang back the next day from the building society.

She thought it odd and probably ominous that Jude didn't want to tell her on the phone, but agreed to meet her after work. The rendezvous was a small wine bar behind her office.

Jude got there first and was halfway down a glass of wine by the time Wendy appeared, once again neat in her building society uniform. The girl chose a vodka and tonic, expecting to need bolstering for the news she was about to receive.

'All right, tell me,' she said after she'd taken a long swallow. 'Was it another woman?'

'No. It was a man.' But Jude couldn't allow time for the relief to flood in; she pressed on. 'Which means I've got to ask you a very awkward question, Wendy.' The girl looked puzzled. 'Do you know if Nigel ever had any gay experiences?'

The answer did not come immediately. Wendy looked pale; the idea was clearly not new to her. 'I don't know, Jude. I really don't. I sometimes wondered. Nigel was certainly screwed up about sex . . . but then he was screwed up about a lot of other things too. I don't know. I think he really loved me.' She clung to this thought, the last piece of the wreckage left to her.

'I'm not asking out of prurient curiosity. There are two reasons. The first – the man whose mobile he kept ringing. His name was Karl Floyd, by the way – I don't know if that means anything to you?'

The girl shook her head. 'Does sound vaguely familiar, but no, nothing to do with Nigel. He never mentioned anyone called that.'

'And the second reason is that a suggestion has been made that Nigel might have been in a relationship with his boss at work.'

'His boss?' Wendy was incredulous. 'You mean Donald Chew?'

'It was suggested.'

'No. Well, I don't know whether there was any attraction on Donald Chew's side. I got a general feeling that round the company they thought he was gay, but pretty much still in the closet. Still, the suggestion that he and Nigel—' The idea was too much for her. 'No. No.' Though forceful, her reaction was one of logic rather than distaste.

'You said Nigel was screwed up about a lot of things.' Jude prompted gently.

'Yes. I think it was part of the depression. I've never been depressed. I've been down or miserable – I'm not great at the moment – but I've never had it the way he described . . . the sort of self-hatred thing. Sometimes he just worried about everything so much, about who he was, what he was doing, whether he should be doing it.'

'You mean professionally, Wendy?'

'I suppose so, yes. In his work. He did have worries in his work, but I'm sure they had nothing to do with Donald Chew coming on to him. It was more . . .'

'More what?'

'He kept saying he was worried about the ethics of what he was doing.'

Jude smiled. 'Unusual for a solicitor to worry about that. But rather heart-warming, I suppose. Was it anything specific? Any particular part of the job – or any particular case that was worrying him?'

'I honestly don't know. Nigel talked so much about everything, after a time it was difficult to keep up. I remember he kept saying there was nothing illegal. "That's what so wrong," he'd say. "No laws are being broken. It's not illegal." But it still worried him.'

'You can't think of any more details?'

Wendy Fullerton gave a rueful shake of her head. 'Sorry. He did just go on about it not being illegal. "There should be a big exposé," he said. "People should know what's going on" and then he'd go back to the fact that it wasn't illegal.'

There was a silence. Behind her mask of make-up, the girl was thinking things out. 'I'm sure Nigel wasn't gay. I'm sure, whatever his connection was with this Karl person, it wasn't that. And he certainly wasn't in any kind of emotional relationship with Donald Chew.'

She looked at her watch. 'Sorry, I must go. Get home, change, put on my make-up. Then go out.'

Jude found it hard to imagine that Wendy Fullerton's face could take any more make-up. 'Are you going somewhere nice?'

The girl grimaced. 'Oh yes. Very nice restaurant. I've been invited out. I'm getting back into the business of dating.'

'Good.'

'I suppose so.' But she didn't sound convinced. 'Has to be done, though. Have to move on. Meet men. Meet *the* man.' She sighed at the effort of it all, downed the last of her vodka and stood up. 'Though at the moment it's as if I'm just going through the motions.'

As she watched the girl leave, Jude got the feeling that Wendy Fullerton would be going through the motions for a long time yet. Perhaps for the rest of her life.

Chapter Thirty-Six

'I'm beginning to wonder if it all *is* coincidence,' said Carole grumpily. The crusading hunger she'd felt for the truth when she last spoke to Barry Stilwell seemed to have trickled away. 'Suppose everything is exactly as it appears on the surface? Nigel Ackford committed suicide; Donald Chew fell down the cellar stairs by accident.'

'I can't believe I'm hearing you say this, Carole.'

Carole looked morosely out of the front window of Woodside Cottage, where heavy grey rain fell, matching her mood. 'Well, we've tried every way to get a logical thread through recent events on the assumption that murder was involved, and we've failed dismally. It might make more sense if we took things at face value.'

Jude's haystack of hair quivered as she vigorously shook her head. 'No. There are too many inconsistencies for us to take things at face value. We've been treated like the Red Queen in *Alice Through the Looking-Glass* – been asked to believe as many as six impossible things before breakfast! Think about it.'

'What?' Carole was being deliberately obtuse.

'First, Suzy covers up – not telling the police about the threatening note.'

'Simply to protect the reputation of her hotel.'

'All right. Then Max lets out the fact that Rick Hendry was there that night, and suddenly we have a whole new set of cover-ups. Kerry drinking with her father and Barry Stilwell – later replaced by Donald Chew. Kerry being very happy to tell me that alibi, and the timing happening to coincide with her passing an audition to be in *Pop Crop*. Max comes back to me and spells out a very detailed scenario which doesn't allow Kerry to be alone with Rick – and, goodness me, it turns out that Korfilia Productions are going to be promoting Max as a celebrity chef. Don't you find all that a bit odd, Carole?'

'Yes, all right. Rick Hendry was trying to divert publicity from himself, and using bribes he knew would work with Kerry and Max. But I still can't find any connection between that and Nigel Ackford's death. Until he heard about the body in the four-poster room, I doubt whether Rick knew of Nigel's existence.'

'All right.' Jude sighed. She couldn't decide whether Carole had genuinely stopped believing in the murder theory, was playing devil's advocate, or was just being bloody-minded. 'Let's look at it from another angle. The information that Max gave me in the Crown and Anchor – which I don't believe for a minute was true – established, as you say, that Rick could not have been alone with Kerry, so no one could accuse him of messing about with yet another young girl. But it also established the same for Bob Hartson. He couldn't have been alone with Kerry either.'

Carole looked alarmed. 'What are you suggesting?'

'You know what I'm suggesting. I've mentioned it before. Every time I've seen Bob Hartson with Kerry, he's been exceptionally affectionate towards her.' Jude rubbed a rueful hand against her cheek. 'He wouldn't be the first stepfather to have found his stepdaughter more attractive than his new wife.'

Carole remembered Sandra Hartson's pained look as she had watched her husband and daughter go arm in arm into the hotel bar on Saturday night. 'You could be right. So what you're suggesting, Jude, is that Bob Hartson might have set up Max to give you all that guff?'

'Possible.'

'But if that were the case, Bob Hartson can't have had anything to do with Nigel's death.'

'How so?'

'Well, assuming that Bob Hartson is the one who's been orchestrating the alibis – or at least he knows they are being orchestrated . . . We are assuming that, aren't we, Jude?'

'All right.'

'Well then, although he's covered himself with regard to his stepdaughter, he left himself completely without an alibi for the time when the conjectural murder might have taken place. Surely that shows he's innocent. It never even occurred to him that he might be a suspect. If it had, he'd have covered himself.'

'True.' Jude nodded. 'He was awake and inside the hotel, so he could have killed Nigel.'

'The same goes for Donald Chew.'

'Which brings us on to yet another cover-up. All that stuff Barry Stilwell gave you about Donald Chew being gay.'

'I think that could actually have been true.'

'But the idea of him and Nigel having been in a relationship. Having talked to Wendy Fullerton again, I just don't buy that.'

'No, Jude. Nor do I.'

Jude looked thoughtfully out into the sheeting rain. Forget April showers, this was more like another Deluge. The good people of Fethering would soon be getting out their B&Q cubit measuring tapes and building arks.

'It's odd,' she said finally. 'All these cover-ups and alibis . . . I'm sure they're being done just for us.'

'Sorry?'

'For our benefit. Nobody else is being given all of this information, because nobody else is interested. Other people either genuinely don't care, or they recognize the fact that it's prudent not to care.'

'Where's this leading you, Jude?'

'Well, we keep being offered scenarios to believe in, and we make it clear we don't believe in them, and then we're offered another one. Maybe if we claim to be satisfied with the latest explanation, there won't be any more of them.'

'So if we let it be known that we believe Nigel Ackford committed suicide because of his difficult relationship with Donald Chew, and Donald Chew topped himself for the same reason, everything'll go quiet?'

'Might do.'

'And if they think we've accepted the explanation,' said Carole excitedly, 'they'll relax, and we'll be able to continue our investigation without so much interference?'

'What is this investigation?' asked Jude ingenuously. 'I didn't think there was any investigation to be pursued. I thought your view was that it was all coincidence.'

'Oh, shut up,' said Carole.

Jude's phone rang just after Carole had gone back to High Tor. It was Suzy with another emergency. A big lunch party and two of her regular waitresses had flu. Would Jude mind . . .?

As she phoned for a taxi, Jude felt good. At least that particular bridge had been rebuilt. She'd never doubted it would happen in time, but was reassured to know that she and Suzy were back on their old footing.

In spite of the bullish note on which her conversation with Jude had ended, Carole still felt restless and short-tempered. The weather didn't help. Nor did the plaintive padding around of Gulliver. His early morning walk had been postponed because of the rain Carole had just taken him onto the waste ground behind the house to do his business – and he felt aggrieved by the omission. Gulliver didn't mind walks in the rain; he enjoyed sploshing about and rolling in puddles; it was only his wet blanket of an owner who was put off by the thought of washing and drying him after they got back. So he was as grumpy as she was.

Carole made herself a cup of coffee she didn't really want and sat in her front room, trying not to listen to the incessant dribbling of rain down a piece of guttering that needed mending. The noise offended her sense of rightness. Carole Seddon prided herself on keeping High Tor in immaculate repair, and the water in the broken gutter sounded a constant reproach.

She tried to think if there was anyone she could phone up. There were Fethering people who would be perfectly happy to exchange social niceties, but she had no real reason, apart from boredom, to call them.

She supposed she could ring Stephen. The afterglow of their lunch at Hopwicke House had faded a little, and it was down to her to maintain contact. Her conversation with the wedding-organizing couple at the auction of promises had made her realize how ignorant she was of the basics of Stephen and Gaby's plans. She should really ring up to show an interest. But that'd have to be later. A call from his mother while he was at work was so unprecedented, Stephen would probably assume she was ringing to announce the diagnosis of a life-threatening disease.

There was a novel by her bed that Carole was quite enjoying, but the effort of going upstairs to fetch it seemed insuperable. She looked out of the window. The rain had to stop soon, then she could take Gulliver on to Fethering beach and blow the grumpiness out of both of them.

Carole found she was hearing the gurgling from the broken gutter again and to block it out, picked up a copy of the *Fethering Observer*. It was the previous week's; the next one wasn't due out till Thursday. She wondered how much coverage would be afforded then to the demise of Donald Chew.

Without much optimism, she flicked through the pages in search of something to divert her. The report of a recent spate of dustbin fires didn't promise to do the trick. Nor did news of Fethering's plans to twin with a seaside town in Belgium. And though a headline about a pensioner being found guilty of causing unnecessary suffering to rabbits intrigued, the subsequent story disappointed.

What stopped her was an article about Fethering town council's successful application for a licence to hold civil weddings in the town hall. Carole did not have any plans to remarry. Nor did she think the grey-fronted civic rectangle opposite Fethering parish church would be a sufficiently glamorous venue for Stephen and Gaby. What interested her about the article was the name of its reporter.

She remembered sitting in Donald Chew's office when his receptionist announced a call from 'Mr Floyd from the *Fethering Observer*.'

The by-line on the town hall article was 'Karl Floyd'.

Carole Seddon had no aptitude for subterfuge. She didn't possess the skills to take on another identity or disguise her voice, but she knew a lie was necessary. While she was in his office, Donald Chew had said that he would fix a meeting with 'Mr Floyd from the *Fethering Observer*.' As she waited for the phone to be answered, Carole just prayed that the receptionist would not recognize her voice.

'Renton and Chew,' the enhanced vowels announced.

Too late Carole wished she'd gone out to a public phone box. The invention of the 1471 last caller identification service must have wreaked havoc with the world of espionage.

She plunged in, hoping – rightly, as it transpired – that no attempt would be made to trace her call. 'Good morning. I'm calling on behalf of Karl Floyd at the *Fethering Observer*. I believe he has a meeting with Mr Donald Chew scheduled for this week.'

'Well, yes, he did, but—'

'I just wanted to confirm the time of that meeting.'

The enhanced vowels at the end of the line sounded bewildered. 'It was for Monday.'

'Yesterday?'

'Yes. And since Mr Floyd didn't come here, I assumed he'd got my message.'

Carole thought on her feet. 'Oh yes, he must've done. Sorry, he's out of the office today. I just found something about the meeting on a Post-it note on Mr Floyd's computer, and thought it needed action. Sorry to have troubled you.'

'No problem,' said the enhanced vowels, perhaps

relieved at not having to spell out again the circumstances of her boss's death.

Carole ended the call. Then, having just claimed to
be ringing from the *Fethering Observer*, she rang the real
Fethering Observer.

Chapter Thirty-Seven

The lunch at Hopwicke House was part of a day-long seminar given by one of the few companies that still realized the value of lavish corporate entertaining. They were an up-market accountancy firm, whose invitation list had only included people the capture of whose business would justify the outlay. A surprising number of these had agreed to turn up; they hadn't made their fortunes by failing to recognize the value of a free lunch. Each one of them had arrived determined to make no change to their existing accountancy arrangements. But they were all duly appreciative of Max Townley's cooking, and listened with apparent interest to the blandishments of the accountants who were trying to ensnare their business.

Because of the tight timetable to which the seminar had been planned, lunch was a relatively short break. Some wine was drunk, but not a great deal. The dining room was clear by two-fifteen; tidying and re-laying for dinner would be complete by quarter to three.

Jude had to go to the first-floor linen room to fetch clean tablecloths. The mobile laundry service delivered everything up there – bedding, towels and table drapery.

The linen room was also the base for the chambermaids and, when the hotel had had one, the housekeeper. (As profit margins tightened, Suzy had cut the full-time post, and the housekeeper's duties were thereafter shared between the chambermaids or added to Suzy's already excessive workload.) As well as stocks of linen, the room's shelves were filled with individual packets of soap, shampoo, shower-gel, shower-caps, teabags, instant-coffee granules, sweetener, long-life milk and cream, shoe-cleaning wipes, sewing kits and all the other impedimenta which form an obligatory part of the twenty-first-century hotel experience – even in a country house hotel.

There was a clipboard on the wall of the linen room for the daily bedroom sheets. On these forms were three columns: for the room numbers, for guests' names to show whether or not the room was occupied, and for the ticks the chambermaids had to put in when the room had been cleaned and tidied ready for the next guest. A form of shorthand was used to show when beds needed new sheets rather than just remaking, when breakages had occurred, and when maintenance work – like replacing light bulbs, retuning television sets or unblocking sinks – was required.

The clipboard gave Jude an idea. There was no fixed schedule for removing its old sheets. Often they wouldn't be cleared until their mass became too great for the new one to be clipped in, which was the case on this occasion. Jude flicked through and found the sheet for the Wednesday in the small hours of which Nigel Ackford had died. The ticking of the form that morning had been erratic. With a police investigation on the premises, the chambermaids' re-tidying of the bedrooms had had a low priority. But the names showing which rooms had been occupied were all in place.

Pushing at the release clip, Jude slid out the relevant sheet. She folded it and put it in her pocket, with a view to checking the rooms against the Pillars of Sussex guest list at Woodside Cottage.

Downstairs, the accountants were leading their prey to the next sales pitch in the conference suite. 'Wish they were all like this,' Suzy confided to Jude, as the last guest left the dining room. 'One of the big downturns of the hotel industry is watching customers lingering over their meals, while all you want to do is move in and clear up.'

'Are they here for dinner?'

'No, thank God. Tea and biscuits at five, then they're off – the company people to plan their follow-up phone calls, and the potential clients to forget they've ever been here.'

'Does that mean you've got an evening off?'

'No, but it's not stressful. Just a private party.'

'Oh?'

'Kerry Hartson's sixteenth.'

'Amazing to think she's that young.'

'I know. She's been fifteen going on twenty-five for a long time.'

'So is it going to be a wild teenage rave here tonight?'

'Good heavens, no. Just an elegant family dinner party. No doubt she'll go clubbing with her mates on some other occasion.' Suzy's shoulders rose in an involuntary shudder. 'Anyway, thank God I no longer have to deal with Kerry.'

'Why did you take her on, Suzy?'

'Oh, she wanted to learn the hotel business. As ever, I needed another pair of hands.'

An inadequate answer, but Jude let it pass.

They were in the kitchen. The other waitresses had knocked off, and Max had gone to do whatever it is that chefs do in the afternoon – in his case, possibly practising television celebrity faces in front of a mirror.

'Do you fancy a coffee?' asked Suzy.

'Please.'

'Come back to my place.'

Jude had been into the barn before, but was once again struck by the elegance of its decoration. As with her wardrobe, Suzy had used only the best designers; everything in the barn conversion was minimalist and perfect.

In the kitchen she produced a couple of cappuccinos from the Italian coffee-maker, and sat down at the long wooden table. The rain had stopped ; the weather was warm enough now for the French windows to be opened, and for the two women to look out to the rolling green curves of the South Downs, cleansed by their recent drenching.

Suzy let out a long sigh. 'I hope things settle down a

325

bit now. I think I've had more than my share of bad luck in the last two weeks.'

'Two deaths in the hotel,' said Jude.

'Exactly. Two too many.'

'And is it your view that there was a connection between them?'

Another, even longer, sigh. 'I honestly don't know. And I'm afraid I don't really care. Sounds callous, but maybe I am. You have to develop a strong core of selfishness if you run your own business. When the first death happened, I was afraid it threatened the hotel. Now . . .' The sculpted shoulders shrugged.

'You think the danger's gone away?'

'The danger of damaging publicity, yes. There are always other dangers to a business like this, mind you, so I can never relax. Recessions, lack of bookings, international crises, Americans still pussy-footing about travelling abroad. If I want to worry, I can always find something to worry about.'

'So why have you stopped worrying about the bad publicity?'

The hazel eyes turned curiously towards Jude. 'I told you. The young man's death was reported in the local paper, and Hopwicke House wasn't even mentioned.'

'And what about the old man's death? Are you confident that will be discreetly reported too?'

'Yes. I am, actually.'

'And is that because the editor of the *Fethering Observer* and Detective Inspector Goodchild were both here on Saturday night when it happened?'

Suzy Longthorne framed her face in two hands, which she swept up through her auburn hair. 'That may have something to do with it. Oh, stop looking at me with righteous indignation, Jude.'

'I wasn't.'

'Yes, you were. If there's one thing my years of the so-called "celebrity lifestyle" have taught me, it's that you need people to fix things for you. And if you get an offer of having something fixed, then you'd be very stupid to turn it down.'

'Even if what is being fixed for you is the cover-up of a murder?'

'If I thought a murder had been committed, Jude, I might feel differently. But I don't.'

'Really?'

'Yes, really. From the moment you found that young man's body, you have been the only person in the world who thought it was murder. Well, maybe you've convinced your friend Carole too. Nobody else thinks it was anything other than suicide.'

'Then why did they all start making excuses and fabricating alibis?'

'For reasons of their own. For self-protection. To avoid bad publicity. Not because they thought they were murder suspects.'

'But—'

'It's you who planted that idea, Jude. And all the questioning from you and your friend Carole just got people more nervous, so they started to make up new stories to get you off their backs.'

Jude's brown eyes returned the hazel stare. 'Do you sincerely believe what you're saying, Suzy?'

'Of course I do.' She laid her long hands palms upwards on the table, pleading. 'God, Jude, how long have we known each other? Can't you tell when I'm speaking the truth?'

'Yes. I can.' But Jude wished she could have said it with more conviction. 'Very well. Say Nigel Ackford did commit suicide – what about Donald Chew?'

'It was an accident. He fell down the cellar steps.' Suzy sounded weary now. 'All right. Maybe I should have checked that the door was locked. But I can't do everything.'

'No.' There was a silence between them. 'Suzy, I can't deny it's very convincing. Suicide and an accident. Certainly a much more appealing explanation than two murders.'

'Then, for heaven's sake,' demanded Suzy, her weariness now turning to exasperation, 'why can't you believe it?'

'I just can't.' Feeble, she knew, but the only answer Jude could come up with. 'Maybe I could if I hadn't heard what Nigel Ackford said the night he died. They weren't the words of someone about to kill himself.'

'And that's all? If you had a reason why he should have done it, then you'd believe the death was suicide?'

'Yes,' said Jude. 'Yes, I would.'

'Right,' said Suzy. She lifted herself out of her chair and crossed to a small cupboard set into the old beams for the barn. 'I'm not meant to show you this, but I think the moment has come when I've got to.'

*

The young man at the end of the phone sounded wary. Yes, his name was Karl Floyd and he did work for the *Fethering Observer*.

'And you're there as an investigative reporter?' asked Carole.

It had been the right thing to say. Whether or not her description was rather overstating his role, there was a note of pride in his admission that yes, he was an investigative reporter.

Now she had to take a risk. The minute Jude had mentioned Nigel Ackford's name to Karl Floyd, their conversation had been ended very abruptly. But then the young man had been on his mobile. Now he was at work. If she just phrased it right . . .

'I might have some information relevant to one of your enquiries.'

'Oh yes?' He was interested, but still cautious. 'Can you tell me who I'm talking to, please?'

'That doesn't matter for the time being.' Another calculated risk. But Carole reckoned she'd got him hooked, and didn't want to give him any excuse to put the phone down. The fact that his informant was a middle-aged retired woman from Fethering High Street might do just that.

Now the biggest risk. She was guessing, and if her conjecture was wrong, she could look forward to a very quick end to their conversation. 'The enquiry I'm referring to is the one you had been talking about to Nigel Ackford and Donald Chew.'

Total silence from the other end of the line. Carole

raised the stakes of her risks further. 'About Renton and Chew?'

Still silence, and she started to worry she'd made a conjecture too far.

Then Karl Floyd spoke. 'What do you know about them?'

Carole felt herself relax. She'd been right. He'd admitted he had been investigating Renton and Chew.

'I'd rather not talk on the phone. Would it be possible for us to meet?'

'I'm not in the habit of meeting people whose names I don't know.'

'Very well. My name's Carole Seddon.'

'Oh.'

His intonation was blank, could have been approving, could have been disapproving. In case he was about to put the phone down, Carole said quickly, 'I am a client of Renton and Chew.'

Thank God, that did it. 'OK, let's meet. I'd better tell you, though, that even if I do get all the facts for this investigation together, there's a strong likelihood that the *Fethering Observer* won't run it.'

No, it'll be spiked by the editor, thought Carole, while he counts down the days to full-time sea fishing. The Pillars of Sussex would close ranks, as ever – particularly now they had a cosmetic presentation job to do on the death of Donald Chew.

'Don't worry about that,' she said. 'There are other newspapers.'

Again she'd hit the right note. Every young journalist still dreamed of the huge international scoop. *All the President's Men* must have been obligatory viewing during their training.

Karl Floyd's flat turned out to be in Fethering, within walking distance from High Tor. He'd certainly be back from work by seven. Carole arranged to go round and see him then.

She put the phone down with a huge glow of satisfaction. This was a breakthrough. There was no question now about her contributing her fair share to the investigation. Immediately she dialled Jude's mobile number.

'Who was that?' asked Suzy as soon as Jude ended the call. 'Sorry, am I being nosy?'

Her friend grinned. 'Well, you are, but that's nothing new. It was Carole.'

'Ah.'

'She's tracked down another link in the chain.'

'Sorry?'

'There was someone Nigel had been in touch with a lot in the weeks before he died called Karl Floyd. I spoke to him once on the phone, then he vanished. But good old Carole's tracked him down.'

'Of course,' said Suzy. 'I keep forgetting it's not just you.' She giggled, 'We've got two matronly supersleuths on this case, haven't we?'

'Less of the "matronly", thank you very much.' Jude's large bosom swelled in mock affront. 'Just because some of us haven't spent our entire lives

331

staying young and beautiful, it's very mean of you to snipe.'

Suzy held up her hands in a gesture of submission. 'Sorry. Take it all back.'

'Anyway, we're wasting time. Show me what you were going to show me.'

'All right.' Suzy removed a sheet of white copier paper from the Hopwicke House envelope she'd taken out of the cupboard.

'And this is going to convince me that Nigel committed suicide?'

'I think it will, yes.'

'Don't forget you've got to convince Carole too. After an entirely characteristic moment of doubt, she's now back fully committed to the investigation.'

'This'll convince her too.' Still Suzy did not hand the piece of paper across. 'I'd better explain how I come to have this. You remember, when you found Nigel Ackford's body in the four-poster room, you came straight down and told me.'

'Yes.'

'And I went up to have a look. I found a letter under the pillow. Before the police arrived' – she waved the sheet of white paper – 'I took a photocopy.'

'Why?'

'I don't know. I was confused and shocked, and I suddenly saw all my hard work building up the hotel being threatened, so I just thought, the more information I had . . .'

'So you never told anyone else about the letter? Like the police?'

'Of course I did. I wasn't in the business of destroying evidence.'

'You say that, but you didn't tell the police about the threatening note Kerry found.'

'No, but that pointed towards a possible murder, which would have been a publicity disaster. This letter pointed towards suicide, which was bad, but not *as* bad. No, as soon as I'd photocopied the letter, I put it back for the police to find.'

'Surely your fingerprints would have been on the paper?'

'I suppose they would. I wasn't really thinking of that. Anyway, when Inspector Goodchild questioned me, I told him exactly what I'd done, so if they did find my fingerprints, they'd know why.'

'But why on earth didn't this letter come out before?' Jude wailed. 'If proof existed that Nigel had a reason to kill himself, then Carole and I could have saved ourselves a great deal of bother.'

With a rueful nod, Suzy agreed. 'I know. But Inspector Goodchild told me not to mention it to anyone, and I've obeyed him – well, until now.'

'Why would he do that, though? Because he's part of the Pillars of Sussex cover-up conspiracy?'

'Jude . . .' Suzy shook her elegant head in aggrieved exasperation. 'There is no cover-up. There's nothing to cover up. Nigel Ackford died on my premises, which was extremely unfortunate. The preliminary inquest was adjourned, to give the police time to assemble their evidence. When that evidence is assembled, Nigel

Ackford will be adjudged to have committed suicide. Inspector Goodchild is a professional policeman. He's not about to show classified information or evidence to two middle-aged women who have fantasies of being crime-solvers.'

In all their long friendship, Suzy had never before said anything so cruel to Jude, and she regretted it as soon as the words had left her mouth. 'I'm sorry. That just came out. I've had it up to here over all this business. As you know, the hotel's been under threat, and this couldn't have come at a worse time. You and your friend Carole have made it even worse.'

There was a cold silence. Jude reached out a plump hand. 'I'd better read it then.'

Suzy handed the photocopy across.

The letterhead was the address and telephone number of a flat in Hove. The contents were hand-written in the elegant italic style favoured by artists, designers and architects. It was dated the day before the Pillars of Sussex dinner.

Dear Nigel

I know you've made up your mind, and I know you wouldn't listen to me on the phone, but I can't just let you go ahead without one more plea to you not to do it.

OK, I'm not pretending you haven't got problems, but I'm sure if you calm down and give yourself a bit of space, you'll be able to deal with them. I know our relationship didn't work out, and I know you've been trying to convince yourself that you love Wendy, but deep down you know you're gay. You always have known it. And you'll only ever find happiness when you accept that fact. To fulfil yourself completely, you're going to end up in a loving relationship with another man. I wish that person could be me. I still can't totally damp down the hope that, once we've spent some relaxed time together, it will be me. But I'm not putting any pressure on you.

What you've got to understand, Nigel, is that nobody's putting any pressure on you – except, perhaps, Wendy, a little. The only person who's really putting pressure on you is yourself. All your worries about the ethics of your personal and professional behaviour are self-imposed. I don't mean by that that they're irrelevant – all the talking we've done on the subject should prove that to you – but they're the kind of anxieties that any thinking person is going to have as he or she negotiates a way through the complexities of life.

For my sake – but even more for your own sake, Nigel – don't do what you're contemplating. I know how bad you're feeling at the moment, but you will come through this patch – I promise you that. You have so much to live for – don't throw it all away.

With love (and that's not written with any view to emotional blackmail – it's just an honest expression of what I feel for you),

Ed

There was a long silence, during which Jude

avoided her friend's eyes. Then she looked up, her face as stubborn as a five-year-old's. 'It could be a forgery.'

'Yes, it could,' Suzy admitted. 'But the man's got a phone number. Why don't you ring him and find out?'

Chapter Thirty-Eight

The flat was in the basement of an old white house in Hove. The space had been well designed and renovated, but too long ago. The exposed pine and the low Scandinavian furniture gave a feeling of the early seventies. So did the white emulsion, which had needed repainting for at least a decade. The grey and white striped curtains, bought from Habitat at its peak of trendiness, now had new stripes where the sun had faded them.

The man who let Jude in also seemed to be a relic of an earlier age: jeans, a faded denim shirt tight over his swelling belly and hair cut long in a style that had been fashionable before the hair became white.

'Edward Dukesbury,' he said, and gestured to the crammed cardboard boxes in the middle of the room. 'You were lucky to catch me. As you see, I'm moving out shortly.'

'Away from Hove?'

Away from Hove. Away from Sussex. London. I'm afraid this place doesn't have very happy memories for me.'

Jude did not ask him to elaborate at that point. She

was still taking him in, forming her own estimation of the man.

'Do sit down. Can I offer you anything? Coffee, tea, or I've got some wine . . .' he offered vaguely.

'No, thank you.' Jude subsided on to a low sofa, which only seemed to promise comfort to those who lay on it horizontally. She perched on the edge of the cushion.

'You said you wanted to talk to me about Nigel.'

'Yes.'

As he lowered himself on to a narrow wooden chair, Jude noticed there was a list on the box in front of him. She saw the words 'electricity' and 'gas'. No doubt things that had to be done before he left. The hand-writing was the same as in the letter she'd seen at Hopwicke House.

'I heard about you through Suzy Longthorne,' Jude volunteered.

Edward Dukesbury shrugged and shook his head. 'Sorry, the name doesn't mean anything to me.'

'What about Rick Hendry, or Bob Hartson?'

'The only Rick Hendry I've heard of is the former rock musician, but I've never met him. And the other name – sorry, never heard it.'

'What about Donald Chew?'

'I know that was the name of Nigel's boss at work, but we never met.'

'So you haven't heard what happened to him?'

'No.' The ignorance in the watery blue eyes appeared genuine. But Edward Dukesbury wasn't interested in the fate of Donald Chew; he was keen to move on. 'You said you wanted to talk to me about Nigel. Did you know him?'

'I met him once. The night before he died.'

'How come?'

'I was working at Hopwicke Country House Hotel.'

'Ah.' The man looked puzzled. 'Then I don't see why . . .'

'I just wanted to be sure that he committed suicide.'

'What?' There was authentic surprise in the voice.

'That there wasn't some other explanation for his death.'

Edward Dukesbury let out a bitter laugh. 'What other explanation could there be? You don't hang yourself by accident.'

'No. But I thought . . . You knew him well. Perhaps you could tell me why you think he did it.'

For the first time there was wariness in the pale eyes. 'Why did you come to me? How did you get my phone number?'

'I happened to see a copy of the letter you wrote to Nigel Ackford the day before he died.'

'Ah.' Her answer satisfied him, and brought a new resignation into his tone. 'Are you police? I've already talked to Inspector Goodchild. I thought that would be the end of it.'

'No, I'm not police. I'm just interested in what happened.'

Her lack of official authorization didn't seem to concern him. 'Well, since you're here, ask what you want to ask. Nigel's dead. Nothing we say can harm him any more.'

'You and he had a relationship?'

Without embarrassment, he replied, 'Yes. We were lovers, on and off, for over a year. Nigel had problems with admitting he was gay. He even moved in with a girlfriend to try and cure himself, but it was never going to work.'

'Wendy.'

'That was her name, yes.'

'Did you ever meet her?'

He shook his head.

'Was the sex thing the reason why Nigel killed himself?'

'Part of it. Like a lot of young men, Nigel was uncertain about his own identity. Sexual orientation was part of the problem, but he was also worried about doing the work he was doing.'

'Being a solicitor?'

'Yes.'

'Why, was there something criminal going on at Renton and Chew?'

Another short, bitter laugh. 'Not so far as I know. No more than in any other solicitor's office, I imagine. But Nigel sometimes thought he should be doing something more useful to the world, something that actually did some good. We used to talk about it a lot.'

'Why? Is your work more useful to the world?'

He smiled cynically. 'Might be, if I had any work. I'm an architect by training. Was quite successful in the sixties and seventies, but now . . .' He gestured feebly, needing no more explanation than the flat around him.

'Trouble is, I started letting my conscience get in the way . . .'

'Oh?'

'Got rather involved in environmental issues. Tried only to do projects that would actually improve the world around us. The nineteen eighties weren't the best time to have principles like that.'

'But surely the climate's better now? There's more awareness of the environmental consequences of development.'

He didn't look convinced. 'There's a certain amount of lip-service, yes. Projects get stopped because they threaten the habitat of some little-known field mouse. And the big developers go through a major charade of environmental consultation before they submit their plans. Some of them even have their own in-house environmental consultants. But, as ever, there's a big difference between the plans that are approved and what actually gets built.'

He sighed. 'Maybe I'm being too cynical. Maybe, if I was starting out now as a young architect, I'd be full of idealism and the belief that I could actually make changes. And maybe I could. Now, though, at my age – I'm too old and defeated.'

'And that was the kind of subject you and Nigel used to talk about?'

'Yes.'

'Because Renton and Chew works with property developers.'

'I'm sure they do. Anyone in business is going to

341

need contracts sorted out, that kind of thing. There's always work for solicitors to do.'

'But you say Nigel never worried he was being asked to do anything illegal?'

'No. I think he just thought he'd reached a cross-roads in his life. He could hang on to his principles, the kind of ideas I talked to him about, or he could just get on with his career, take the money and close his mind to the consequences. And that was exactly paralleled in his private life. He could ask this Wendy to marry him, and spend the rest of his days pretending to be some-thing he wasn't – rather as he implied his boss did. What's his name? Donald Chew, that's right. Appar-ently he's gay, but has maintained the facade of a marriage for a long time. Anyway, those were the pres-sures Nigel was under. And the fact that he couldn't cope with those pressures was the reason why he killed himself.'

'Had he talked about suicide to you?'

The white head nodded, and the blue eyes became even more watery. 'Yes. He did get bad moods. Well, he was a depressive. I kept telling him to go to his doctor, get professional help, but Nigel could be very stubborn at times.'

Jude stayed perched in silence on the edge of the sofa. Then she asked, 'Was the letter you wrote the last communication you had with Nigel?'

'No.' He was almost weeping now. 'I wish it had been. I could have done without the phone call.'

'What phone call? When did that happen?'

'The night . . .' Tears trickled down his lined face as

he tried to get the words out. 'The night he was at the hotel, the night he . . . Nigel phoned me in the small hours. He woke me up.'

'What time would this have been?'

'About four o'clock. I don't know exactly.'

'And what did he say?'

Again the words didn't come easily. 'That he was going to kill himself. He said he'd just woken up and realized things were never going to get better. He'd made up his mind.'

'But he was incredibly drunk. I don't think he was capable of—'

'I wish you were right, wish he had just passed out that night. But no, Nigel was coherent enough to do what he had to do.'

'Didn't you think of calling the police?'

'No,' the architect replied flatly. 'By the time they got there, it would have been too late. Anyway, if that was what Nigel had decided to do . . . Also, quite honestly, I've had enough tangles with authority in my life. When I was growing up, just for me to express my sexuality was illegal. I've been through plenty with the police over the years, so after Nigel's call I didn't fancy the idea of picking through my most painful emotions with some insensitive flatfoot.'

'But the police did talk to you?'

'Of course they did. They saw the original of the letter that brought you here. There's no way they weren't going to talk to me after that. Oh yes, I did my time with Inspector Goodchild. I'd love to have escaped that pleasure, but I didn't.

'I'm afraid, you see, I'm not one of those people who regards the truth as the most important thing in life. I would say, over the years, I have generally received more comfort from lies. Sorry, not a very public-spirited citizen, am I?'

Jude's mind was moving fast, trying to find some logical objection to what she had just been told. 'The phone call!' She clung to the thought. 'If Nigel called you that night, the call would have registered on the Hopwicke House switchboard.'

'He used his mobile.'

He hadn't got a mobile! He'd given his mobile to Wendy Fullerton! But before she could produce that clinching argument, Jude remembered Wendy saying that Nigel had been planning to buy another. Presumably the new phone was now in the hands of the police, yet another piece of the evidence that would be used to help the coroner arrive at a verdict of death by suicide.

Which was the truth. Jude looked back at her past weeks of speculation and excitement, and could only see the wreckage of her false logic. She had never felt lower.

Chapter Thirty-Nine

It was about a quarter to seven when Jude knocked on the door of High Tor, but there was no reply, so she went disconsolately back into Woodside Cottage. She poured a glass of white wine, but forgot about it as she buried herself deep in the draperies of an ancient armchair and gave herself up to gloomy thoughts.

She and Carole had been guilty of breaking one of the most basic rules of investigation: they had ignored the obvious. Once she had found out from Wendy Fullerton that Nigel Ackford had been a depressive, she should have realized that they were on a hiding to nothing. She should have guessed that the police had evidence to justify their ready acceptance of a suicide verdict, and she should have recognized that the many cover-ups she and Carole had encountered were merely symptoms of naturally secretive people trying to avoid damaging publicity for reasons which had nothing to do with their being guilty of murder.

The way she had behaved, in retrospect, appeared naive and melodramatic.

For Jude, who prided herself on her good sense and

345

mental equilibrium, that knowledge hurt deeply.

The gloomy thoughts did not lift.

Karl Floyd was as Carole would have expected him to be – young, earnest, full of uncoordinated enthusiasm, and also a bit frightened.

His flat, which he told her was rented, gave the impression of being a transient resting place. He was living out of suitcases and, from the evidence of his small kitchen/diner, out of tins and polystyrene take-away boxes. He looked as though he'd dressed in a hurry too – shabby suit, top button missing from the shirt, randomly chosen diamond-patterned tie. He had thick ginger hair that refused to lie down at the back.

And yes, he did see himself as a crusading journalist in the mould of Carl Bernstein and Bob Woodward. He confided to Carole that his father, also a newspaperman, though not a great speller, had named him Karl as a homage to Bernstein. This could have prompted interesting speculation about the young man trying to live up to parental expectations, but Carole didn't have time to go into that.

'And it was,' she asked, 'in connection with an inves-tigation that you were in touch with Nigel Ackford and Donald Chew?'

'Yes. Nigel approached me first. He was very troubled about things that were going on.'

'Inside Renton and Chew?'

'In a way, yes. I think Nigel's anxiety was more about the way things ran generally, the amount of backhanders and back-scratching that are involved in all kinds of business deals. He saw himself at a cross-roads. He could either try to fight to expose the system, or he could close his mind to it and get on with his life.'

'Continue working at Renton and Chew, get put up for the right golf clubs, become a Pillar of Sussex?'

'I guess so. When he first got in touch with me, he was very keen to expose stuff like that.'

'You imply he changed his tune?'

'Yes, he did seem to back off. He became gradually less enthusiastic.'

'Do you think someone was getting at him?'

'That wasn't the impression I got. More that he'd assessed his options and come down on the side of the easy life. Rising through the ranks at Renton and Chew, getting married, living a well-cushioned middle-class life.'

Exactly the sort of prospects Nigel Ackford had talked about in his drunken ramblings to Jude the night he died.

'So, Karl, to what extent had Nigel backed off?'

'What do you mean?'

'Was he actually regretting having got in touch with you in the first place?'

'I think he probably was. Difficult to tell with him. He was very volatile. Sometimes when he rung, he was full of crusading zeal. A few hours later, he was down in the dumps and thought it was pointless to try to do anything.'

Which could be the behaviour of a potential suicide, thought Carole. But before she made a final decision on that, she had to know more.

'Was it because Nigel was going cold on the idea of the investigation that you got in touch with Donald Chew?'

'Yes. There were questions I wanted to ask him.'

'And he agreed to see you?'

'He did. I mentioned one or two things that seemed to set alarm bells going with him. We fixed a meeting for this Monday.'

'Which, sadly, he was unable to make.'

The young man nodded gloomily.

'Right, Karl. I think it's time you told me what it was Nigel Ackford started you investigating.'

Jude's mood hadn't improved. Her wine glass was still untouched, its contents long risen to room temperature. Restlessly, she was zapping through television channels, which for her was a sure sign of low spirits.

Though she'd occasionally worked as a television actress in the late sixties, the medium had soon lost its interest for Jude. And now that every programme seemed to involve ordinary members of the public, she found it even less alluring. The trend may have been very lucrative for Rick Hendry, but it didn't do anything for her. Jude met quite enough real people in her daily life; she didn't feel the need to see them humiliated on television.

Previously she'd had a very basic portable TV with a snowstorm picture and an indoor aerial, but she'd installed a new one with satellite channels for the benefit of Laurence Hawker, a friend and lover who had lived out his last months with her at Woodside

Cottage. Since he died, the infinitely wide range of options the television offered had remained unexplored.

Though Jude had been upset by Laurence's death, this was the first time she had felt low enough for mindless flicking with the remote control. But she couldn't settle to anything else, and the constant changes on the screen gave her the illusion of something happening.

She was amazed at how little there was on offer that anyone might want to watch. Anyone, that is, who wasn't interested in sport, make-over programmes, music videos, movies that had failed to strike a chord with cinema audiences, and repeats of cop series that long before should have been allowed mercifully to expire. After the first twenty channels, the challenge of finding something watchable became almost interesting.

At first she didn't believe what she'd seen. She'd already zapped on to another station; she zapped back.

No good. It was no longer on the screen. She stayed with the channel, watching some dire early seventies British espionage series. The sets were cardboard, the actors more so. The men tried to look tough and gritty, in spite of ridiculous sideburns. The women, with short skirts, lacquered hair and black-lined upper eyelids, seemed to be there only to stick their bottoms out and look winsome.

The scene changed. And she saw it again. This time there was no doubt.

Chapter Forty

They both had so much to say that it was some time after Jude had opened the door before either of them could hear the other. The Renault was parked directly outside Woodside Cottage. Carole must have been really excited to forgo her customary ritual of putting the car in the High Tor garage.

She managed to get in first with what she had heard from Karl Floyd.

'I thought something like that must have happened,' said Jude.

'There remains some doubt over whether it's actually illegal, but Karl's still on the case. He's got all enthusiastic about it again now. And his boss at the *Fethering Observer* has definitely gagged him on the story, so he's convinced there is something to hide. He's going to open out his investigation to the whole Pillars of Sussex network.'

'Great.'

'I've given him your phone numbers as well as mine, so if you get a call from him, you'll know what it's about.'

'That's good, Carole, but listen to what I've got!' The

defeatist lethargy was gone. Jude's whole face sparkled with animation. 'You know, this man I went to see this afternoon—'

'No, I'm sorry, I don't know what you're talking about.'

Jude realized she hadn't spoken to Carole since her emergency summons to the hotel that morning. Briefly she brought her up to date on the letter Suzy Longthorne had shown her, and the subsequent meeting in Hove with Edward Dukesbury.

Then she revealed her new discovery.

'There are details that need checking,' Jude concluded, glowing with excitement, 'but I'm sure we're on to something.'

'Well, you must ring Wendy Fullerton.'

'I know that. I just wish there was some way I could check what I saw on the television. I don't have any contacts in that world any more.'

'No,' said Carole, with sudden complacency, 'but I do.'

'What!' Jude couldn't have been more surprised if her neighbour had announced she was taking up bungee jumping.

'This is an area in which my future daughter-in-law-to-be could prove very useful indeed.'

She rang Stephen straight away. If he was surprised by a sudden call from his mother asking to speak to Gaby, he disguised the fact. Soon Carole was connected. And yes, Gaby thought she could help. Would be delighted to help. A bit of research on the internet would be required, but it should be possible. She'd ring back. Or, in fact, emailing the results would be simpler.

Jude didn't use a computer, but she still had the laptop upstairs which had belonged to Laurence Hawker. Within minutes, the machine was switched on and attached to a printer.

Jude rang Wendy Fullerton, and got the information she had hoped for.

Then she and Carole sat and waited. Seeing her still untouched glass, Jude offered Carole a drink. But no, they were both too tense.

After twenty minutes that felt like an hour, Jude had a sudden recollection and found the chambermaids' sheet she had filched from the linen room at Hopwicke House. She checked the bookings through against the Pillars of Sussex guest list she had kept. Her hunch had been right. Jude had just found the confirmation she required, when her land-line rang. It was Gaby, asking to speak to Carole.

Yes, she had found the information and Stephen was emailing it through as she spoke. 'Don't bother to explain, Carole. You're clearly in a hurry. Tell me about it when we next meet.'

Carole just had time to register the warming thought that they would be meeting again, before she and Jude rushed upstairs to retrieve Gaby's email.

They were looking at the printout when Jude's phone rang again.

'Carole? Did you say Carole? Yes, she's here.'

Jude looked anxious as she passed the phone

across. 'I don't know who it is. I can hardly hear what he's saying.'

Carole couldn't recognize the voice immediately, there was so much wheezing and groaning. Then she realized it was the young man to whom she'd been speaking only an hour before.

'Karl, what on earth's the matter?'

'He came round . . .' the boy managed to gasp. 'Beat me up. He's . . . coming round to get you . . .'

As she heard the words, Carole heard a shuddering crash. She and Jude moved to her bedroom window. A large car was parked outside High Tor. And a man was using the garden birdbath to smash down the front door.

'Quick,' hissed Jude. 'Into your car! We'll get away!'

Carole abandoned her customary caution, and drove the Renault like a rally car.

There was no sign of pursuit, but both women knew that, when he found High Tor empty, the man would come after them.

He didn't need to keep the Renault in sight. He knew that they both had the same destination.

And Carole and Jude knew they wouldn't have long before he arrived to do what they had to do.

Chapter Forty-One

Hopwicke Country House Hotel was just as good at small private parties as it was at larger events. The one laid-up table in the dining room had a cloth of exactly the same colour as the Dolce & Gabbana dress that Kerry had been given by her parents as one of her presents. The table centrepiece was a cake out of whose surface Max Townley had conjured a number sixteen in spun sugar. And the menu had been specially designed according to the birthday girl's wishes.

The invitation list had been drawn up by her step-father. He'd booked a London club for the Saturday night party Kerry was going to have with her contemporaries. On the birthday itself he was, as ever, in sole command.

He'd chosen to have an intimate dinner party. Himself, Kerry, her mother, Suzy Longthorne and Rick Hendry. Though the last two did not seek out each other's company at social events, Bob Hartson knew they'd do it for him. Kerry had wanted Rick Hendry there, so she could discuss her pop career, and Suzy would be on the premises anyway. Since, as well as being involved in a business relationship with him, she was also his friend, Bob Hartson had decided she should be one of the dinner guests. And since she was the hotelier, she could do any serving at table that might be required. Not that there would be much. The menu and wines had been pre-ordered. All Suzy would have to do was collect the dishes from Max in the kitchen and take back the empty ones. Bob Hartson enjoyed having the money and power to lay on nice treats for his stepdaughter.

The party had started with vintage champagne in the bar. Bob Hartson watched with indulgent pride the speed at which Kerry could put her drink away. For as long as he'd had any influence on her, he'd brought her up to relish the good things of life. He luxuriated in the prospect of her attaining pop success, of seeing his stepdaughter's photograph and lifestyle splashed across celebrity magazines. Bob Hartson liked being in charge. He liked having power over everyone around him. And that evening, in that company, he felt good. He looked round the hotel bar, and every face he saw gave him a good feeling.

Except for the face of the woman who'd just walked in from the hall.

'What the hell are you doing here?'

'Jude.' Suzy had risen to her feet in alarm.

'I had to come,' said her friend. 'I owe you an apology, Suzy.'

'What is this?' said Rick Hendry.

Suzy knew his question was directed at her. 'I don't know.'

355

Jude provided the explanation. 'I wanted to apologize not just to you, Suzy, but to anyone else about whom I may have harboured false suspicions.'

'Look,' said Kerry, 'this is my birthday party. It's private. I don't want it disturbed by—'

But a raised hand from Jude silenced her. 'I went to see someone this afternoon. An architect called Edward Dukesbury. A former lover of Nigel Ackford. And Edward Dukesbury was good enough to explain to me exactly why that poor young man hanged himself here in the hotel. His explanation was entirely convincing.'

She looked covertly round the room to see if anyone had visibly relaxed at this news. But no, they all stayed tense, as if they were all expecting more.

'So what we were talking about this afternoon, Suzy – whether I'd be satisfied if I was given a reason why Nigel Ackford committed suicide – well, I guess now I have that reason. I should be completely satisfied.'

'Thank God.' Suzy did relax.

'And I would be completely satisfied,' Jude went on, 'if I did not know Edward Dukesbury to be a fraud.'

'What?' demanded Sandra Hartson.

'He's an actor called Lionel Greaves.' There was no point in spelling out to them how she'd recognized the face from the old television show, how Carole had asked Gaby to check out the name, and how Gaby had emailed back a photograph taken from the website of the *Spotlight* actors' directory.

'A very good try,' Jude went on. 'Nearly had me fooled. But I got a break of good luck. So I don't know who tried to set up that little treat for me . . .' She looked round the room. Suzy would not meet her eye. 'Anyway, whichever one of you it was who briefed Lionel Greaves, I should tell you he got one detail wrong. As a clincher on selling me the suicide theory, the so-called Edward Dukesbury told me he'd been woken by a phone call from Nigel Ackford shortly before he killed himself. The young man apparently rang on his mobile – which is strange, because Nigel Ackford didn't at the time have a mobile. He'd given his to his former girlfriend Wendy Fullerton, and though he'd talked of buying another one, according to Wendy, he hadn't got round to it. So . . .'

Jude's brown eyes gave the room another circuit. Suzy still wouldn't look at her, but none of the others cracked.

Kerry Hartson, though, was annoyed. 'Listen, this is my birthday party—'

'Ssh!' It was Rick Hendry's hand that had gone up, and the girl was instantly silent.

He turned to face Jude. The beam of his smile was as big as ever, but there was little warmth in it. 'Listen, sweetie. I know you've always been a bit flaky. Suze always had some friends who were a few joss-sticks short of a bundle. But I want some explanations. Presumably what you're talking about makes sense to you, but I got lost a long time ago. Edward Dukesbury – Lionel Whatever – who are these people?'

'Someone here knows very well,' said Jude doggedly. 'Or maybe you all do?'

'What do you mean by that?' asked Sandra Hartson.

'I mean I think there's been collusion between all of you. The efficiency with which Carole and I have been fed ever-changing stories – someone's been orchestrating that.'

Sandra Hartson still didn't understand.

'When you're threatened,' Jude went on, 'you all close ranks, just like the Pillars of Sussex.'

'I have nothing to do with the Pillars of Sussex,' Suzy objected.

'Nor do I,' her ex-husband agreed.

'Not directly, no. But you're all part of the same thing, or you've all become part of the same thing.'

'And what's that?' Sandra Hartson posed the question as if she really did not know the answer. Which she possibly didn't. Sandra was the only person present Jude reckoned might be genuinely ignorant.

She had their attention, so she started to spell out what Carole had relayed to her. 'There's a journalist called Karl Floyd, who works for the *Fethering Observer*, and he got rather interested in the business dealings of some of the Pillars of Sussex. All right, low-power threat. Not too dangerous. He could be controlled by his editor who, like so many important people locally, the Pillars had in their pocket. He could be gagged and sacked if necessary. But Karl Floyd was persistent and, once Nigel Ackford started feeding him information about Renton and Chew, he became more of a threat. Still, he hadn't got much, and if Nigel could be stopped from giving him more, the threat would go away. That, in my view,' said Jude boldly, 'is why Nigel Ackford was killed.'

'He wasn't killed. He committed suicide.' But Suzy no longer sounded as though she believed her own words.

'That wasn't the end of it, though. Nigel was out of the way, but Karl Floyd wasn't. And he was persistent. He started working away at a new source of information, someone much higher up in Renton and Chew, Donald Chew himself. And Donald was getting increasingly unreliable. He was getting less cautious about hiding his homosexuality. Maybe he liked the idea of talking to a young male journalist. And he was also drinking more than ever. He was becoming more of a potential liability every day, and life would be a lot easier if he were off the scene, which of course, conveniently, he now is.'

There was a derisive laugh from Rick Hendry. 'I've heard of conspiracy theories . . . We're spoilt for them in the rock business. Who sabotaged Buddy Holly's plane? Did the CIA kill Jimi Hendrix? Who was the actual body in Elvis Presley's coffin? But yours, Jude, seems to take the biscuit. What is this awful deed that the Pillars of Sussex were perpetrating? And that this intrepid boy reporter was about to unmask. Gunrunning? Drugs? Illegal immigrants?'

'Nothing so dramatic as those. And indeed something that may not even be illegal – though it could engender some bad publicity – and I don't need to tell you, Rick, how nasty that can be. What Karl Floyd was investigating concerns the business practices of Bob Hartson.'

There was no change of expression on the property

developer's corrugated face, though both his wife and stepdaughter looked anxiously towards him.

'As we all know, Mr Hartson, you've been very successful.' He bowed his head in acknowledgment of the compliment. 'You have a vast property empire all along the South Coast. You're very well in with the local planners and all the other great and good of Sussex.' Still he seemed to think he was being flattered. 'And as a result, you have a lot of money to invest in new developments and, on occasions to help out people in trouble.'

Bob Hartson seemed to be enjoying this paean to his success and philanthropy.

'Just as you have helped Suzy here at Hopwicke House.'

As Jude went on, the hotelier gave her a sharp look.

'In his researches, Karl Floyd found out that what you've done for Suzy follows a pattern. You look out for businesses in nice old properties or on attractive sites, and you particularly look out for ones that are having financial problems. Then you offer to invest in the properties, help the people out, offer them loans at advantageous rates. All above board, proper contracts sorted out by your friendly solicitors, Renton and Chew.'

Bob Hartson smiled. 'You haven't said anything yet that I wouldn't be happy to see in the *Fethering Observer* – or the *Sunday Times* Business Section, come to that.'

'No, I agree,' said Jude. 'You've been very supportive to local businesses. It's when you withdraw the support that's significant. The contracts Renton and Chew draw up for you have very specific timing clauses, giving you options to pull the plugs whenever you choose.'

Bob Hartson shrugged his large shoulders. 'Normal business practice.'

There was the crunch of a large car drawing up on the gravel outside. Jude flinched, recognizing the significance of the sound. But none of the others reacted, so, swallowing down her fear, she continued to outline her argument.

'But, Mr Hartson, it's striking in how many cases you've withdrawn your financial support at a very bad time, and as a result the owners have been forced to sell up, and then – remarkably – their properties have been bought by one of your companies.'

He still couldn't see anything wrong. 'I always offer well over the going rate. Otherwise they wouldn't sell to me.'

'And then you sit on the properties until your friends in the planning departments get change of use agreed, and you develop them into housing.'

'In exact accordance with current government policy,' said Bob Hartson complacently. 'The south-east needs more houses. I bet the prime minister wishes there were more developers like me around.'

'I don't know. I think the prime minster likes to keep all the power to himself. He might not like you having as much as you do – or indeed the way you use it.'

'How do you mean?'

Surprisingly, the answer came from Suzy. 'Like the way you've used your power over me! Constantly threatening to take your investment out of Hopwicke House unless I do exactly as you want. Making me take cut-rate bookings for functions like the Pillars of Sussex dinner, so you can show off to your friends!'

Rick Hendry joined in. 'And the way you've manipulated me! Encouraging me to invest in your companies, then threatening to expose my involvement with you. Constantly asking for favours in return!'

'Favours like getting Kerry through the *Pop Crop* auditions?' suggested Jude.

'Yes,' said Rick Hendry.

'Oy!' the girl wailed. 'That's not the reason. It's because I'm good!'

All her idol responded to this was 'In your dreams.' Kerry burst into tears.

'Favours like building up Max Townley's hopes for his television career?' Jude went on.

'Yes,' Rick Hendry admitted. 'And the worst of the lot was making me agree to be auctioneer for that bloody auction of promises!'

'I'm not so sure, Rick,' said Jude. 'Don't you think the worst was actually using your showbiz contacts to persuade a beat-up actor like Lionel Greaves to spend a little time in one of Bob Hartson's unconverted flats in Hove, taking a very small part for a very large amount of money?'

But that was an admission too far for Rick Hendry. He looked bemused. 'I don't know what you're talking about.'

Kerry Hartson was now weeping bitterly. Her

mother leant across to comfort her. But her stepfather was enjoying himself too much to notice. He was positively glowing with confidence.

'I don't deny anything you've said, Jude.'

'And you don't deny that, if it appeared in the press, a list of all the deals of that kind that you've done would look pretty bad?'

'Sure, it'd look bad, but it's not going to appear in the press.'

'Because Nigel Ackford and Donald Chew are both dead.'

'Yes. Conveniently, they are.' Bob Hartson's smile was almost smug now. 'And no one will ever be able to find any connection between me and either of their deaths. Anyway, if I wanted to keep that stuff out of the press, I wouldn't have gone after Nigel or Donald. I'd have silenced the journalist – this Karl whatever-his-name-is. And I notice nobody's yet made an attack on him.'

'Oh, but they have,' said a new voice, as Carole Seddon stepped into the bar.

'What?' Bob Hartson's demeanour changed completely. He looked as if he had just received a heavy punch in the stomach.

'You should be careful,' Carole went on, 'when you use someone else to do your dirty work. There's always a danger they may go freelance and start doing things off their own bat. Like attacking Karl Floyd. Like trying to attack me – and breaking down my front door!' she added indignantly.

'Where is he?' Bob Hartson gasped.

'In the kitchen. Where do you expect him to be?' asked Carole. 'That's his proper place.'

'I'll go and get him,' said Suzy.

A moment later, she returned through the dining room, and resumed her seat. The man who had followed her from the kitchen stood framed in the doorway, looking in amazement round the group in front of him. Finally, his eyes rested on Bob Hartson.

'What is this? What's going on?' he asked.

The developer seemed to have recovered some of his composure. 'Oh, it's very simple. You've just been accused of two murders.' He turned to Carole. 'Or is it three? You didn't say whether Karl Floyd was dead or alive.'

'Alive. Badly beaten, but alive.'

Bob Hartson turned back to the man in the doorway. 'Two murders and one GBH, I reckon it is then.'

'But there's no way I could have done the first one. I was fast asleep in the stable block.'

'No,' said Jude coolly. 'You were supposed to be in the stable block, but when I checked the chambermaids' check sheets for that night, it turns out you were actually in one of the rooms inside the hotel.'

'I didn't know anything about that,' said Suzy.

'No. But I think I know who organized it.'

Under the probing beam of Jude's look, the way Kerry Hartson turned away her tear-stained face was sufficient admission of guilt.

The man in the doorway appealed to Bob Hartson.

'It's rubbish, isn't it? They can't prove anything, can they?'

The property developer smiled a hard smile. 'I could say I saw you do Nigel Ackford.'

'But you didn't. You weren't there. You'd got an alibi with Donald Chew. That was the whole point.'

'Hm.' Bob Hartson's self-confidence seemed to be returning very quickly. 'I certainly didn't see you kill Donald Chew. And the attack on Karl Floyd – the first I heard of such a thing was when this lady mentioned it a minute ago.'

'But I thought it was what you'd want, Bob. Suzy rang to the car while you were on site. She told me that woman Carole was going to meet Karl Floyd. I thought you'd want to stop that. I thought that was what you'd want, Bob.' The was pathos in his repetition of the line.

The developer shook his head sagely. 'Very risky, to try and imagine what other people might want, Geoff.' He looked his driver straight in the eye. 'Next thing you'll be telling these good people that I wanted Nigel and Donald dead.'

'But you did. You told me to get rid of them.'

'Doesn't sound like me.' Bob Hartson turned to his wife. 'Does it, Sandra?'

'No,' she said weakly.

'Not my usual style at all.' He rose from his chair and moved towards the bewildered chauffeur. 'I think you must have got the wrong end of the stick, Geoff. And that's a dangerous thing to do when you've been inside twice for GBH.'

'But, Bob, you told me—'

'I don't think you've got any proof of that, Geoff.'

'You bastard!'

Quick as a flash, a gun appeared in the chauffeur's hand.

Even quicker, Bob Hartson's hand bunched into a fist and shot up into the man's jaw.

The bullet hit the bar-room ceiling before the gun smashed into the wall.

As his chauffeur crumpled on to the floor, Bob Hartson looked back at his guests and gatecrashers. 'Well, say thank you. I think I saved at least one person's life there.'

Then he looked up as Inspector Goodchild came into the room. 'Reg, good to see you. I'd assumed Carole would call you over here.' He pointed to the heap on the floor behind him. 'There's your murderer.'

Chapter Forty-Two

The pub was full, but Carole and Jude felt a distinct atmosphere of disappointment around the Crown and Anchor when the news came through that Bob Hartson's chauffeur Geoffrey Gardner had been charged on two counts of murder and one of grievous bodily harm. The police knew they'd get him on the last count, because Karl Floyd had identified Gardner as the man who attacked him, but they were surprised when the driver admitted to the murders of Nigel Ackford and Donald Chew.

The accused kept insisting that he had done the killings under the express instructions of his boss, Bob Hartson, but could produce no proof to back up his assertions. Since Geoffrey Gardner had a prison record for violent crime and Bob Hartson had never been charged with anything, the police were inclined to the view that Gardner was simply trying to shift the blame. And since Bob Hartson would certainly engage the best lawyers money could buy, the police view was unlikely to change.

As Carole and Jude sat over their Chilean Chardonnay in the bar that evening they tried for the umpteenth time to think of a single scrap of evidence against Bob Hartson. 'There must be something we've forgotten,' Jude insisted. 'Something that hasn't been explained.'

Carole removed her rimless glasses and polished them thoughtfully with a handkerchief. 'Well, I suppose the only thing that hasn't been explained is what happened to the note Donald Chew left in Nigel Ackford's bedroom.'

'That's true.' Jude perked up instantly. 'Yes. Kerry found it, and gave it to Suzy. She showed it to me, and then later in the evening it had disappeared from her apron pocket.'

'There's probably some perfectly simple—'

But before Carole had time to defuse the idea, Jude had her mobile phone out and was moving excitedly towards the pub door. 'I'm going to ring Suzy. Too noisy in here.' And she was gone.

'You look like a cat that's had its mouse taken away.'

At the sound, Carole looked up to register that Ted Crisp had joined her.

'Yes, I'm sorry, I . . . Jude's just finding something out for me.'

'Oh yeah? Well, if you're trying to nail Bob Hartson, you have my full support.'

Carole looked puzzled. Ted nodded his head towards the old milk depot behind the pub. 'Work starts on that site Monday week.'

'Oh yes?'

'And it's one of Bob Hartson's companies that'll be doing it.'

The landlord's news did nothing to improve Carole's mood.

But at that moment, Jude came rushing back into the pub, and her bubbling manner suggested that maybe all hope was not completely lost.

'I talked to Suzy. She knows what happened to the missing note!'

'Really!'

Ted Crisp hadn't a clue what was going on, but he wasn't about to interrupt their euphoria by seeking explanations.

'Yes. Kerry talked to her about it some time last week. It was Kerry who removed the note from the apron!'

'Why?'

'This is the good bit . . .' Excitement sparkled in Jude's brown eyes. 'Kerry mentioned to her father she'd found the note, when she saw him at the dinner, and Bob Hartson insisted she should take the note back and destroy it. Well, don't you see what that means?'

'What?' asked Carole, confused, but beginning to catch her friend's childlike elation.

'Bob Hartson didn't want anything suspicious connected with Nigel Ackford's room! That apparently threatening note was bound to alert the police to something funny going on. The fact that he asked Kerry to destroy the note means Bob Hartson knew that the murder was going to take place!'

'Yes,' Carole sighed with satisfaction.

'Yes,' Jude echoed.

'Erm . . .' Ted Crisp broke into their microclimate of

mutual bliss, 'I don't fully know what you're talking about, and I don't want to put a damper on proceedings or anything but are you saying you've now actually got proof against Bob Hartson?'

'Yes.'

'Proof that would stand up in court?'

'Well . . .' But Jude was in no mood to have her enthusiasm dented. 'Yes, we have. If the police only use their imagination and —'

'Inspector Goodchild use his imagination?' asked Carole, beginning to absorb the moisture from Ted's wet blanket.

'Of course,' Jude brazened on. 'Then if we can get Kerry to stand up in court and repeat what she told Suzy . . .'

'And what's the likelihood of that happening?' Carole's question was bleak. 'Kerry shopping her own father, after all this?'

The sudden flare of excitement had fizzled out. The atmosphere of disappointment reasserted itself. All three of them found themselves looking out through the pub window to the old milk depot.

Seeing the site of Bob Hartson's next highly profitable project served only to turn the knife in their wounds. There had to be some way they could nail him.

Karl Floyd was out of hospital when Carole and Jude went to visit him, but he moved with difficulty, his arm was still in plaster, and the healing scabs on his face would leave him scarred for life.

He hadn't been keen on the idea of a meeting, and pretty soon after their arrival he made clear why. As soon as Carole mentioned the names Bob Hartson and Geoffrey Gardner, Karl stopped her. 'I don't want to have anything more to do with that.'

'What? But come on, I thought it was your ambition to be a crusading journalist?'

'Yes, it was. It's not now.'

'Why ever not?' asked Jude.

The young man made a painful, open-armed gesture, as if his broken body was answer enough.

Carole tried to bring him back to a proper sense of duty. 'You've got all that information. All that stuff on your computer about Renton and Chew, about the Pillars of Sussex and—'

'I've wiped it.'

'All?'

'Yes. I'm giving up journalism.'

'What does your father think about that?' asked Carole. 'I thought you were named after Carl Bernstein.'

'My father doesn't know yet.'

'But, Karl,' Carole insisted, 'you've got nothing to be frightened of. The man who beat you up is in prison, and will be staying there for a long, long time.'

The boy looked at her sardonically. 'And you think Bob Hartson isn't capable of finding another heavy?'

There was disbelief in Carole's voice as she asked, 'Are you actually saying the beating you received has frightened you off?'

'That's exactly what I'm saying.'

There was a silence before Jude spoke. 'What are you going to do instead of journalism?'

'Nothing for a while.' Karl Floyd spoke with new confidence. 'I'm going to buy a couple of flats – live in one, get rent from the other – and spend a bit of time working out the next stage of my career.'

'And where are you getting the money to do that?' asked Carole huffily. 'As I recall, you told me this flat was rented.'

'Yes,' he replied coolly. 'I came into some money.'

'Where from?'

'An aunt died.'

However much they questioned him further, the dead aunt was the story he stuck with. And in that way maybe the career of another fledgling property tycoon began.

The one unarguable fact that came out of their encounter with Karl Floyd was the sad reality that bullying – and, come to that, bribery – are often very effective.

So Bob Hartson thrived. The Pillars of Sussex and all his other local connections closed ranks around him and, as ever, by the judicious application of influence and incentives, his profits continued to grow.

Local business continued to be conducted in the way it always had been conducted. Very little was done that was actually against the law, nobody was so indelicate as to use words like 'bribery', but the skills of knowing and nurturing the right people continued to work their timeless magic.

Suzy Longthorne kept on running Hopwicke Country House Hotel and gradually her hard work turned its fortunes round. Max Townley continued as her chef, and continued to complain that his talents were under-appreciated. Rick Hendry had fulfilled the promise to help Max's television career through Korfilia Productions, but after one screen-test had been shown to the BBC, Max was dropped as being 'too like all the other television chefs'. So he had to confine his tantrums and his cheery singing to the audience of his own kitchen.

Kerry Hartson didn't fare much better in the new series of *Pop Crop*. The format had been changed so that, though a hundred hopefuls were shown in the first programme, a mere ten went through to the next stage. Only the chosen ten were seen and heard singing on television. Kerry was not one of them. She was just in the ensemble shots, queuing for her precious audition.

But failure to achieve pop celebrity did not change Kerry's life much. Her stepfather continued to buy her everything she announced she wanted. He was assiduous in going round virtually every day to her Brighton flat, 'to see that she was all right'. And Sandra Hartson continued to worry about the precise nature of her husband's relationship with her daughter.

Rick Hendry milked pop-wannabee television for everything it was worth, and shrewdly got out when he saw the bubble was about to burst. He retired to count his money and work out in what form he would reincarnate himself for his sixties. He almost completely lost touch with Suzy Longthorne.

Wendy Fullerton continued to work at the building society and to put on ever-heavier make-up. She continued looking for Mr Right, though with an increasing conviction that the man she had once lived with was probably as near as she would ever get.

Barry Stilwell, after his daring foray into the possibilities of extramarital sex, stayed at home more than ever under the thumb of Pomme. But he still got out now and then to vilify women at Rotary and Pillars of Sussex meetings.

Brenda Chew, greatly relieved no longer to have Donald around, threw herself ever more vigorously into charitable works, for which she was never as well appreciated as she should have been. Much of her effort was directed towards Pillars of Sussex events. Because, as its members never ceased to tell people, the primary purpose of their organization was charitable. The fact that members might make useful business contacts at Pillars of Sussex meetings was just a serendipitous by-product of their activities.

Jude's friendship with Suzy survived the lies. And she still received regular SOS calls from Hopwicke Country House Hotel, when yet another of the waitresses had defected.

Carole Seddon got to know her son's fiancée. Through Gaby, she began to get to know Stephen. And increasingly she dreaded the moment when she would have to meet David again. As for the wedding scheduled for the fourteenth of September, she viewed that prospect with trepidation, but also with a little excitement.